MW00609417

CALCULATED RISK

ENDORSEMENTS

Laurie Westlake is a top-notch writer. Her writing and storytelling abilities will keep readers satisfied for years to come.
—Larry J. Leech II, author, coach

An exciting read and page turner!
—Anne Gressett, reader

Fans of Rachel Decker are in for a treat with Calculated Risk. L.G. Westlake's heart-pounding debut is a suspense ride you won't soon forget!
—Lori Bates Wright, author

L.G.'s unique gift of creating fearless, compelling characters and weaving a suspenseful story escorts the reader on this thrill ride.
—C. B., reader

Calculated Risk is a fun and fast novel. The characters will stick with you long after you've finished the book.
—Jill West, reader

CALCULATED RISK

L. G. WESTLAKE

ELK LAKE PUBLISHING INC
PUBLISHING THE POSITIVE
Plymouth, Massachusetts

Copyright Notice

Calculated Risk

First edition. Copyright © 2021 by L. G. Westlake. The information contained in this book is the intellectual property of L. G. Westlake and is governed by United States and International copyright laws. All rights reserved. No part of this publication, either text or image, may be used for any purpose other than personal use. Therefore, reproduction, modification, storage in a retrieval system, or retransmission, in any form or by any means, electronic, mechanical, or otherwise, for reasons other than personal use, except for brief quotations for reviews or articles and promotions, is strictly prohibited without prior written permission by the publisher.

This is a work of fiction. Names, characters, businesses, places, events, locales, and incidents are either the products of the author's imagination or used in a fictitious manner. Any resemblance to actual persons, living or dead, or actual events is purely coincidental.

Scripture taken from the New King James Version®. Copyright © 1982 by Thomas Nelson. Used by permission. All rights reserved.

Cover and Interior Design: Derinda Babcock

Editor(s): Mel Hughes, Deb Haggerty

PUBLISHED BY: Elk Lake Publishing, Inc., 35 Dogwood Drive, Plymouth, MA 02360, 2021

Library Cataloging Data

Names: Westlake, L. G. (L. G. Westlake)

Calculated Risk / L. G. Westlake

354 p. 23cm × 15cm (9in × 6 in.)

ISBN-13: 978-1-64949-277-7 (paperback) | 978-1-64949-278-4 (trade paperback) | 978-1-64949-279-1 (e-book)

Key Words: Best Christian Suspense Books; Inspirational Suspense Books; Christian Suspense Books; Christian Fiction Suspense Authors; Top Christian Suspense Authors; Christian Mystery Books; Inspiration Mystery Books Authors

Library of Congress Control Number: 2021939937 Fiction

DEDICATION

For the superhero buried deep inside
each of us ordinary people.

ACKNOWLEDGMENTS

Thank you, Mom, for always supporting me.

Thank you, Steve, for patiently listening as I verbally dreamed a story, developed a plot, and fashioned characters. You are my rock.

And thank you to all the family members, who at holiday gatherings, politely asked how the writing was going and spent the next two hours hearing a story they now have no need to purchase.

Gratitude must also go to my original critique group in Waxahachie. You beat me up and made me a better writer. Thank you. I miss you all.

I am grateful, as well, for my editor M.H. who reads dictionaries, rides motorcycles, and is from a galaxy far, far away.

Finally, thank you to all the women I've studied the Word of God with over the years. Your wild examples of valor encourage me to inspire others to be brave.

PROLOGUE

At the distinct sound of formidable boots pounding the floor in the hall, Isa looked up from the spreadsheet on her computer screen.

In her wing of the building, heavy or rushed footfalls were nothing new. Urgency filled the hallways here, even on slow days. Sometimes expletives accompanied the hustle outside her door. Once she heard an officer yell, "Drop your weapon," followed by the *pop, pop, pop* of rapid gunfire.

That's why she kept the door shut. Not out of fear, but for focus.

Seven times out of ten, the sarge's footsteps led to her door. Any second, he'd burst into her office without knocking.

Sure enough, his large shadow appeared through the crooked blinds covering the half-glass door. Isa pulled in a breath. He'd visited once already, pushing her to find that crucial piece of evidence. The sarge wanted to pound that final nail into the bank president's indictment coffin. The DA said they couldn't hold the arrogant banker on the thin proof she'd given them last week.

But this time, her tarnished brass doorknob didn't twist in his hand. The sarge, silhouetted behind those blinds, stood as still as stone.

She glanced at Mac's picture on her desk. He was due home last night but didn't show. Sure, theirs was a rough relationship, but Mac usually called when his case was going to take longer than predicted.

CALCULATED RISK

Looking back at the door with her sarge still frozen on the other side, she realized Mac just might be the biggest challenge of her life.

And she'd had plenty.

Odd, the sarge's shadow pulled away, and the signature *click, stop, click, stop* of his steps echoed back down the hall.

She pulled her pony tail tight. Closed one of the folders on her desk.

What she desired was the frustration release of a mat and a jiujitsu sparring partner.

What she needed was another set of eyes on these figures.

What she had was a pile of work and no one but herself to manage it.

Working alone eighty-two percent of the time, she didn't have the luxury of multiple opinions on a case. She led, investigated, sat on witness stands, and wrapped up financial crimes as the sole forensic accountant. The junior bookkeeper they'd finally hired two months ago had left last week for a position at the bank under investigation. One of the bank's on-the-prowl officers discovered the girl possessed more than math talents.

Refreshing the screen on her desktop, she scanned the bank's financial transfers, comparing them to the spreadsheet on her laptop.

I can do this single-handedly. After all, she'd managed *life* with almost no support.

And that thought brought her back to Mac.

Which distracted her from the footsteps that had circled back her way.

The sarge didn't bust in, but slipped through the door, gently pushing it shut behind him.

Before he turned to face her, he let go a substantial sigh.

The abnormal tilt of his head. The eyes cast down at the floor as he turned. Something—

A dry lump rose in her throat.

"Mac's dead," the sarge said. "I'm sorry."

CHAPTER 1

Isabella Phillips counted the red venules crisscrossing Sergeant Caba's nose.

Eleven.

When the sergeant's blood pressure rose, the tiny, webbed veins were exacerbated, turning his whole nose crimson. Today, the sarge's globe glowed raging red. She hadn't seen it that color since he'd told her Mac wouldn't be coming home that night. Or ever. Albuquerque police had found his body in an arroyo on the southeast quadrant of Albuquerque three long months ago.

"What's this?" The sarge waved the paper around she'd left in his office.

Scooting her chair tighter beneath the desk, she chose careful words. "It's self-explanatory, but—"

"I can read." He narrowed an eye. "What is this *really* about?"

What this was *really* about, she couldn't say. Partly because she didn't want the sarge's blood pressure to spike. The man was the perfect model for a stroke—drinking sodas, eating fries and a good twenty pounds overweight. But mostly she couldn't say, because she didn't want to give him the chance to talk her out of the plan.

She opened her mouth, but he cut her off again. "You're an accountant, you know. Not a homicide investigator. If that's what you're thinking."

True. But neither the Houston Police Department nor Albuquerque's tough-guy murder investigators had come up with any answers as to who had killed Mac or why he was in Albuquerque that day. Before he left home, Mac had told her he'd be gone two days tops, pulling an all-nighter with a cartel lead north of Houston.

Isa pressed her hand against her chest. Cleared her throat. "I want to start my own business. Something less stressful." She tried an infomercial smile. "Make some muffins, sell some coffee. Human depravity is getting old."

"You think coffee drinkers are angels? Corruption is everywhere." He sucked in a breath. "Don't I know." The sarge adjusted his belt beneath his midlife belly. "You need to stay here where you're needed. Where I can keep an eye on you."

He'd kept an eye on her since she'd joined the department four years ago. Finding solid, court-admissible evidence was her gig, and she had a knack for it. He had told her this sixteen times in the last 1,462 days—an average of once every three months. Sarge seemed like a dad at times. The one she never had.

"You don't need to keep an eye on me. I know what I'm doing." She tried a smile.

The old guy threw his arms in the air and let a profane word slip out.

"I thought you were done with cussing and drinking."

"I said I was done with liars, too, but looks like I'm staring at one right now." He bent towards her, hands landing on her desk. "This isn't about coffee or doughnuts."

She edged her chin up.

"You can't leave me with a backlog of cases." He pushed off the desk, dropping the crumpled letter in front of her.

She cleared her throat. Again. "As I explained in the letter—"

"Like I can't read through this?" He crossed his arms. "This is about Mac."

"No." Her stomach backflipped. Saying *no* wasn't a total lie. She wasn't going *only* to get answers about her husband's murder. She was going with the fantasy notion she might open a real coffee shop, too. If she could get all the variables to fall into the right columns.

4

"Yes, it is." His red nose throbbed. "You need to be patient. You know how investigations need to go."

She did know. But this one wasn't going the way it should. Every time she asked homicide investigators about progress, they coughed or pretended to need something from another room.

The sergeant thrust his finger at her. "Let the law do its work. Your place is to wait behind this desk. Let real investigators handle this. You'll get yourself killed snooping around a bunch of drug dealers."

What he didn't know was that before Mac died, he had insisted she carry a weapon. A Glock 19. Being married to an undercover cop, Mac believed, presented risks, and HPD didn't issue guns to the auditors in the white-collar crimes' unit.

Isa shifted in her seat. "First, I am a real investigator, and I've solved more crimes than those gun-toting lug heads you have working undercover. Plus, I find plenty of forensic evidence when I wrap up a case, so you, Sarge, can get a conviction. But you're wrong on this. I'm starting a business." She glanced at her briefcase already packed with files. "That's all."

"Well, you don't fool me." The sergeant straightened.

She let go of her chair. Leaned back. Counted off the seconds, waiting for him to blow up again.

"I know." The light bulb going off above his head was nearly visible. "Take a leave. Go to some Caribbean island and get wasted on martinis."

"I think you mean margaritas."

"I mean whatever the heck it takes to get your brain out of your butt and back where it belongs." He tapped his temple. "In your smarter-than-average head." Stepping back, he put himself next to the door. "I won't accept the resignation. Take three weeks' leave. Then you'll come back here." He pointed at the floor. "By then, we should have more information from New Mexico." He nodded quick and stepped out the door before she could offer a rebuttal. The blinds rattled against the glass pane when he pulled the door shut.

CALCULATED RISK

Isa stared at nothing for a moment, and then slid her eyes over to look at a photograph on the edge of her desk. Mac on their wedding day. In the last three months, every time she walked into an HPD office, voices hushed, coworkers exchanged glances or got busy at their computers. Something wasn't lining up. She slapped his picture face-down on the desk.

She could line up a thing or two. Crime solving took brains, not just muscles, guts, and guns.

The decision to leave had been made the day the bank called with the surprising information that she'd inherited a safe deposit box loaded with its own enigmas. She would pull the chaos surrounding Mac's murder into neat rows and orderly columns, wrap the loose ends up with an accounting-tape bow. Finding solid, court-admissible evidence, after all, was her job. If she could track down the mastermind behind a complicated financial scheme and bring them in, she could find answers to a murder on Albuquerque's drug-infested streets.

As long as she didn't get herself killed in the process.

CHAPTER 2

Isa shoved Mac's picture into her stuffed briefcase. The sergeant's directive to get to a beach was slightly short of hilarious. No way sun lovers deserved what she might unleash. She'd be as much fun as a beached shark. A live one.

The lack of information between New Mexico DEA and Houston had created an empty space in her gut. This gave the normally dormant, but fire-breathing, creature that lived inside her room to expand, get out of his cage, and fester up old feelings. Over the last few years, she'd been able to contain her beastly temper by mentally organizing a room's clutter, or counting objects, or taking on a jiujitsu opponent. But not so much lately, and she felt the dragon clawing at her nerves today.

Isa quickly counted the accounting books on her shelf—something she'd done 103 times before—and the itch to let go a frustrating scream subsided.

She needed to stay on task. Collect data to solve the mysteries. First problem to crack—Mac was not supposed to be in Albuquerque, but that's where they found his body. Second, the creepy message someone left in her car. Then third, the building he'd bought in downtown Albuquerque that no one knew anything about.

Who buys a building and doesn't tell someone—especially his wife?

She ran her hand across the wide pocket on the outside of the briefcase. Felt the edges of that worn folder peeking out. That flimsy file folder guarded the spreadsheet of questions she'd been compiling since before Mac had died. Helped keep her thoughts logical. And dragons at bay.

She heard hushed voices outside her door.

Was word of her resignation already out?

Isa grabbed her purse from the desk's bottom drawer and checked inside it for the note. Still there. Time to go before rumors started to spread.

She lifted the briefcase, eyes burning. This would be her last time in this office.

As she glanced around, guilt wrapped its fingers around her throat. This office had been home for six almost-great years.

The guilt fist tightened.

Looking back at her desk, she could envision Mac leaning over it and hear his husky laugh. A little more than a year ago, he'd entered her office with the force of a hurricane, circling her with wild energy. When the Mac tide washed back out, he'd left her little to hang onto.

Isa swung the briefcase strap over her shoulder and slipped to the door. Determination was a fickle thing— came and went with almost every breath.

She stared at the light switch. Reached for it, then stopped. Had she made the right decision? At the edge of the life-changing cliff now, she had only to jump—leap into the abyss on a quest. Resign from HPD.

She flipped the switch. Pulled the door closed. Heard the blinds rattle behind her.

CHAPTER 3

Head down, Isa kept her gaze on the 1980s-style black and yellowed linoleum floor that some local secretary-slash-decorator had recommended thirty years ago. She'd always found eighties decor fascinating—in your face, but orderly. She'd counted those squares every morning on her way to her office. Thirty-eight black and yellowed vinyl tiles.

Mac had sauntered these halls. Teased her about laying black and white faux squares in their own kitchen, though that would never have happened. He had an eye for the upscale, and upscale was something a lowly-paid undercover cop could never afford.

Hand on the case, she turned for the side door to the parking lot. Just thirty seconds more and HPD and hall whispers would be in her rearview mirror. Was she ready? When she walked out those doors, she would obliterate her hard-earned and stable career. And the biggest risk? Putting herself back in the middle of the kind of chaos that had sent her to her closet when she was young. That could force her to face the ghosts of her past. Something she'd avoided since finding the surety of spreadsheet cells.

The double doors stood within arm's reach. Before her fingers felt the cool metal of the push bar stretched across the glass, Claire Washington yelled Isa's name from somewhere behind her.

Isa stopped. Looked out the door. So close. Pulling in a breath, she turned.

Hands on her hips and frown on her face, Claire looked ready for a rumble.

CALCULATED RISK

Claire investigated crime-scenes. Isa investigated money trails. Their work rarely crossed paths, but they'd managed to become good friends. In the heavy testosterone-laden environment, girls tended to stick together.

Claire marched toward her. "You're resigning and didn't tell me?" Her five-foot nine, broad-shouldered frame towered a good five inches over Isa.

Crossing her arms, Isa sighed. "I was going to call you."

"After? After you walked out?"

"Caba tell you?"

Claire lowered her chin, leveled her coal-black eyes. "Yeah, he did. The man left my desk minutes ago saying you tried to resign. But he's giving you some time to think about it." She shook her massive, black curls. "What the heck, Isa?"

Isa had prepared a sellable answer in case she ran into Claire. Even rehearsed it. "I need a redirect."

"Let's go get a beer and talk about it." Claire stepped between Isa and the door.

Isa looked past her friend, through the glass. Another cop scurried up the outside steps. The guy opened the door, shot the two an awkward smile, then headed down the hall to the HPD inner lair.

"I gotta go, Claire."

Claire clicked her tongue. "Girl, where you got to go?"

"Away."

"Away?" The coal-eyes burned through her. "Away like a beach vacation? Or, away like outta-here for good?"

"Don't make this more difficult than it already is."

"You make me wanna yank that black ponytail of yours. I never figured you for a runner."

Inside, the dragon's breath scorched. Heated up a couple of degrees. Isa almost told Claire to bring it on but stuck with the rehearsed script. "I'm not running. I'm changing direction, all right?"

"Come on, Isa. Slipping out in the middle of the day without telling anyone? Without telling me?" Claire's arms dropped to her side, her mocha face appealing for answers.

"You haven't been yourself. I am trying to help you."

Isa crossed her arms again, eyes still on the escape hatch. "I need some time."

"Don't be making rash decisions. Everyone says wait a year before you make life changes. Mac's only been gone—"

"My husband is dead. Don't pretend to understand this." Hot flames inched up inside Isa's throat.

"Hey, I just want to talk." Claire's voice softened. "I know it's been hard."

"Until I know what happened, I can't let this go."

"You gotta let real investigators do their stuff. Let the law do its work, Isa."

Similar words had left Caba's mouth moments earlier. Funny how the department creed now sounded shallow. "I'll call you later." Isa brushed past Claire and pushed the door open.

Claire, surprisingly, let her by, but called after her, "You faint at the sight of blood, girl. How you gonna handle real crime?"

Street noise rushed in, making it easier to keep going. She took the steps, six of them. Another 140 strides and she'd be to her unofficial parking spot where her Corolla waited.

She could feel Claire's stare through the glass door the whole way across the parking lot. Opening the driver's door, Isa added up the reasons to blow up a life—hers.

1. Death. Two of them. Her brother and now Mac. Murder by drugs in both cases.
2. Life. According to what Mac said during their last fight, she needed one.
3.
4.

CHAPTER 4

Isa opened her car door, stepped out of traffic and up on the curb to face her inheritance—a single-story standalone nestled between two taller buildings in downtown Albuquerque. India Magic's sign hung sideways on the wall of the deserted building. The single-pane glass door had a crack that ran the length of it with silver duct tape holding it together. The white-stucco restaurant trimmed in hot pink could have rivaled a hooker's dress on New Year's Eve. From what she'd seen so far, most Albuquerque business owners painted their buildings the ever-popular tan, as if bringing the lifeless desert into every aspect of their lives. But not the Asian entrepreneurs who'd owned this restaurant before Mac obtained it. They'd chosen to stand out in the sea of sand-colored high rises. And they'd chosen to serve up their chicken masala in a tiny space where the green chilies of New Mexican cuisine ruled. They had guts, but from the looks of things, zero consideration for curb appeal.

The deed showed Mac had bought this property from a man named Raj Khartri about the time they started to date. So he'd had it a while and evidently hadn't done anything to fix the place up. Could she make this eyesore a cover business for an investigation? Could selling coffee become a reality in the future? She told herself to forget about the coffee dream. That wasn't something she should even think about at the moment.

Plotting to pose as an entrepreneur while drilling into Albuquerque's drug crime scene seemed heroic in the wake of Mac's death. But the reality of the shoddy building put a knot in her gut right next to the dragon. She stared at her desolate, pink-and-white surprise.

A guy on a bike appeared from nowhere. Yelled, "move!" He swerved, narrowly missing Isa. She jumped toward the door, fought the desire to start adding up losses before she knew what they were.

She did this for Mac. She did this for answers. She did this to prove a few things, if not to the world, then to herself.

Digging around for the building keys in the purse at her hip, she touched the envelope. The envelope with the note. That final nudge that launched this fact-finding scheme. Not that the scribbled sentence divulged anything. Far from it. Its eighteen words compounded the unknowns.

She pulled the paper from the envelope and unfolded it, taking care not to tear at the already worn creases. For the thirty-ninth time, she read it. For the thirty-ninth time, the words gave her pause.

> But there is nothing covered up that will not be revealed, and hidden that will not be known.

Though oddly phrased and a bit creepy, she understood the intent of the note. Someone had secrets about Mac. There was no doubt whatsoever about that. Everything else was a crapshoot.

She looked up at the silver duct tape holding the broken door together. If only a strip of duct tape would hold her and these plans together.

"This place is no longer open."

Isa whirled around to find a woman with a face the color of New Mexico's endless desert. This gal had seen some interesting life, and the deep wrinkles in her cheeks proved it. Long, gray braids cascaded down both shoulders, and she wore a multicolored skirt that reached her ankles, revealing army boots—one olive green and one black. She leaned against a cane carved with symbols and sayings.

"They left and took my job with them." A bottom tooth was missing.

Isa pointed her thumb back at the door. "You worked here?"

The woman nodded. "Thirteen months ago."

Maybe a fluke, but it looked like Isa's day was about to turn—and she would be able to fill a couple of cells in her spreadsheets with data. "So." Isa bent toward the woman, shoving the note back into her purse. "You knew the owner? Raj Khatri?"

The woman dropped her head. "No. I worked for this man, but never *knew* him. There are many that never knew *him* either." The woman pointed at the sky. "They'll come in his name, but he'll say he didn't know them." With that strange statement, she spat on the cement leaving a puddle the color of dark tea.

Isa's temples started to throb, but she probed anyway. "I hoped to talk with the owner, find out a little about who bought this place from him."

"He went back to India. Why you need to talk to him? You hungry? There's a taco stand there." She pointed her cane to the left. Isa's gaze followed the woman's cane. That's when she saw a man the size of her car leaving a bar—the place she'd flagged early in her research. It couldn't be a coincidence that Mac bought a building one block away from a bar known to attract drug dealers and buyers. That pit was called, appropriately, the Drake's Horn.

The woman pulled her back into the moment. "The pulled chipotle pork is good there. Made with citrus."

"Pardon?" Isa asked, watching the giant man mount his bike.

Before he fired the Harley up, he glanced her way. Did a double-take that ended with a wicked stare.

When the woman didn't respond, Isa looked back to see her walking away. "Wait."

Turning, the old gal eyed Isa suspiciously. "Yes?"

"I have a couple of questions." Isa adjusted her purse strap. "Could I buy *you* a taco?"

"No. Taco place isn't open yet. It's morning."

"But I thought you said ... never mind." What did

investigators do when they had a wacky witness? "Well, then, could I ask you a couple of questions now?"

The woman shot a stream of tobacco at the cement again and squinted skyward.

Isa tried another time. "Just a couple of—"

"Shish." She held up an age-spotted hand. "I listen."

Okay, maybe fluke encounter expressed the wrong idea. Maybe "freak encounter" described this interaction better.

Still squinting, but with her eyes back on Isa, the woman spoke. "I must go, but will stay to answer one question for you today … because the sun has smiled down on a young woman staring wistfully at an empty café."

One question? What kind of game was this? Isa tapped her foot. If she had merely one question, it had better be good.

The woman folded her arms, the satisfaction on her face said she was rather pleased she'd stumped Isa.

This had to be the strangest conversation Isa had ever had, and she couldn't decide if she should ask if the woman knew the owners of the biker bar down the street or inquire if she had information about local drug trafficking. Or maybe she should ask if the old woman had seen a man who looked like Mac in India Magic. She settled on none of these and went with an out-of-the-blue impulse instead.

"If I have but one question, then I will ask you this." She crossed her arms to mirror the old lady's stance. "Where are you going?"

A flat smile stretched across the weathered face. "Ah, daughter of the sun, you have asked wisely." The woman shuffled around to face Isa straight on again. "I will give you my answer." She reached into her bottom lip and pulled out a small wad of spit-laden tobacco, then removed a snack-sized baggie from the leather pouch hung at her hip. She placed the lump into the plastic. "In my long journey, I go to a place no one has seen. Tomorrow, I go to the laundry mat to worship." The woman started to walk away, shoving the baggie back into her pouch.

Isa's shoulders slumped. She started to count the woman's steps before the old gal stopped and looked back

at her. "But, today, I go to the Dollar King down the street."
The cane pointed north.

"Isn't that interesting," Isa said, her shoulders slipping
back into place. "I need to go to the Dollar King, too." Why
not? Who couldn't find something they needed at the local
catch-all?

The woman's eyes sparkled. "And is this the time that
you wish to go?"

"Why, yes. It is." Isa grinned.

"Do you wish to walk with me and ask me more of your
questions?"

"Indeed." Isa's smile widened.

"We pass a Herbert's Diner on the way. You look hungry."

Oh, brother.

"No, I'm fine. I want to get to know the neighborhood."
She shrugged. "That's all."

"It is good that you come when I go, anyway." The
woman looked skyward again.

Isa studied the sky, too, shielding her eyes with her
hand. The white-hot sun of the mile-high city was too
intense to eyeball for long, and she looked back to the
woman to find her staring into India Magic's window. She
leaned toward Isa and whispered, "You will do well to walk
away with me."

"Excuse me?"

"There is a spirit in that place." She gave a quick nod
toward the windows.

The hairs on Isa's arms sprang upright. "I'm sorry?"

"And he wishes to consume you."

CHAPTER 5

Consuming spirit?

The hairs standing at attention on Isa's arms started to quiver, and she rubbed at them. Three months ago, she would have disregarded this spirit-seer's comment and backed herself out of the conversation. But because there was a tip-off note about hidden things being made known, she wanted to hear more. Still, rather than explain, the elder woman scrutinized Isa like a lawyer eyeing a witness on the stand. Isa knew the feeling. More than once she'd been in the witness chair.

The spirit-seer stood her ground, waiting for Isa to respond to the outrageous, but hair-raising, claim that she'd seen a spirit through the window of Isa's building. The calculator in Isa's head evaluated the chances that the old gal was delusional or had a certifiable case of crazy. Totals hovered at eighty percent for crazy. How do you logically answer insanity?

Isa attempted humor. "So, there's only one of them?"

The woman narrowed her eyes, looked like she took the remark seriously. "Like roaches, were there is one, there will be more."

The crazy percentage moved up to eighty-nine percent.

"Ma'am? Are you sure you saw something?"

The woman frowned. "I am not Ma'am. I am Awena, a daughter of the sun." She started walking.

Isa remembered reading something in her research of Albuquerque, one of the local tribes had worshipped the sun. "Are you from the Zia Tribe?" she asked running after the woman and thankfully away from the issue of a supposed spirit in her building.

The woman glanced over, confusion at her brows. "I am not Zia. What makes you think I belong to the Zia?"

Isa shook her head, afraid she'd made a cultural blunder. "I ... I don't know. I'm sorry if that offended you."

"I'm Navajo. My name is Awena Johnson." She winked at Isa. "Maybe all Indians look alike."

Isa decided to keep her mouth shut long enough to regather the wits the old woman's antics had scattered.

A group of young women came toward them, each with hair a different shade of purple. They passed on either side of Awena like an aubergine sea parting before a goddess. Awena eyed the girls as they passed. "The purple-hairs are not in harmony."

"What do you mean?"

"The Navajo walk the Beautiful Trail, a journey of harmony with creation. We prefer natural beauty." Awena's olive green and black boots were hitting the pavement quicker. "What trail do you walk?"

A trail of frustration.

"Um," she muttered, digging around in her brain for a better answer. "I have been on a journey of ..." She stopped. "Of resolution." She repeated the word, liking the way it felt in her mouth. "Resolution."

"Ah." Awena nodded and motioned for Isa to pick up speed.

"I've just moved here," Isa said catching up. "I have questions. I am curious about the area."

"Your brown skin speaks of the south."

"Yes, I am part Latina. My mother was born in El Paso and my birth father is from California."

"The Navajo originated in the east. You eat food from the east? From India? India is the largest subcontinent in the world. Lots of curry over there."

For a tiny thing, the woman was into her foods.

"Yes, I eat Indian food. But I have lots of questions I'd like to ask you about Albuquerque and some of the locals."

"There are other restaurants I can show you that serve curry." The woman slowed, keeping her gaze forward. "I know of a food that you can eat, and you will never hunger again."

Isa scratched her head. "That's great, Awena—and a little weird. But what I need is information about who bought India Magic from your old boss. What can you tell me about that?"

"I can tell you that an unclean spirit abides there."

Redirecting Awena was a bit like redirecting a fast-moving snake. Isa gave up.

They reached a cross-street and Isa stopped but Awena stepped off the curb and kept walking. Right into oncoming traffic.

Isa gasped.

A female driver behind the wheel of a silver SUV laid on her brakes and horn coming within inches of Awena who kept walking, head forward. Isa flew into the street between Awena and the oncoming cars, jutting her arms out wide to stop traffic. The woman in the SUV presented Isa a middle finger.

Fighting the urge to count the cars piling up behind the SUV, Isa looked around for her new friend.

Awena, evidently, had ignored the ruckus and made it to the curb on the other side.

Isa mouthed, *I'm sorry,* toward the driver and hustled over to Awena. "You cannot cross the street until the lighted sign tells you—"

"Why you interested in the history of the India Magic building?"

The woman walked through heavy traffic, unscathed. Maybe *she* was the spirit. Isa shook her head. "I own it now and want to put a coffee shop in there."

"I would not open a coffee shop with a bad spirit inside."

"Well, I didn't know there was one inside until you told me."

"People avoid drinking their coffee with demons."

The senseless conversation made Isa's head hurt. "I've never seen a demon. How was I supposed to know?"

"Now I have told you."

Isa sucked in dry desert air then pushed it out long and slow. "So. What do I do with a ..." Legitimizing the idea by speaking the words seemed insane. "A demon in my coffee shop? Can I get rid of it?"

A man in a dirty shirt and tattered pants stopped to ask the two for money for food. Awena told him to meet her at Dollar King in five minutes and she'd buy him some crackers. He walked on, and she watched him closely. "It's not food he seeks."

Isa opened her mouth. Then shut it. The little sage saw right through people, and that made her squirm. She should turn, walk back to India Magic, put her key in the door, and get started with cleanup. That, or get in her car and drive back to Houston.

Awena studied Isa's face. "Perhaps, there is a solution."

"To the spirit or the homeless guy?"

"Your spirit."

Isa almost hated to ask. "What then?"

"I will get you some HO." The woman looked across the street. "Ah, there is Dollar King. You hungry?" Awena headed straight for the street again.

Isa shot her arm out in front of Awena like a mother protecting her child in the passenger seat. "What's HO?" she asked, looking both ways and blocking Awena.

"Holy oil." Awena stepped around Isa's arm and walked across the asphalt.

Again, Isa halted cars so mystic Awena could pass. From routine-driven accountant to amateur investigator to traffic cop, and it wasn't even 11:00 a.m. yet. "Holy oil?" she asked when they'd both reached the other side of the street.

"I will bring to you tomorrow."

"Okay, then." She'd let Awena do this so she could continue the probe. Fitting for the beginning of a resolution journey. "I'll be there. Want to meet at, say, eight in the morning?"

"Sometime."

"Sometime?"

"Yes, sometime tomorrow I will come." Awena reached for the broken handle dangling from Dollar King's glass door.

"Also." Isa touched her arm to stop her. "I'd love to know what people say about the Drake's Horn bar down the street from India Magic. I've heard it's a rough place. Maybe you can tell me about it tomorrow."

"You coming in?"

Isa eyed the plastic flower display flanking the Dollar King's doors. "No, I need to get going."

Awena looked down and studied her two different-colored boots. "I can tell you something about the Drake's Horn now."

"Please." Anticipation sped Isa's heart up.

"Likely," she said, lowering her voice, "it's where your demon's master lives."

CHAPTER 6

Without the courage to walk into a demon-infested building, Isa came back to sit in her car. The near-noonday sun had turned her black Corolla into an oven. Not two hours into her secret mission and a petite Native American with mix-matched army boots had thrown a demon wrench into her investigation.

She reminded herself for the sixth time that demons were not real. Awena, although completely lovable, must suffer from a mental disorder.

"Mac," Isa said, hands on the wheel. "What have you done?"

He'd never mentioned the building. Not once. She'd discovered the legal document the day the bank called about Mac's safety deposit box. He'd never mentioned that either. After death certificates, probates, and a court appearance, she'd been allowed access to the box where she found the deed to a commercial building and $25,000 in cash.

How could she have married someone with mysteries deeper than the Grand Canyon? A memory flashed across her already-strained brain. Her stepfather. On one of his drunken nights, he'd seized her on the staircase, and she had cried, threatening him with the wrath of her real father. But they both knew her actual father would never come to Isa's rescue. To her best recollection, she had visited her birth dad three times in her life. That night, her stepfather laughed, then told her her real father didn't love her—that no one could love her. And then he dragged her up the stairs.

Isa held her breath. Counted to six. But the memory wouldn't fade back to the place she kept locked.

Maybe she didn't know anything about love. Maybe Mac was the first thing to come along that seemed like love, but she neglected to read it right.

She started counting again and made it to forty-three when her thoughts turned back to the problem at hand. That building ten feet from her car hosted answers.

She opened the car door, slung her purse across her shoulder, and stepped out.

For good measure—just in case—she crossed herself. Darn those prickles at the back of her neck.

She fumbled for the front door keys in her purse. A week earlier, she'd called a locksmith to put a new lock on the door. From the looks of the deadbolt, someone had tried to jimmy their way in already. Great.

As she stepped into her new possession, the smell of molds and curry rushed at her senses. She squinted, wiped at her nose. An Indian party bomb had exploded here. Emerald-green chairs lay scattered across the Saltillo-tile floor. Someone had emptied a box of gold, silky napkins in a corner and dumped white plastic forks and knives on a table. Broken glass glistened from the floor.

Had Mac made this mess? He'd certainly made one of her life. Her marriage had been challenging from day six, the day the honeymoon ended and Mac went back to work. He hadn't come home night six. Or called.

Isa kicked a chair to the side, its rattle unsettling the one nerve that held her inner dragon at bay.

Stepping across a sticky floor and behind the counter, she found the backside littered with plastic serving utensils and trash. An empty liter bottle labeled Shasta Strawberry Soda lay on the floor covered in rat droppings.

She shuddered. Then gagged. Felt the smolder of hot coals in her esophagus.

Moving through a half-open door at the back of the dining room, Isa stepped into the kitchen. A stand-alone metal pantry sat to the right, its door dented in a couple of places. Several Costco-sized spice canisters lined a shelf above a grease-covered stove. A couple of the canisters were tossed to the side, their contents spilled across the shelf. There had been a struggle in here.

To the left sat the ovens. Two stacked beauties with the word *convection* written across the top one. Isa sank her teeth into her bottom lip, biting back an unexpected eagerness. Baking. She loved the science of it—the exactness in measuring and timing. A half-teaspoon difference, or a minute too long, and you could take a potential masterpiece to complete disaster. She pulled the oven door down. Enthusiasm rose again. Inside, the oven appeared somewhat clean.

Her nerves took a break—visions of muffins and cappuccinos materializing. In the chaos of murder and mystery, business-building dreams had become the sweet spot in the plan, and the inherited building presented an unexpected opportunity.

She backed up to a chair next to the three-compartment sink full of pots. Maybe this was doable. Easing down into the seat, she tried to imagine herself solving Mac's murder, then starting a new life. Perhaps her days as a forensic accountant *were* over, and a coffee and bake shop lay ahead.

But getting this place fixed up as a front to her investigation, let alone as a full-fledged operation, would cost more cash than Mac left behind. And then there was that other colossal negative. Undercover work could be deadly. Drug lords frowned upon moles.

She pulled her mini notebook from her purse. Flipped to the page with the list of expenses she'd anticipated for this risky endeavor. Fifteen items lined the page, each with a precise bullet point made from the tip of her mechanical pencil. Soft lead.

Her hand hovered over the page as she considered expense number sixteen.

And then ...

Glass crunched.

Isa's head jerked up. She stiffened.

A rat?

The sound repeated.

The hairs that had bristled earlier jumped to attention on her arm again.

Alarms rang in her head. She started to reach for her gun but knocked the notebook to the floor. Isa's mouth went dry knowing that whatever she was hearing now would have heard her drop the notebook. Plus, there was no gun. She'd left it in her new and mostly empty apartment. Stupid move.

A creak.

Someone crept across India Magic's dining room floor.

CHAPTER 7

Three choices rushed to Isa's mind. She could find the back door and run like crazy or hide in the oversized pantry and hold her breath. Or lastly, face whatever creeped around the dining room.

Considering that last option threw her heart against her chest so hard, she guessed the *whatever* heard it.

A squish noise—the sound of a rubber sole connecting with a sticky floor.

Something in her brain grabbed a lucid idea and she shoved her hand into her purse, found her phone. Instead of tapping the 911 code into the screen though, she thrust her cell into the waist of her jeans. Concealed phones had rescued many a fast-thinking victim, according to HPD training videos.

She reminded herself to breathe. Force rational thoughts. Act in confidence. Fear had the power to put victims on the defense and keep them trapped there. "I'm a real cop. I'm a real cop." Isa whispered. "I can handle this."

The phrase didn't instill avenger-type superpowers, but it did give her the confidence to take the lead in introductions.

She silently counted to three. "Hello." She stood.

No answer.

"Hello," she said again, stepping next to the door but not opening it.

Still nothing.

Isa pulled the door toward her and surveyed the restaurant.

Empty dining room.

She looked left. Nothing.

She looked right—right into the barrel of a gun.

Her lungs collapsed as if someone on the jiujitsu matt had kicked the air out of them.

Holding a revolver pointed at her forehead was a frying-pan sized hand attached to an arm the size of a tree trunk. One carved up with devils, numbers, and skull tattoos.

Pure bulk stood before her—way too much volume for any amateur jiujitsu move she could pull. Not that she should consider busting a move anyway. That gun aimed for her brain and she would be as still as possible until the giant's weapon pointed elsewhere.

She raised her hands in the air.

"Who 'er you?" He slanted the gun sideways. The kind of sideways killers in movies used as a warning that they were about to blow someone's head off.

She hadn't made up an undercover name yet. Saying *nobody* was the best she could come up with. "No ... body."

The answer didn't satisfy him. He asked louder. "Who 'er you?"

From the corner of her eye, the gun looked like a toy in the giant's oversized hand. "I'm ... I'm ..." She couldn't get her tongue to work.

As if prompting her with the right answer, he broke in. "You're Sicily."

"No. No. I'm not Sicily," she said, trying not to shake her head and bump the gun. She slid her eyes as far right as she could get them to check his reaction.

He frowned, emphasizing the tear drop tattooed at the outside corner of his left eye.

"I'm the auditor."

He flinched.

Isa cinched her eyes shut. She'd meant to say *owner*, not *auditor*.

"Auditor?" He tilted his head back and the gun dropped slightly. "You that bookkeeper El Padrino is waitin' on?"

El Padrino. *The Godfather*. Had to be a high-ranking Mexican gangster and not someone she'd be anxious to meet. But she couldn't get her brain to come up with an answer, so she stood there.

The giant glanced toward the front door. That's when she saw the red snake tattoo that moved up the right side of his neck, wound around his ear, and ended with its fangs bared, on the man's temple. Not a comforting sign.

Lowering his gun, the intruder seemed to relax a little. "They've been looking for you. Waiting for you to count up some expenses or somethin'."

Count? Did he say count expenses? She went with it. "I am counting expenses." She'd never guessed she would be jumping into an undercover role on the fly.

His brows met in the middle of his forehead pulling the snake's fangs closer to his eyes. "They got you working *here*?" He lifted the gun to the side of his head and rubbed the barrel up and down his temple. "I mean ... what?"

The giant beside her didn't seem so threatening with his gun upside his own head, so she took the lead, motioning around the dining room. "Here I am trying to open a coffee shop and first thing I get is a guy with a gun in my face. Things are off to a bad start, I'd say." She took the opportunity to get her arms down where she could use them if needed.

"A coffee place?" He stepped back, giving her a little space to breathe. "Nobody told *me*."

His gun was far away enough to give her room for a quick nod. "I didn't realize you were on the need-to-know list." The nervous chuckle that followed the humor-fail comment was as equally lame. So she tried the truth. At least some truth. "This, um, this is ... my place."

He brought his gun down to scrape at his elbow. "You kidding?"

"I know, right? I own this mess."

"That ain't right." The wobble of his head said he found himself lost in the dialogue. "I'm missing something."

Boy was he ever on cue.

"Look," she said and faced him straight on. "You're obviously in the wrong place. Think you could leave now? We can forget you were here."

He longingly beheld the escape hatch—the front, broken door.

That's when near-death shock wore off and her default mechanisms showed up. When things got chaotic, Isa could get them in some sense of order by mentally organizing a room or counting off things most people ignored. Like the jumble of dishes beneath the counter. "Seriously, I've got to organize the pile there." She pointed. "I'm looking at sixteen dirty glasses right now."

He followed her gaze to a shelf beneath the counter.

"That's where I'll put the seven-hundred paper cups. I did the math already. Do you have any idea how much paper cups cost?"

He looked up. Took a step back. "I don't know 'bout no cups."

"That's only the twelve-ounce cups. I'll have to order at least five-hundred ten-ounce."

He made for the exit. "I'll tell the boss you're here."

"Espresso cups too," she called after him. "Probably two-hundred or ..."

He got through the taped glass door, shoving the gun into his pants.

"Yeah," she said, quieting her voice. "Two-hundred espresso cups."

Isa blinked.

Did that just happen?

That giant was the same man she'd seen mount a bike outside The Drake's Horn earlier.

Isa ran to the door, locked it, and scooted back behind the counter, dropping to her knees. Then lowering the rest of her body to the floor, she put her cheek to the gummy, dirty tile. Seeing plastic forks scattered on the floor beneath the counter, she counted them. Eight times. Felt like the old days hiding in her closet counting dust bunnies along the baseboards.

She groaned and thought about getting up. But that's when the wobbling breaths started followed by a sharp pain in her forehead. Her chest contracted.

But she fought back the waterworks. She was a real cop now.

CHAPTER 8

At 2:30 a.m., and back in her new apartment, Isa gave up on sleep. It could have been the cheap mattress on the floor, or the pressure of a couple of unpacked boxes, but in truth, it was probably images of the giant with a gun to her head in her pretend entrepreneurial start-up. Was she cut out for undercover work so close to Albuquerque's drug scene? If the encounter with the snake face was an indication of what would be coming through the door of her faux coffee and bakery bar, then she was going to have to carry her Glock 24-7.

She made a decaf latte and made her way to the balcony, such as it was—the terrace was hardly wide enough for a chair. She'd found the studio flat on Albuquerque's West Mesa, a good fifteen minutes from downtown. But it was affordable, offered a short-term lease, and had mountain views. She gazed at the quarter moon in the cloudless sky. Unlike the heavy, humid air back in Houston, a dry but cool breeze kept company with the Albuquerque lights in the valley beneath her. Isa lifted her face to the gentle, rustling air. Welcomed the deep night's affections.

But it was a fleeting peaceful moment. Memories she had tried to forget her entire adult life found her. Again. She could smell her werewolf stepfather's beer breath, hear her brother Angel's curses after a clash with that monster, and visualize the secret world she created in her closet when everything downstairs went into chaos. Isa shut her eyes to block out the past. But she could still hear the creak of her bedroom door followed by her stepfather's whisper, *Where are you, Isabella?*

Eyes flying open, Isa counted a few sparkling buildings in the valley below.

She'd had a few good years, she reminded herself. College had opened a world of new possibilities and eventually, a job she loved. She'd even begun to forgive herself for letting Angel die.

But then came marriage. And with marriage, Mac's secrets and another death, then all the attained ordinance and order slipped through her fingers again. Okay, so her bad memories outweighed the pleasant ones. She would change that, though, once she got a few more things figured out.

Her undercover-coffee-house plans were still viable. That's why she had finally gotten up from India Magic's dirty floor yesterday, and driven to Dollar King, where she purchased a few unusual items.

Isa contemplated the patio rails next. Snake Face had stated he would tell someone she was there. Who? Her eyes widened, recalling the name. She yanked the patio door open. Found her laptop and opened it. Isa googled "El Padrino."

Three hours later, Isa put on her Dollar King purchases of a faux straw beach hat, wanna-be Ray-Ban shades, and an oversized tie-dyed tunic. She hardly recognized herself in the mirror. Forgoing her standard tight pony tail, she let her hair fall loose across the shoulders. She donned the one pair of ragged jeans she owned. Had pulled those rarely worn throwbacks from the bottom of a still-unpacked suitcase. The black flip-flops on her feet were, as a rule, reserved for the shower. But considering her other footgear consisted of either black and navy pumps or athletic shoes, she'd added them to her camouflage. The Glock in her nightstand drawer got moved to the outside pocket of her purse for easy access.

A jolt of confidence accompanied her third cup of joe as Isa drove back to India Magic's neighborhood. Somewhere along the way, her sureness slipped a little, so when she parked and checked the rearview mirror, her disguise looked dumber than ever.

But with the sun rising on an innocuously empty downtown Albuquerque, she decided to at least take the next step. Then, she'd allow herself to quit. *One more,* she told herself. *One more action item.* It would be like getting another numeric column totaled before calling it a day at the office. She could go back to her apartment, or Houston for that matter, if she pushed herself to do one more step to move forward.

She hurried along, the flip-flops reprimanding her of the poor footgear selection. Reaching India Magic, she crossed the street to Tattoo You.

The tat parlor had an adjacent alley that ran the length of it, graffiti covering the walls. She couldn't view the Drake's Horn from inside the alley but figured she could watch her own building and record the comings and goings of unwanted people. Like the giant with a snake on his face and the woman named Sicily he'd been looking for.

Fifteen minutes passed. Isa grew tired of staring at India Magic's glass and duct-tape door and moved to study the images covering the alley walls. Two skulls, one white and one red. Three deep-purple silhouettes of well-endowed, faceless females. One two-digit number, 96, spray-painted in black. Over her head were two side-by-side black spiders, fangs bared. She grimaced. Scooted away from the wall spiders. When the smell of urine hit her nose, she slid back to the sinister insects again.

Great. *But I am a real cop taking one more step.*

Isa pulled the synthetic straw hat down around her ears. Pushed the shades up the bridge of her nose. Settled her shoulder against a spider leg.

She aimed to disappear from anyone's curiosity. Which was something she did well and consistently. Learned that skill when the stepfather arrived. Unlike her brother Angel, who had fought his way through those years while she blended into the closet.

At a rustling noise from behind. Isa whirled.

Nothing but trash scattered around at the back of the alley.

She turned to face India Magic again and checked her watch: 7:02 a.m.

Isa glanced down the alley again, stretching her neck to watch a shadow cross. She pulled her shades down the bridge of her nose to get a clearer view.

"Daughter."

Isa nearly jumped out of her flip-flops, spinning back to come face-to-face with Awena. Goodness, the woman materialized out of nowhere. "I didn't see you." Isa put her hand over her heart.

"Daughter," Awena greeted again.

Isa straightened. Adjusted her hat. "How did you know it was me?"

The corners of Awena's wide mouth dipped in confusion. "I met you yesterday. Remember?"

"Yes, I know, But I—"

"Nice hat."

Isa smoothed her tunic. "You startled me."

The little sage reached into her bag. "I brought the HO." She lifted out what looked like a bottle of essential oil. Isa had seen plenty of those popular little vials. Claire kept a diffuser full of lavender oil blowing serenity into the back office at the HPD. Claimed it calmed her nerves and made the guys agreeable.

Isa fumbled through her purse and pulled out the keys to India Magic's front door. "Here, you go ahead. I'll cover you from here."

Awena put her empty hand on her hip. "It's a two-person job."

"You go do whatever it is you're going to do. I need to stay here." She rattled her keys at Awena. "I'm keeping an eye on the bar down street."

"But he will want you there."

"Who?"

"The sun."

Again with the proverbs. Isa sighed. "Okay, can't you simply sprinkle some of that holy oil around inside over there and call it a day? I'm watching for a man who put a gun to my head yesterday."

Awena stiffened. "Who has done this?"

"A guy from the Drake's Horn, I think. Mistaken identity, but I want to make sure he isn't going to bust in the building again."

"You're afraid." Awena put her HO back in her pouch. Leaned against her cane.

Isa shook her head. "No. I'm not afraid. I'm making sure all appears safe out here."

"You look afraid."

Isa pushed her sunglasses closer to her face. "You can't even see my eyes."

"I feel your fear."

Oh, brother. "Fine. I'll walk you over, but it's best I keep a watch on the street." Isa stepped out of the alley, looked both ways, then started across.

"Tell me about the man with the gun." Awena said, close on Isa's heels.

"He's a giant, and he came in the building. Thought I was someone else and put a gun to my head. I talked him down."

"A giant? Like Goliath?"

"Huge guy."

At the broken glass door, Awena grabbed Isa's elbow. "Every giant is an opportunity for a David."

"Never mind." Isa slipped the key into the deadbolt. Turned the lock. She pushed the door open and the scent of curry welcomed them into the mess.

Awena pushed past her like a horse heading to its barn. Stepping across the broken glass, she positioned herself in the center of the dining room. Studied the ceiling for a few seconds. "Okay." She laid her cane across a table. Rubbed her hands together. "We start."

CHAPTER 9

"El Padrino," Oso called from the door.

He never tired of hearing his title. Lifting his eyes to meet Oso's concerned face in the door, he answered, "I am not done yet."

"Snake wishes to speak with you. *Rapido*. Says it's urgent."

El Padrino looked across the wide game table and made eye contact with his makeshift financial specialist, Juan. He then shifted his focus to Coyote Blanco, the new pup who hadn't yet proved himself. El Padrino nodded. "Five minutes."

Oso closed the door.

Ah, Oso, his loyalist member, so unlike the other two beside him now. Oso had been with him from the beginning, back in their village of discouraged men, disillusioned women, and starving children. His friend had been a ravenous youth then, smaller than the other boys their age. In those days, Oso reminded El Padrino of a bear cub scouring for waste in the night. That's why he'd given his wiry friend the title. Didn't fit physically, but oh, did it describe his friend's disposition. He didn't scavenge garbage cans anymore. He protected El Padrino like a mamma grizzly guarded her cubs.

But at this early hour and with another meeting before noon, he didn't have time to consider the loyalties of his extended family. He needed to get a little problem checked off his list and the two financial geniuses with him now were giving him a headache.

"Explain to me again," he said, putting his forearms against the edge of the table and making a temple with his index fingers. "How I find myself in this situation." His temperature hadn't risen high enough to make his blood boil—yet—but could if this flickering matchstick wasn't snuffed out. Trivial flames were a risk to singe the deal he planned to present to Miguel Lopez, the leader of his competition and the oversized La Liga cartel.

As a rule, El Padrino let his wife and his financial advisors take care of details. Delegating finances to professionals made him unique in the cartel world. It gave El Padrino more of a business image than the mob-boss persona the ruthless Miguel Lopez carried. But with an IRS audit looming, word could get around and make him look like he didn't take care of business properly. To form the powerful alliance he dreamed of, he would need to prove his business savvy unquestionable. He needed to put the IRS audit to bed as soon as possible.

El Padrino's newest advisor, Jay Hernandez, had been with him just shy of six months and was a crapshoot. The newcomer could be a miracle or a misfortune—El Padrino had yet to decide. That's why he'd dubbed the new man Coyote, the trustless dog.

Juan tucked his hands beneath the table. Not a posture of confidence. The sweat beads gathering across his forehead proved it. But Coyote—the wild card in this new game of chance—leaned back in his chair, crossed his arms with cocky arrogance.

"It's a small thing," Juan claimed, leaning in closer but beneath El Padrino's eye level. "It is customary for the American IRS to audit small businesses, Señor." Juan's sweat beads multiplied.

El Padrino looked at Coyote.

"No one *I've* worked for has ever drawn an audit. Something's suspicious. They've been tipped off, and let me tell you, with one single wrong entry in your books, the alarms are gonna blow." Coyote smirked. "This is big, and you need big help."

Juan's head wagged back and forth like a bobble doll.

El Padrino leaned back in his chair. "But this accountant you promised hasn't shown up yet. I question the validity of your connections, Coyote."

"She will show."

Coyote's grit rivaled that of his best men. El Padrino liked confidence, but something about Coyote's coolness annoyed him.

The new white dog continued, "She needs big money, and that puts her and us in a beautiful relationship."

El Padrino pushed down the urge to show this fledgling member where he belonged in the pack. *Coyote Blanco is not part of "us" yet.* The American Ponzi schemer would need to prove himself.

"We don't need her," Juan cut in, his voice unsteady.

Coyote leaned forward, met Padrino's stare head on. "Not just anyone can cook the books. My accountant is a master chef, an expert at hiding dollars. Like I said, I've seen her work."

"Then where is your master chef?" El Padrino asked, flipping a coaster on the table.

"She'll show." Coyote rested on his elbows and intertwined his fingers. "I'll make it happen."

"You've promised her for two days. Tell me, how do I know she is real? Maybe you stall, waiting on the Feds to swoop in and catch El Padrino."

Coyote cocked his head to one side. "And why would I want that?"

"Perhaps to take over my empire." El Padrino chuckled at the impossibility.

Coyote patted his chest. "I'm here to work for you. The rest of my crew went digital with a hacker. I'm with you all the way, and my book cooker will be too. She's from outside the US and held up at a border, that's all. It's safer using a nonresident."

"El Padrino," Juan pleaded. "A new accountant will not know our ways. A woman is not a good idea."

"Unless she's greedy," Coyote quipped. "I wonder if your guy here," he pointed at Juan. "isn't up to something. Why doesn't he want my professional to help you, Padre?"

"Shut up," Juan shot back. "You have a big mouth."

"Maybe you don't want my girl coming in because she'll blow your little racket, Juan." Coyote looked at the nails on both hands like accusing Juan of treason was no skin off his nose. "Maybe you're a snitch for the Feds and want the IRS to find your planted evidence."

Juan sprang to his feet, eyes pleading with El Padrino. "You going to let this gringo talk to me like that?"

El Padrino drummed his fingers on the table. "This is a grave accusation, Coyote."

"Just saying." He tilted his head, eyed Juan. "Something doesn't smell right, and Juan's the only one you've let handle your finances so far. Why has the IRS suddenly come calling?"

The door cracked opened and Oso stuck his head in. "Snake, El Padrino."

El Padrino nodded. "Send him in." He scowled at Juan. "You are dismissed, but you should not go far."

Juan's lower jaw went slack.

Coyote rose from his chair, his chest swelling more like a lion than the hungry half-bred he was.

"Not you." Padrino pointed at Coyote. "Sit."

Of course, he obeyed.

Juan disappeared out the door.

Nodding to Oso, El Padrino said, "Follow him, and you will know what it is you should do."

Oso nodded, and after stepping aside to let Snake enter, he exited behind Juan.

El Padrino nodded at Snake. The brother had little in the way of brains but possessed many other assets, allegiance being his greatest. The giant had come to him lost, in need of acceptance, two years earlier. El Padrino had provided by taking Snake into his own home.

He checked his watch. "You worked late into the night, Snake, and here you are at this early hour. What have I done to deserve such loyal effort?" It was a rhetorical question. One he asked subjects often. His best men knew the answer well, and Snake repeated the line loud and clear so Coyote could hear. "You have given me the chance to live, El Padrino, and live well."

"Thank you," he said, glancing to Coyote. "What is this urgency so early in the morning?"

"She is back."

"She?" El Padrino tilted his head. "The woman you met yesterday? The auditor who claims she owns our building?"

"Yes."

"Bring her to me."

He turned to obey.

"Take Coyote with you."

Snake looked from El Padrino to Coyote and back.

El Padrino motioned for Coyote to follow orders.

But the dog, smooth as his stone face, said, "I told you, Padre, I'm high finance. Kidnapping is not my MO."

El Padrino sucked in his breath and closed his eyes. Counted down from five to one, then allowed himself a little laugh. "I wish to borrow her for a little while, not long, so put away your conscience. You won't be needing it." The corners of his mouth lifted in a generous smile. "Because when you work with El Padrino, I decide what is right and wrong."

Coyote got to his feet. "Let's go see what the little woman is up to, then."

This pup would not be so hard to tame. Not if El Padrino put him on a short chain.

CHAPTER 10

The pale light filtering through India Magic's dirty windows seemed to speak of descending darkness rather than a dawning new day. In the past twenty-four hours, she'd come face-to-face with the abandoned restaurant Mac had bought for no apparent reason, met a pushy little shaman who insisted the building hosted a demon, and had a gun put to her head by a giant with a snake on his face. If you added the lack of sleep, then there were not a lot of plusses to help uplift her less-than-sunny disposition.

Isa stayed near the front door to keep an eye out for giants. She left the door unlocked because something about bolting herself in with an unpredictable exorcist and supposed provoked demon felt unwise.

If there was a demon.

Mostly, she wanted to pick Awena's brain about the previous owners and find out how Mac had come to buy this building. But if she got a free demon extraction out of the deal, then, what the heck. Nothing about her life had been normal and by now, she should be used to out-of-the-ordinary encounters.

Awena circled the dining area, eyeing the ceiling and peeking beneath tables. "It's not in here," she whispered. She picked her way across the rubble to the counter.

"No demon?" Isa asked loud enough to let Awena—and whatever else might be listening—know this was her preference. "Good. I'm going to keep an eye on things from across the street. You ready to go now?"

"No. It is in this building. But not in *here*." Awena got to the counter and looked beneath the lip. Shook her head. Next, she ran her hand across the top then studied her index finger closely. Again with the head shake. She moved behind the counter. "Oh, my."

The flesh on Isa's arms quivered like the time she watched that horror movie with the ax-wielding psycho. *There are no such things as demons. There are no such things as demons.*

"What are you 'Oh my-ing' about over there?" she asked, her neck already turning her head away from whatever Awena found.

"What a mess." Awena made a *tisk* sound. "I am dishonored to say I worked here."

Inside, Isa wanted to scream. "Let's go, Awena. I'll clean this up later."

"In there." Awena pointed to the door that led to the kitchen. "It's got to be in there."

Isa pulled away from the front door. Patted at her purse. Felt the outline of the Glock's handle in the outer pocket.

Awena frowned. "You won't need that."

Isa raised her hands in innocence. "Need what?"

"The gun."

"Who said I had a gun?"

Awena rolled her eyes. "You can't shoot a spirit."

"I don't know what you're talking about."

"The gun in the pocket on your purse. I got all the power we need, right here." The old woman fished around in her bag and pulled out a tiny leather book the size of her palm. She flipped a few pages.

A sorcerer's guide? Her odds were better with a gun.

"Ah, here," Awena said putting the tattered book out to arm's length. She squinted. "Exodus forty, verse nine."

Isa's chin dropped. "The Bible?"

Awena peered over her book. "What else would it be?"

Isa pulled at her cheeks. "This is so ... so ... unreal."

"It is real. It is right here." She cleared her throat, looked at her book. "Then you shall take the anointing oil and anoint the tabernacle and all that is in it, and consecrate it and all its furniture, so that it may become holy." Awena laid the Bible on the counter. "We anoint." Out came the essential oil.

"Now wait a minute." Isa put her palm against the gun again. "I'm not saying I believe all of this, but what will a demon do when you throw oil on it? Does it melt like the wicked witch, or does it dart out of here like a banshee? Do I get a mop, or do I stand clear?"

Awena chuckled. "Stand clear." She looked back to her Bible. "We do not see with our eyes. We trust with our hearts."

Isa tilted her head sideways. "Then, how did you ..." She pushed the brim of her hat back. "How did you see this spirit yesterday?"

Awena poured the oil into her palm. "With the eyes of my heart." She ran her hand down the center of the kitchen door and stepped back.

Okay, Isa should have seen this coming yesterday. She should have recognized delusion in the woman the moment they met.

Awena put more oil in her hand and moved it perpendicular across the first streak. She stepped back and examined her oily cross. "That's it," she uttered. "In the name of the sun, we declare this coffee shop clean, uncontaminated by evil."

Standing as still as a mannequin, Isa glanced from one side of the room to another. Nothing had changed. Except the light of day now filled their space.

"We must be in agreement." Awena looked back at Isa. "Say amen."

Isa pulled in a shallow breath, shot out a quick, "Amen."

Awena disappeared behind the kitchen door.

"We done?"

Pots rattled, then Awena let out an, "Oh." More rattling. "Oh, my."

Isa took a step toward the counter. "What is it?" She stopped. Did she really want to know what *it* was?

"Come," Awena commanded.

Isa glanced back at the unlocked front door, then scooted around the counter. Dreading more hocus pocus, she pressed her hand to the oily cross and pushed the door open nice and slow.

The old woman pointed at the dented metal cabinet. The one Isa pegged as a pantry but hadn't bothered to open yesterday. "What?" she lifted her palms. "It's in the cabinet?"

"He guards this cabinet. There is something of value there."

Isa gulped. Why hadn't she bothered to look inside when she was standing in this spot yesterday? But then, maybe she should be glad she hadn't.

Awena reached out. Wrapped her fingers around the pitted stainless-steel handle on one of the cabinet's dented double doors.

Like she watched a scene from *Friday the 13th*, Isa wanted to scream *don't open that door*, but counted the dents instead. There were six small dents, four medium sized dimples, and one impression the size of a human head.

Awena tugged at the door.

Metal screeched.

Isa stiffened.

The door didn't budge.

Giving Isa a quick glance, Awena said, "You try."

There was no logic in fearing something that didn't exist. But logic was nowhere to be found at the moment.

"No way." She stepped behind the woman, who was a good two inches shorter.

Awena reached for the cabinet again.

Isa clinched her eye lids shut. Heard the door rattle and heard Awena suck in a breath. "Oh, my."

Isa opened one eye.

Curry. She opened the other eye. Saffron. Shelves of curry and saffron and coriander. A disarray of plastic bottles with cinnamon and ginger, too. The pent-up air in her chest expelled through her puckered-up lips. "It is just a pantry." And just a couple of fools making like exorcists.

Something creaked.

Uh-oh.

Swooshed.

Good grief. Someone or thing was near the front door. The unlocked front door.

The sound of glass crunching beneath a heavy foot let her know a person or spirit snooped around in the dining room. Déjà vu.

Neither woman moved.

"She's not here." The voice speaking from the dining room belonged to a man.

Isa let out some air. It didn't sound like the snake-faced giant.

"Try the kitchen."

She sucked the air back into her lungs. That voice belonged to the giant.

Awena glanced up at Isa then reached for the kitchen door.

Isa pulled at her arm. "I think there's a back door," she whispered.

Awena didn't pick up on Isa's social cue to keep her voice down. She blurted, "I know this. I worked here, remember?"

Cover blown.

Squish, squish went the rubber soles quickly across the sticky dining-room floor, and the freshly oiled kitchen door flew open.

Snake Face. Isa could see the outline of his gun handle beneath his T-shirt. He had a friend, too—a tall but slender one. This guy had a head full of shaggy, sand-colored hair, several days' growth of a dark beard, and one visible tattoo on his forearm—a sword with orange and red flames jutting from the blade.

Isa fixated on the tattoo, counting tense seconds.

Four passed, before the guy with the sword tat gestured at Isa. "A scrawny, throwback hippy?" He pointed at Awena. "An old homeless woman?" His laugh came straight from his belly. "Are you kidding? One of these is the menacing auditor?"

CALCULATED RISK

The humorous expression on his face should have relieved some of the pressure rising in Isa's chest.

But no.

His insults awakened her dragon.

CHAPTER 11

Isa narrowed her eyes and lowered her chin. "Excuse me, but you're trespassing on private property," she told the shaggy-headed guy standing next to Snake Face. What a jerk.

Snake Face's friend chuckled again. "The boho chick's got some feist." Then he gave her one revolting look up and down- the body, neglecting the dirty glance his giant gave him.

Isa crossed her arms.

"That one." The giant lifted his T-shirt and pulled his gun out. Pointed it at Isa. "The one with the gun in her purse. Outside pocket. She's the auditor who says she owns the place."

Isa's shoulders slumped. So much for amateur disguises and weapon concealment. Her undercover prowess needed some sharpening.

The new and insulting guy had his hand in the side pocket of Isa's purse before she could blink. He slipped the gun out and shoved it in his own pants. "It was obvious, Babe. We could see the outline."

Awena wagged her finger at Isa. "I knew you shouldn't have a gun."

Seriously, this couldn't be happening. Two thugs and a nagging little woman.

The giant, Snake Face, wiggled his gun at Isa. "You come with us."

"That is not happening." Isa pressed her heels to the floor.

"No. Not happening," Awena echoed, crossing her arms, too.

The Snake Face took a step for Isa, but his friend put his sword arm out. "Wait. Let me persuade the lady."

"These ladies," Awena piped in. "Anywhere she go, I go."

Snake Face growled but stayed put.

The new guy moved in close to Isa. Which made her blood pump wild, because he had to be a good eight inches taller and looked to be solid, hard-core muscle. Could she take him with a jiujitsu kick? Her right foot inched back.

"The owner of the Drake's Horn would like to speak with you about an issue with this building. My friend and I have been sent to escort you to him." He grinned then winked. "My pleasure, of course."

Isa threw her hands up. Like his condescending wink and patronizing words would have any effect on her.

Awena inched closer to Isa. "She not go anywhere without me."

"Fine by me." The insulter shrugged. "You can come, too."

The giant objected to his friend's generosity. "But the boss said bring the auditor who thinks she owns the building."

"And what is this owner of the Drake's Horn's name?" Isa interrupted, slipping her arm through Awena's and pulling the woman closer to her side.

The two gangsters exchanged glances, but it was Snake Face, the giant, who answered, and he did so with a tone that might as well have been announcing royalty. "El Padrino."

She already knew the owner's title—her earlier research had revealed that much. This could be the opportunity she'd imagined when she'd decided to come to Albuquerque and penetrate the drug industry. Yep, the doors were opening, but at the sound of his name, her knees nearly buckled anyway.

CHAPTER 12

El Padrino waited in the back room for his macchiato. Most mornings, he drank his coffee black and at home with his wife. But with a dollop of steamed milk on top, this morning's fix would feel like dessert—a special reward he allowed himself after every extermination. Not that he ever got his hands dirty. He hadn't pulled a trigger or shoved a knife in years. He sent his loyal men like God sent angels— to do his bidding.

Carlos, another of his loyal employees, stuck his head in the door. "El Padrino, they've brought her."

Carlos's small frame fooled most. He was a master with a knife.

El Padrino asked, "Have you word from Oso?"

The nod Carlos gave him told him all he needed to know.

"Good then. And my coffee?"

Carols glanced behind him, rattled off a little Spanish to another trusted family member. "He says a couple of minutes. We were out of cream."

El Padrino went to the table, rolled out a chair and wiped the seat down with his handkerchief. The one his mother embroidered his initials on. A reminder of where he'd come from and how far his conscience had exceeded the tiny thoughts of his spiritually abusive mother in rural Mexico.

He motioned at Oso. "Send her in."

Snake entered first, followed by the woman—a Latina who looked like she should be standing on a beach and not at the edge of the Chihuahuan Desierto. Coyote came in behind the woman, and the nonchalant smirk on his face forced El Padrino to consider teaching this newcomer a few additional rules. Carlos shadowed the three with El Padrino's macchiato, which made the unremarkable rank and file before him more palatable.

"Please sit down." El Padrino motioned across the table and the three rolled-out chairs. The woman examined the room with eyes wide and blinking. Her nerves were right where he wanted them. He watched her, knowing she felt his scrutiny.

"Thank you for coming." El Padrino nodded, showing her the respect she needed to sense.

Subjects waffling between fear and respect were subjects one could control.

Once in her chair, the woman put her hands under the security of the table. A good sign.

"Hey, can I get one of those?" Coyote's whining disrupted his thoughts. El Padrino shifted his gaze to the white dog.

"The coffee. Smells good." Coyote rubbed his hands together. "I don't usually work this early, and I could use a cup."

This pup would need obedience training. "Get our guests a cup of coffee, Snake," El Padrino said, his eyes fixated on Coyote.

Snake was on his feet and at the door, when Coyote yipped, "I'll have what the Padre is having."

Snake stopped in the doorway but didn't turn around.

"You don't know what you're asking for." El Padrino sipped at his hot brew. "This cup is reserved for special favors."

"What kind of favors?"

Yipping, yipping. Coyote Blanco didn't know how to sit dutifully and wait upon his master. "You shall soon see." El Padrino leaned back in his chair, his macchiato perched near his chin. "Coyote will take his black." He nodded at Snake and the large man closed the door behind him.

But the girl shifted in her chair, suspicious and uneasy. Determining who was in charge and who was not.

El Padrino smiled at her. "Tell me your name."

"Tell me yours," she shot back.

Ah, she tried to sound brave and strong. But he'd unnerved her and wanted to keep her that way until she learned what most of his closest friends discovered—El Padrino could be their best ally. "*Me llamo es El Padrino.*"

"The Godfather." Her gaze dropped to the table. Then she looked up and met his with courage flashing. "That's a title, not a name, and you cannot force me here without giving me direct answers."

Direct answers? Interesting that she pursued something more than an easy way out. This was not someone Snake had simply pulled out of his empty building. She had an agenda and a reason to be there.

"Do you speak Spanish?" He'd fine-tuned the art of being *indirect*. It kept those around him guessing.

"I speak enough," she said, glancing to see if Coyote observed her boldness.

"Then you will understand me when I say, '*Estoy a cargo.*' And because I am the one in charge of this meeting, I will not proceed until I know to whom I speak."

It took her a second too long to consider his statement.

"Isa," she finally answered, with a raise of her chin. "Isadora Padilla."

She lied. Her eyes said so. Not a problem. He'd play along. "I knew we would understand each other. Now, Isa, there seems to be confusion about the building you have visited the last two days."

Snake entered again with two paper coffee cups.

"Leave them, then leave us."

Ever obedient, Snake placed the cups on the table and shut the door behind him.

Coyote appeared to like being on the inside, now being the only employee in the room. His chest puffed out ever so slightly when he grabbed one of the cups.

"Please, drink," El Padrino gestured to Isa.

She ignored his offering but said, "I own that building. There's no confusion on my part."

"Oh, you see, we do have a dispute. I've been in a rent-with-purchase contract with India Magic's owner, a man from India who accepted my down payment and one year's rent up front." He took another sip of coffee so that could sink in. "I'm to send him another substantial payment at the end of one year."

Puzzlement set her brows low over her eyes. "But I have the deed," she said.

"May I see it?"

Her brows shot back up. "May I see your contract?"

Her quick reaction showed grit, naïve as it was. His pulse quickened ever so slightly as she, oblivious to what she initiated, challenged him.

"Of course." He licked at his mustache, relishing the aftertaste of coffee and cream and control. "I'll have it sent to you later today. Now, when can I see your deed?"

She shot a glance at Coyote, clearly checking his temperature. Smart. Being outnumbered, she should most definitely proceed with caution.

"I don't have it with me."

And Coyote—he'd hardened his mask, but something about the way he watched her didn't set well. His stare showed the faintest concern for the prey climbing her way into El Padrino's web.

He looked back to this Isa. "Where is your deed? We will send for it."

"It's not here ... not in Albuquerque." Her shifting gaze betrayed her. She made up lies on the spot.

He nestled back into his game table chair, enjoying this human sport. "Is there someone who can email you a copy?"

"No." She opened her mouth to add a lie or two but must have decided against it.

No woman taken against her will would engage this way, unless—he smiled more to himself than to her.

"Now we have a dispute because I have a contract on file and you, you have nothing to prove ownership. I will have to ask you to refrain from entering my building until you can offer me documented proof that the establishment in question is yours."

The woman's lips parted, but her by-the-seat-of-her-pants plan wasn't formulating fast enough.

Oh, but his blueprint to IRS liberty was coming together quite nicely. He drained his coffee cup, enjoying the surge of anticipation. "If you actually have the documented proof, that is. Otherwise, we'll consider some alternatives."

"Okay, Padre." Coyote Blanco slapped the table. "Looks like she's willing to cooperate. I'll make sure she doesn't come around again. Come on," he said, motioning to her. "I'll escort you out."

"That is the second time you've called me Padre." El Padrino leveled his eyes on Coyote. "It is disrespectful."

"Understood," Coyote countered, letting his hardened mask melt into a carefree smirk. "But you've never called me by my name, and that's okay." He shrugged. "No offense. But for the record again, it's Jay Hernandez."

El Padrino decided to temporarily ignore the yapping fool beside him. He turned back to Isa. "My associate has informed me that you have accounting experience. Is this true?"

She leaned forward, alarm working the magic he intended. "I ... I used to be an accountant." Her words came much too quickly. "But not anymore. I'm opening a coffee shop."

"I see."

She entered the trap, so unsuspecting—like an innocent bird pecking at a deceptive line of seed.

He continued. "Perhaps we have common ground. I would enjoy having a coffee shop near my bar. You see, I do not drink alcohol." He smiled at the woman. "It will be my pleasure to purchase coffee from you. We'll create a partnership."

The woman straightened, checking to see if the Coyote would wag his tail for her again.

But Coyote looked to be a baffled as she was.

She spoke up. "Are you saying you'll give up your rental agreement, so I can sell you coffee?"

CALCULATED RISK

"We can make an arrangement, yes." He sat his empty cup on the table, taking time to draw out the expectation of an offer. One should never be too keen to make quick proposals. "I need an accountant."

Coyote straightened in this chair.

CHAPTER 13

Isa's mind considered the possibilities while her insides twisted with anxiety.

This was the kind of opportunity the undercover investigators back at HPD dreamed of. How often does a detective get a one-on-one with the leader of a drug cartel?

But ... but.

There was no data to analyze. She couldn't, no, *wouldn't* simply feel her way through whatever he was about to propose. She needed a brake pedal to push and an analytic chart to consider.

"What type of accounting have you done?" the drug lord asked.

The man called Coyote shook his head in the faintest manner. She barely caught it, but felt he signaled something. It was anyone's guess who that gesture was for.

"Hmmm?" El Padrino pushed. "Are you a CPA?"

El Padrino's eyes were wide and his smile a little too plastic. Isa studied spreadsheets for answers, not faces. Was she reading him correctly? The kink in her gut squeezed tighter, but she nodded.

"El Padrino—" Coyote broke in.

El Padrino held up a hand to stop him, never taking his eyes off Isa. "A CPA with auditing experience. Excellent. What have you audited in the past?"

An unnerving job interview ... with a drug lord. Not only was it giving her major stomach pains, but it all seemed too opportune—too coincidental.

CALCULATED RISK

Somehow, she managed to have a few words form. "I've subcontracted with several agencies. Primarily bank audits."

"Very impressive." El Padrino licked at his lips. "I happen to be facing an audit with the Drake's Horn and we need an expert to oversee ..." he hesitated, glancing at Coyote, "things."

Beneath the table, Isa rubbed the top of her thighs with sweaty palms. "Maybe I could take a look." *Good, good, no commitments, keep exploring, gathering facts.* "But first, I'd like to see your rent-to-own contract on the India Magic building."

He almost seemed pleased that she wanted to negotiate. "Tell me, my new business neighbor, are you married?"

She winced at that one. "What difference does that make?" Perhaps she should say yes, as part of her cover, but then she'd have to come up with a name, and—

"I simply wondered if I should be dealing with your man. Men understand each other when it comes to business. Right, Coyote?"

Coyote perked up a little. "That's right. Where's your husband?"

"I am not married. I do not have a *man*, and I can handle this myself. Can I see the contract?"

The drug lord overlooked her growing irritation. "I wonder if you have family we might consult with?"

Okay, the guy was tiptoeing into some inner dragon-stirring territory now. She'd been making it on her own all her life and didn't need some out-of-the-ditches-of-society scumbag insinuating she couldn't handle a little real estate discussion. The pain-inducing coil in her belly unraveled and the dragon sat up. "Do you have a problem dealing with me? Like I said, I, me, myself, own that building down the street." She pointed in India Magic's direction. "I am the person you deal with."

El Padrino lifted his hands in surrender. "Okay, okay."

Coyote slumped in his chair.

Placing his palms back on the table, El Padrino said, "You must remember that I know nothing about you, and I am about to show you my personal papers, ask you to work with me, and make you an incredible offer in partnership. Being a businessman, I make sure there are not others I'll need to deal with."

She knew she shouldn't say it. But she was going to say it anyway. With an angry inferno burning her insides, she was at the edge of no return. She'd come to Albuquerque for answers. A man full of them sat before her. *Three, two, one.* "I just moved here. I am alone. And I am able to make my own choices."

"She's not alone," Coyote said, shaking his head.

El Padrino ignored him. "All right, Accountant. Here is what I am willing to do. For one or maybe two weeks you will prepare my books for an audit, and I will rip up my rental contract when your work is finished."

"Wait," Coyote broke in. "I have someone in the wings."

El Padrino chuckled. "Coyote is noisy, but valuable. He has worked with large-scale businesses like mine that know how to cut through legal red tape. You understand what I mean when I say red tape, correct?"

Isa pursed her lips but nodded.

"Coyote will oversee your project."

She told herself to keep all doors open and options on the table. Keep him guessing and making offers. "I didn't say I'd work for you. I said *maybe* I could take a look at your books after I see the legitimate rent-with-option contract. A lot hinges on the contract."

"Really?" El Padrino leaned across his coffee cup and getting closer. "Why is that?"

"Fraud."

Nodding methodically, El Padrino rolled that statement around in his head. She'd hit a nerve.

"You don't believe what I am telling you?"

"Third party real estate contracts can cover a lot of dirty money."

"That's enough." Coyote stood. "I'll escort her out and see to it she's no longer a problem."

Motioning at Jay, El Padrino told him to sit. "I am intrigued." He nodded at Isa. "Please continue and explain what you mean."

"It's quite simple, really." Element—she was in hers, bigtime. "Hypothetically, you could own the India Magic building, but use a third-party you trust as the lessor. The funds you've paid as the lessee would go back into your own pocket, looking like you are spending money on rent when in reality you are covering a money trail."

"Hypothetically?"

She nodded, feeling more confident by the second. "Hypothetically."

"Fascinating. You are obviously qualified for the job we need. You will start today." He tapped the table. "See, Coyote, how things have a way of working out? And you were so worried."

Coyote threw his hands in the air. "What am I supposed to do with *my* connection now?"

Isa cleared her throat. "My scenario was hypothetical, and I'm not helping you or anybody that isn't AML compliant." She held her breath, hoping she hadn't taken the ruse too far.

"What is AML?" El Padrino looked at Coyote. "Do you know AML?"

But it was Isa who answered. "Anti-Money Laundering. Regulations used to prevent international fraud."

"Your knowledge is vast. Give me your address, and we'll have some personal items picked up."

"I'm not interested in this deal." She started to stand, hoping like heck she'd shaken him up with her expertise and would soon have him eating out of her hand. "But you can come by for coffee anytime."

The corners of his plastic smile leveled into a straight line. "I do not offer you an option. This is what will happen."

Dropping back into her game-table chair, the truth of what he implied dawned. "I ... I don't think I like what you're saying."

"I am sorry you have misunderstood some of the things we are discussing. Let me speak more clearly. You and I are entering into an employment agreement. I will keep my end of the arrangement and rip up my contract on the India Magic building as payment for your services."

"I don't think so," she said, her stomach recoiling again.

His brows were up, looking like he didn't understand her opposition. "Look at this as your duty—part of the rapid response team to a neighbor in crisis. And of course, we'll host you and cover expenses. I'll take care of your every need while you're—" he cleared his throat—"while you are helping with this crisis. Now, your address? We'll need to get a few of your things."

"This isn't a good plan." Coyote pointed at the door. "She has another woman with her." He shook the pointing finger. "Out there in the bar."

El Padrino gave Isa a side glance that said she'd already betrayed him. "Who is this woman that accompanies you? You said you were alone."

"A—"

Coyote cut her off. "Her mother."

"She's not my mother," Isa snapped. The last ... the very last ... the absolute last thing she wanted to do was get Awena involved in this going-downhill-fast predicament.

"She called you 'Daughter,' didn't she?" Coyote's eyes were bugging out of his head.

"Stop." She fisted both hands on the table. "I just met this woman. I am not her daughter, and I'm not going to oversee any audit."

El Padrino's smile returned, and behind it, she could see he carefully gauged this latest development.

Isa tightened her lips to try and sound calm. "She calls me daughter, but that doesn't mean anything. She wandered into *my* building down the street while I was there. She said she used to work at the restaurant."

"Your friend will come, as well. I cannot have loose ends in the neighborhood." He rubbed his hands together. "Oso," he said in a loud voice. "Is Oso back?"

Coyote glared at Isa, and Isa glared back before speaking through clenched teeth. "She's an old woman with dementia."

"Oso," El Padrino called again, "Bring me the gift."

CHAPTER 14

El Padrino smiled in satisfaction. The little accountant had no idea that by demonstrating a protective nature, she had given him a tool he could use against her. Little heroes were the easiest to blackmail.

"Oso!"

Coyote scrambled to his feet, his composure evaporating like mist in the heat. "We're taking two women on? Not a good idea. They'll expose us. What ... what if the old woman has family near?" He gestured at Isa. "What if she is lying?"

El Padrino stood. Ignored Coyote. Waited for Oso.

Coyote tried another tactic. "This is abrupt. We need time to discuss it."

Oso entered with a large silver tray, covered by a caterer's stainless-steel dome.

"Oh, no," Coyote whispered, proving he was familiar with deadly games. His previously red face drained of all color.

He knew Isa was confused. She looked from the tray to Coyote and back again, her brown eyes large with question.

El Padrino loved winning.

"Juan won't be joining you, Coyote." He nodded to Isa. "Juan was our last auditor, and he was unable to achieve his objective." He nodded at Oso.

"That isn't ... what I think?" Coyote backed up, uneasy.

Every orifice on Isa's face opened wide as she pushed herself up off her seat. He wished he had a slow-motion camera on hand. He'd like to replay that scene.

Oso lifted the dome.

Coyote cursed.

Isa gasped.

On the tray, a saturated-with-fresh-blood shirt.

Coyote dropped his head back saying, "Juan's shirt."

"Juan won't be needing it any longer," El Padrino stated in a flat tone.

Isa tugged at her hat.

El Padrino watched it float to the floor. All color slipped from Isa's face before her forehead landed on the table next to the untouched cup of coffee. Clearly unconscious now, she slid out of the chair and hit the floor. El Padrino shook his head, hoping she hadn't bruised anything on the way down.

"Point made," he said to Oso, who then put the dome back over the shirt.

Coyote cursed again.

The bloody message had made a most excellent point, indeed.

CHAPTER 15

Kidnapped—hooded, tied, and put in a car, with barely any memory of it. She laid her head back against the seat, seeing nothing but passing rays of light and shadows as they drove.

She should have fought—kicked, screamed, dove for ... what ... a weapon? Where was her Glock?

She patted the seat around in search of her purse. Nothing.

When ... when did she lose her gun? Before the bloodied shirt on a plate? She was unsure of several details and needed to throw up to get her stomach to settle down.

Awena. *No, no, no.* Had they taken Awena? Or maybe ... *oh God, please* ... maybe El Padrino let her go.

What a mess she'd made of her noble intensions.

She hated that she'd fainted.

She should have been clever—made a deal so they would let Awena go.

She sucked in oxygen along with some of the hood's black fabric and started to count, getting her equilibrium back in place.

One, one hundred.

An idea emerged as the nausea waned.

She could count minutes as they drove, then compute the time into miles.

Two, one hundred.

Awena. Why hadn't she refused to let the woman accompany her into The Drake's Horn? Stupid move.

CALCULATED RISK

Three, one hundred.

Isa pushed her flip-flop into the front passenger seat.

The guy in that seat said something incredibly rude in Spanish and laughter erupted.

She kicked it. *"Donde es la mujer vieja?"*

"The old woman is fine, Chica. Do not worry about her."

She started to count again. Any forensic evidence, even calculated time distance, she would use on a witness stand.

One, one hundred.

If she lived to be on a witness stand.

But she couldn't get Awena out of her mind. "What happened to the old woman who was with me?" A cold sweat rippled across her forehead. She might explode if she didn't get this hood off and lay eyes on innocent Awena.

"You'll see your crazy old lady." The guy snickered.

Okay—so they had Awena. Or, could the lug in the front seat be suggesting they planned to return Isa to Albuquerque?

She fell back in her seat, realizing that bound and hooded and in a fast-moving car, she could do little. Isa sucked in more air and fabric and resumed counting. When she reached 3,725 the car slowed, beginning up an incline and easing through ruts in a road. They were in the mountains, which still didn't tell her much. Albuquerque was surrounded by mountain ranges. But considering 3,725 meant they'd been driving for about sixty minutes, she figured they entered the Sandia Mountains far north of Albuquerque somewhere outside of Santa Fe.

Another 780 counts and the car stopped. The goons in the front seat exchanged some Spanish, and then her door opened. She was told to get out of the car.

She didn't budge. She didn't know what else to do except resist.

But she was no match for the man with taut muscles who reached and pulled her from the car.

Her loud protest went unanswered as he swung her over his broad shoulder.

"Hey. I can walk, you imbecile," she said trying to wiggle out of his grip.

He didn't respond, but she heard doors open and shut and felt him strain when he started up a staircase.

"You better be taking me to see my friend," she warned. "Or you will be sorry."

Another door opened and closed. Voices echoed from somewhere beyond the room they'd obviously entered. The carrier sat her on her feet.

What's next? It didn't matter. She would find Awena, and they'd walk back to Albuquerque if they had to. And then, she would figure what Mac had in mind when he got involved with a drug lord outside his jurisdiction.

The man who'd carried her in untied the hood and pulled it from her head.

Bright light slammed her face, and she stepped back. The sun streaming through windows behind this guy created the look of a radiant saint. Until today, Isa had put spiritual matters far behind her. But with Awena's exorcism and subsequent kidnapping, she hoped the distant God who'd ignored her own childish cries for help and refused to protect Angel from the teen drug scene would choose to watch after Awena.

God, if you're out there ... Awena.

"Hello? You with me?" Her carrier snapped his fingers in her face.

Coyote.

He reached behind her and that's when she saw the knife in his hand.

Isa hopped out of his reach, losing balance.

"Be still," he snapped. He grabbed her elbow to keep her upright. With one smooth pull of the knife, he cut the plastic ties at her wrists. Then, with little effort, he pulled her towards the bed.

"No," she stated and planted both feet on the floor. Threw a fist and aimed at his chin.

He ducked.

Her effort bounced off his upper arm.

Coyote's grin widened. "I misjudged your strength." He folded the knife, slid it into his front pocket. "Just sit. I want to talk."

Isa kicked off her flip-flops, took the jiujitsu defense stance with one foot back and palms out front. "No."

"It's a little late for a fight." He chuckled. "You're locked away in El Padrino's fortress now, Accountant." He dragged a wooden armchair from across the room. Put it next to the bed.

Isa held her position. She could take him. One kick to the chest and he would hit the wall and give her the chance to get out the door.

As if he read her thoughts and wasn't the least impressed, he said, "Won't do you any good to make a run for it. The boss has a guard at the door. Let's say you get past him. There's two more down the hall. After that? There's a squadron of gun-toting druggies surrounding this compound. You're going to have to deal with me, like it or not." He plopped down in the chair.

Feet still firmly in place, Isa did a quick survey of the surroundings. The room hosted elaborate New Mexican décor with a single door on one side and two side-by-side windows on the other.

Coyote put his hands behind his head and crossed his legs. "If you gotta be a captive, it's nice to do it first class, right?"

This certainly didn't look like typical hostage digs. Not that she'd ever seen any. But this space was nice. Real nice. Shades of sienna and umber covered the walls and a bronze chandelier hung above the bed. Definitely not the gangster hideout she would have envisioned.

"This is how we're going to do this," Coyote said, pulling her attention back to his teacher-esque smirk. "You follow my orders, and I'll see to it you don't get hurt." He dropped his arms to his lap, leaned forward in the chair. "Understand? You need to get this right, and you need to get *this* through your head—you do not have options."

"Where's the woman who was with me?"

"Of course you're concerned about your friend. I get it."

"She's here?"

"She's in possession. That's all I can tell you."

"Is she here?" Isa demanded.

"Okay, I get it—"

"You keep saying, 'I get it,' but I don't think you do."

He let go a burdensome, impatience-packed sigh. "I can tell you this much. She's on the property and in better care than she's ever been. You need to do as I say, and she will be okay."

"I want to see her."

"No can do. It's not my call. I take orders just like you will."

"Then take me to El Padrino."

"Can't do that either." He rolled his head around his shoulders as if life was stressful and he, in need of a massage. "Look, I'm the guy who stands between you and one dangerous dude who uses death as a means of discipline. You don't want me on your bad side because ..." He glanced up to the corner of the room. Isa did, too and that's when she saw the square device with a round lens in the middle. The camera pointed right at them. Coyote lowered his voice. "... because I know your real name."

"You don't know anything." At least she didn't think he could know much yet. But it wouldn't be long before he did, seeing as in her purse was a tell-all cell phone and every identification source known to man. She should have never had that purse with her and by carrying it, she'd obliterated a couple of basic undercover rules.

Not a good way to get started.

Good grief, was she going to have to trust this guy? She glanced at the floor and noticed Coyote's high-dollar Urban Street leather tennis shoes. Made her think of Mac—Mac, always living above his pay scale like this jerk.

Coyote got to his feet, putting one hand in his pocket.

The muscles across her back tightened, and she mentally rehearsed her next move, should he pull a knife. *Lunge for his shoulders. Lift the knee aiming for the gut.*

Ignoring her stiffening stance, he moved closer. "You're not Isadora Padilla. You're Isabella Phillips. I've got your wallet and phone."

So what was he going to do about it? She narrowed her eyes. "And?"

CALCULATED RISK

Seconds passed in a silent stare-off before he said, "I'll get the information I want on you. I have a network of rats out there in the gutters." He moved back, looked her up and down, humor in his eyes. "You're not as tough as you think you are." He waved his hand in front of his face. "And relax. I'm not a snitch." He got to the door and reached for the knob. "You need to remember there are two of them." He nodded towards the ceiling.

Isa jerked to look in the opposite corner. He was right. Another camera.

Coyote shut the door behind him, and she heard the deadbolt slip into the latch.

Jerk.

Shoulders easing back into place, she looked around again. On the desk in the corner lay her purse, her stupid Dollar King hat, and ridiculous fake Ray Ban shades. Her undercover game had blown up before it started.

And if she didn't figure a couple of things out quick, her foolishness could bring harm to innocent Awena.

CHAPTER 16

El Padrino watched his wife place the thick, cobalt-blue glass on the coaster at the edge of his desk. She'd remembered the lime. Tucked it next to the glass. He loved her philosophies—her insight into the human psyche. He'd discovered this beauty not long after arriving in America. She reminded him of a magnificent panther back then, slipping around the dark corners of the Drake's Horn, amber eyes aware.

Not just any woman could marry into the cartel. His first wife certainly hadn't adapted. She never transitioned from her impoverished mentality. Wife number one had given him both grief and a baby at every turn, and he had left her in Mexico where she belonged.

But Sophia, his lovely and exotic cat, had been satisfied to have but one child. She'd also become a major asset in building his kingdom.

He could conquer the world with Sophia at his side. In those glowing eyes, he'd seen all he could be. Her praise took him to the heights he had dreamed of in the villages of Mexico. Aspirations became reality with Sophia spurring him on.

But her compliments and encouragement had waned in the last month. Her mother in Italy had died, and he'd refused to let her fly back for the funeral. As the wife of a hated and sought-after man in two countries, both El Padrino and Sophia were targets for rival gangs or worse. El Padrino made sure his bride stayed within his organization's reach at all times. Perhaps she carried a bit of resentment. He shook off the thought. Whatever bothered Sophia in the past, today she had apparently put it behind her.

She was the one who encouraged him to explore an alliance with Miguel Lopez and the La Liga cartel, pushing at this objective harder than any other.

His wife slid next to him behind the desk.

"My love," she purred, "Have you spoken recently with Sicily about property transfers?"

She held the allure of a thousand beauties, and he welcomed her interest in his affairs.

"Is there a problem?"

"I cannot locate a couple of your property deeds."

"Hm," he said, enjoying the feel of her cool hand on his warm neck. It'd been days since she'd touched him this way. "They are missing?"

She moved to stand in front of him, her arm lingering around his shoulder. "I've interrupted you before an important initiation. Never mind me now. I'm sure it's an oversight." Cupping his face, she kissed his forehead. Making no further sound, she crept away and gently closed the door behind her. Perfect exit. Perfect wife.

He gazed through the window that framed the front of his property like a fine piece of art. Evergreen bushes dotted brown hills that seemed to roll on forever. He likened himself to those determined bushes clinging to the desert mounds. Neither the droughts of hard years nor the pursuit by pestilent police had uprooted his vision.

A knock at the door interrupted his thoughts. The day proved to be more interesting than anticipated. First, Juan's treason revealed, and now he had to deal with the dog that had forced his hand.

Before he had the chance to open his mouth and summon Coyote through the door, the dog sauntered in and up to the front of El Padrino's desk. "Nice hacienda," Coyote said, a look of approval covering his insipid face.

As if what *he* said to El Padrino mattered. He wanted to pull the gun from his drawer and watch Coyote quiver. But El Padrino controlled such urges.

"Our new accountant is in her room?" He lifted his brows, knowing the answer. With a tap of his computer touchpad, he could see the accountant tucked away in the folds of his mountain compound.

"She is."

"Good." El Padrino glanced at the blue glass. "This is good."

Coyote's took in the opulent room, drool nearly dripping from his lips. Greed gripped this man, a flaw that would work in El Padrino's favor.

"Oso," El Padrino called.

Coyote walked to the window. "Nice view."

El Padrino smiled inside.

Oso entered flanked by an associate. One of the big ones, Nick. The two men split up and stepped to either side of Coyote.

The pup was a lot of things, but he was not stupid. He seemed to recognize what lay ahead. "Hey, what's this about?" he blurted, whipping around to face El Padrino. "We don't need your tough guys to talk over our financial plan."

Men should never feel so comfortable they forget to esteem their leaders. "I have concerns." El Padrino said.

"Is roughing me up going to put those concerns to rest?"

"We shall see. Where is the gun you took from the girl?"

Oso inched closer to Coyote.

The dog narrowed his eyes. He snarled at Oso before saying, "Safely stashed." He swung his glare back to El Padrino. "I've always wanted a Glock. Is that a problem?"

"All merchandise retrieved belongs to me." El Padrino put his elbows on his desk and tented his fingers. "You will see that it gets to me."

Nick grabbed Coyote by the elbows.

Coyote flinched but held his gaze on the boss. "You going to do this over a gun?"

"I am going to do this over respect," El Padrino answered.

"I think Juan's fate today taught me all I need to know about respect. You have mine, El Padrino, I assure you."

"Then this is my insurance you don't forget it." El Padrino nodded at Oso.

Oso pulled his fist back and pounded Coyote's gut.

Coyote doubled over. Coughed.

Maneuvering Coyote's elbows, Nick forced him to straighten.

Coyote grimaced but choked out a response. "Remember ... you need my head working ... to keep the girl working. Don't scramble my brains."

"You're full of advice. I prefer a quieter servant." El Padrino stood up. He wanted a closer look and stepped to the front of his desk. He nodded at Oso again.

This time, Oso went for the face. Knocked Coyote's head back so far El Padrino thought his neck might snap. But that blond head bounced back up. Blood ran from Coyote's nose and down his lip.

"Oso, Maria has cleaned today already." El Padrino sighed. "Lessons are so messy."

Oso pulled the bottom of Coyote's shirt upward and wiped it across his chin.

"Thanks," Coyote muttered, sarcasm dripping with the blood.

Oso reared back and landed another blow to Coyote's midsection."

The dog's face scrunched with pain. He groaned and bent low. This time, Nick didn't yank him upright but left Coyote bowing before his new king.

"Now, tell me, did you get the girl's identification? Her phone?"

Coyote shook his head. Finally, El Padrino had shut the dog up.

"Oso, bring me her purse."

Coyote coughed. "Nothing ... there."

"No identification? You've had her searched?"

Coyote nodded.

"And her car, have we located a car?"

He wagged his head from side to side.

"So, we don't know who she is, where she lives, or what she drives. How will I vet her, Coyote, if I don't have facts in front of me?"

"Will ... will ... get it."

El Padrino circled the threesome. "You like the accountant, don't you." He stopped in front of Coyote. "It is not wise to get personally involved with my guests." He bent to look into the dog's eyes. "I watched when you were with her. I always watch."

Coyote did not respond—a sign the day's lessons were sinking into his skull.

"Enough," El Padrino said.

Nick let go of Coyote's arms.

The beaten man stumbled forward. Rubbed at his face and tested his jaw.

Walking back to his desk, El Padrino picked up the blue glass and lime and carried it back to Coyote. The dog eyed him, suspicious.

"My cup," El Padrino stated, lifting the glass to eye level.

Coyote's red face clouded with question.

"A covenant of sorts. Please accept my offering." He gestured the glass at Coyote.

The dog pursed his swollen lips. Perhaps he recognized the ritual. Didn't matter. El Padrino demanded loyalty. It was how his empire worked.

"Take of my cup."

Coyote stared at the liquid, the crossover moment at hand.

"It's tequila for your pain—and considering your offense, this is a compassionate offer."

Coyote reached out his hand.

The corners of El Padrino's lips lifted.

Coyote drank.

CHAPTER 17

Sophia slid up next to her husband's office door and leaned against the wall, straining to hear the voices on the other side. First, she heard José's voice, and then grunting—Jay's beating well underway.

Shaking her head, she thought about the bizarre ceremonies she'd witnessed in the last couple of years. José tied peculiar rituals to his business practices. But if that was what it took to keep him making money and buying up real estate, then fine. She'd play along.

"Now, there is understanding between us," she heard him say. He must be at his desk, which wasn't far from the door.

Next, Coyote coughed. She listened to him say, "You gonna trust me now?"

She pressed her ear closer. Next, José spoke. "Oso, take Coyo—I apologize. I think you prefer to be called Jay. Take Jay Hernandez to his room, where GT can pay him a visit."

GT, the tattoo artist, must be there to brand Jay. Another ritual. Her husband didn't have his men tattooed solely for the show of loyalty, but also to keep them unemployed. Men with frightening tattoos up and down their bodies didn't find jobs easily. The gang members' dependence upon El Padrino was key to his success. So he had them painted up like pages in a Halloween coloring book.

Keeping members unemployable was a new lesson she'd learned. In Italy, the syndicates recruited with wealth and retained their workers with fear. But Italy was a long time ago and far, far away.

CALCULATED RISK

José talked on. "Oso, after showing Jay where he will be living for the next few weeks, bring me the old woman."

The old woman—the American Indian. From a window upstairs, Sophia had watched the men escort her from the car, perplexed as to why her husband would bring a frail woman into their home. But José had explained that the old woman would be the collateral to make sure his new accountant did as she was told.

And the new accountant? Sophia had seen her, too, immediately determining she would need to do some checking on that one.

Ear still to the door, Sophia heard movement. Feet shuffling.

Sophia pulled away, rushed around a corner just as the office door opened. She pressed against the wall, hoping no one had seen her.

If her husband knew the plans she had made ... well, that was something she didn't need to think about now. Her focus would stay on each of the timely steps that would bring her closer to the glorious goal.

Like her daddy had taught her.

CHAPTER 18

Isa positioned herself beneath the cameras near the windows. Wasn't this a grand development. Second day in New Mexico, and she'd managed to get herself and an innocent old woman kidnapped. She studied the dark round lens of the camera. Thoughts of Awena consumed her. She should have never let Awena into her building. Why hadn't she realized the dangerous position she'd put the woman in? It all started with the ridiculous spirit notion Awena had in her head.

No. This all started with Mac.

No. This all started with an innocence-stealing stepfather.

Isa slapped her own face to get that thought back in its mental vault.

She shuffled left then right to see if the lens rotated to follow her. It didn't.

"Hey," she said, and pointed at the camera. "I hope you work because I've got something to say." She rolled her bottom lip beneath her teeth. Then spoke to the camera again. "You need to let Awena go."

Silence answered.

Marching back to the middle of the room, she paced in front of the bed, arms crossed and dragon inside stirring. She stopped. Pointed at the other camera. "I refuse to do anything until I'm assured she is released." She stuck her hands on her hips. "I'm serious."

Six different times she roared at the boxes on the ceiling, and six times she received nada in return. She wanted to kick the skillfully plastered, terracotta-colored wall and leave a nice flip-flop imprint as a memento. How dare they use the silent treatment against her. That ace belonged in her deck of cards. She'd played it plenty as a kid when child protective services came calling. And considering that in college, an MBTI personality assessment determined she was an ISTJ, she wasn't surprised she'd learned to use silence as a weapon.

Isa stared out the window ... walked around the room again ... stared out the window ... plopped down on the bed. Her dragon's heated breath made her throat sore. She wanted to scream—yell demands at the uncommunicative cameras. So much for her silent, introverted tendencies.

She defaulted to a guaranteed form of control. She fisted a handful of hair and started counting split ends. She tallied them out loud, the numbers short and clipped with anger. By the time she reached the twenty-fourth fractured end, her breaths were even, but her chest still tight. She counted off another thirty-two, and all bodily functions and temperature returned to normal. "I need a hair tie," she mumbled. "And a spreadsheet." She fell back into the oversized comforter and replayed each misstep she'd made in the last two days, starting with the crazy notion that a spirit lived in India Magic and ending with the truth that she'd blown it. Blown any chance of skillfully extracting information about Mac while pretending to be an entrepreneur. What an idiot. What a predicament.

And, *Awena better be okay, or—*

The door opened.

Isa sprang upright.

A tatted goon in a black do rag stepped in. He laid a yellow pad and a handful of hair ties on the desk next to her empty purse. He started back for the door but stopped when Isa said, "Hey." She scooted to the end of the bed. Planted her flip-flops on the floor. "When, exactly, do I get to go to the bathroom?"

Led down the hall past several hand-carved doors, Isa and Do-rag came to the guest restroom. The double-sink layout had another door at the other end. Probably opened to a bedroom.

After relieving her aching bladder, Isa lathered up with the lemon-scented soap she pumped from a Talavera dispenser. Other details like the perfect matching towels, the spotless counter top, and oversized glass shower with two seats, initiated thoughts of Mac again. Had he been continuously exposed to this kind of luxury while working undercover? If so, she could understand how he'd developed an eye for the upscale.

She slipped off the hairband she'd put on her wrist and wound it around her hair. Pulled at the strands until she felt the familiar tug at her temples.

That's when the door at the other end opened.

Obviously unaware she occupied the space, Coyote barged in. With a swollen eye and a flattened nose, he looked like he'd been on the receiving end of a prizefighter's workout.

He stopped short when his good eye got a glimpse of her. "Pardon me," he stammered.

She stared, mouth open. Though shocked at his appearance, Isa saw something unexpected. Beneath the facial rearrangement, his expression held a hint of embarrassment. In the span of a moment, she saw a human. A real human void of the harshness the other gang members carried like trophies. This guy demonstrated some manners—common courtesies, like apologizing when charging in on someone in the bathroom.

She glanced down, looking for a wedding ring on his left hand because it seemed he should have one.

No ring around the marital finger.

Jay backed his way out of the tight spot and pulled the door closed.

Isa turned back to the mirror. Blinked. Something didn't add up here.

CHAPTER 19

From his laptop, El Padrino examined Isa's empty bedroom. He had watched her tirade from his desk before one of his men escorted her down the hall. Who was this woman strutting about yelling threats? With the accountant's claims that she owned one of his buildings, and with his wife's mention that a deed or two were missing, El Padrino wondered if there wasn't a little side game underway within his organization.

If owner Raj Khatri had pulled a fast one on him, there would be payback. The eight-thousand miles between El Padrino and India were mere steppingstones when it came to executing revenge.

He ran his finger across the touch pad. Switched to Camera 2. Surely the vinyl purse, cheap hat, and sunglasses on the desk indicated a low financial status for Isa. Lack of resources always worked to his advantage. Dangle a dream at impoverished fingertips and one could lure in a willing participant. And her coffee shop in downtown Albuquerque's rough side? A cruel joke.

But how convenient to have an accountant show up in one of his buildings just when he needed one. He doubted she'd given her real name, and he knew she hid secrets. He'd find out soon enough. Not that this mattered. He could make one spirited little accountant disappear when it came time.

Oso stuck his head in the door. "She's here."

El Padrino looked up, then glanced back at the empty room on the laptop screen. Watching Isa Padilla stomp her way through the coming days would be entertaining enough. If she lasted. He guided the laptop lid down to close. Smoothed the front of his shirt. Pushed back his chair and stood. "Yes. Bring her in."

The second woman to ever cause him to do a double take walked in. The first was Sophia. Now he had to take an impromptu second glance at the American Indian.

Her eyes followed some invisible path to the ceiling.

El Padrino blinked. Unbelievable. She looked so much like her. Or what she would have looked like if she'd lived to this lady's age.

The woman dipped her head in greeting while transfixed on the ceiling.

He rubbed his hands together. "I hope Oso has made you comfortable in my home."

"I've never seen Legion before."

"Legion?" El Padrino frowned.

She nodded. "He is many."

The similarities between this Native American woman and the one he buried years ago disturbed the lunch digesting in stomach. If he hadn't attended her funeral, seen them put her in the ground, he'd believe her alive and standing before him. "Many what?"

She made her way to the center of the office. Then took little side-by-side steps using her cane, moved in a tight circle, her eyes dancing with awe. When she made her away around to face El Padrino again, her smile revealed a missing tooth. "Many of *them*." She pointed at the ceiling.

El Padrino tilted his head and studied her for a moment. He decided not to try and follow her point, and he plastered on a smile. "If I may introduce myself, I am called El Padrino, and this is my home." He slid into his office chair and gestured at her. "And you are?"

"I am Awena," she said, her eyes investigating his face.

"Awena," he said, pointing to her feet. "You'll have everything you need here. We can start with getting you a new pair of shoes."

She folded her hands atop the cane. "My shoes take me wherever I am called to go." She looked at her feet, then back up at El Padrino. "On my path, many things are revealed."

Surely the woman suffered from dementia or similar challenges. "Is that so?" He chuckled low in the chest. "Tell me, then, what has been revealed to you this day?"

"The condition of your soul."

Now she looked like her and *sounded* like her.

He ignored her statement and redirected by asking, "Tell me about your friend Isa Padilla."

"I have no knowledge of Isa Padilla."

He frowned. "This is troubling because she is the woman you were with today."

"Oh," Awena said, putting her finger to her lips. "I never asked her name. I called her *Daughter* as that was the name revealed to me. She is a daughter."

He shook his head to make sure he was getting this conversation straight. "She has told me she has no family here. Whose daughter is she?"

"The king's."

He sighed. "What king?"

"The king of all, but I don't think you know that yet."

"Is this king in Albuquerque?"

She let a giggle. "No."

"Who is this king, then?"

"Your maker."

No one, no god, was El Padrino's king. "Let me start again. Until I told you her name, you didn't know the woman's name you were with earlier today. Is that right?"

"Where is she?"

El Padrino didn't know how long he could sustain patience with the table tennis conversation. "She is here. Already at work for me. I've hired her to do some bookwork and when she is done, you and she will be returned to Albuquerque. I'll be taking good care of you while you're here. So tell me, what else do you know about our Isa Padilla?"

"If harm should come to the girl, you will be held responsible."

El Padrino raised his brows in naivety. "Harm? No harm shall come to either of you. But it is best we keep our work private."

She stared at him. Didn't even blink.

The sides of his mouth dropping in frustration, he said, "How do you know her?"

"The Lord connected us yesterday."

His jaw tightened the way it did on the rare occasions when he lost control. "Then tell me, where is she from?"

She jerked her head up to look at the ceiling again, her eyes darting from one corner to another. "Heaven above. There are big plans for this one."

"So you think she's an angel dropped from the sky?"

"No. Of course she is not an angel. Angels are different beings all together. She is a chosen vessel, one chosen to reveal as I am chosen to reveal." Her eyes latched on to something. She seemed to follow an invisible line across the back of the room.

He ignored her wandering eyes. "What were you doing with Isa today?"

That seemed to register. She looked back at El Padrino and took a step closer to his desk. "We looked for a demon."

"A demon?"

"Indeed."

He tried something different to ensure his tracks were covered and no one would come looking for his guests. "While you are my guest here, will your family be looking for you?"

"My father knows where I am."

"How could your father know this? Has he followed you here?"

"My father knows all things." She dropped her gaze to meet his. "God knows all."

Okay, okay. He was starting to feel the same frustrations he'd experienced at home in Mexico when his mother would start in on her godly warnings. "Did Isa mention any family to you? Does she have a sister or brother?"

The woman squinted. "May I say something?"

He threw his hands up, impatience growing. "Of course." Maybe he'd get more information if she took a turn at leading the conversation.

"Control is an illusion. You control nothing, but it is *something* that controls you." She pointed to the ceiling.

He clasped his hands together. Squeezed them tight to keep them from forming fists—fists that wanted to pound the desk. "I have need of Isa's services, and your presence ensures she gives me her best."

"I am an insurance policy for you then?" Her smile widened, which was odd. Maybe she didn't comprehend the truth of the words. But before he replied with a better illustration of the situation, she said, "I understand," and appeared to be pleased.

He'd have to extract information little by little with this one. There was only so much nonsense he could tolerate in a day. "I am happy we have an understanding." He rose.

But she spoke on. "I have longed to travel to Africa or minister in the jungles of the Amazon. My desires have been for the mission field, but you, sir, have brought the mission field to me."

The woman unsettled him for two reasons. He suspected she communicated something deeper than the obvious nonsense tumbling from her mouth, just like his mother. There was a spiritual fear in his shack in Mexico, and his mother made sure it never left. That's why he did leave. Yes, she sounded and looked like his mother—could be her twin.

El Padrino pulled from his chair, done with the thorn-filled memories. "Oso," he called.

Awena watched him closely. He found it hard to admit she unnerved him, but she did.

"I have work to do, so it is good that I go now," she said as Oso came through the door.

"But you're staying here. I hope you understand this."

"The work I have to do, you know nothing about," she said. "I can do it anywhere in the world."

"And what is this work?"

"Prayer."

CHAPTER 20

At her desk, Isa scooted the little purple potatoes across the dinner plate to sit next to the chunk of medium-rare sirloin she'd cut from the larger piece. She stabbed at a grilled asparagus and shoved it in her mouth. Not that she had an appetite, but there wasn't anything else for her to do.

She felt like one of those silly fairy tales where the girl gets locked in a palatial ivory tower—the well-plated meal, the oversized bed, the layers of lavish cotton bedding. Even the cushions in the desk chair felt like silk. But how would she know?

All wasted on Isa. They might as well have thrown her in a cement dungeon, because she refused to let El Padrino's niceties soften the truth that he'd kidnapped an old, helpless woman and held her prisoner to blackmail Isa.

She sampled the salad. Butter leaf lettuce, avocado, and jicama with what tasted like tangy lime and mango vinaigrette. Why would she even notice?

Because someone wanted her to, that's why. Lure the poor little accountant into the wolf's den with things she couldn't afford out in the real world. Clever. It was becoming evident why Mac was drawn to sparkling Pellegrino on a tap-water budget.

The blush-colored rays of late afternoon light spread across the wood floor. Isa got up and moved to the window. Raised the blinds. A ponderosa pine obstructed her view, but light seeped between the evergreen's limbs and branches. To her left, she could see more pines teetering atop a cliff of rock.

Her posh prison seemed to be tucked into the Sandia Mountain range, confirming her timing exercise under the black hood on her ride up.

The serene scene, far from city fumes and musty HPD halls, threatened to lull her outrage right into apathy if she wasn't careful.

Isa pushed her cheek against the window for a better angle on the view below. A stucco wall rose up a good ten feet and most likely surrounded the perimeter of the house. She guessed the ground to be around thirteen, maybe fifteen, feet below. Running her hand across the top of the lower window, she located the lock latch. Flipped it. Found the second latch and flipped it, too.

Isa closed her eyes, counted to three, and raised the window an inch. She braced herself for the blaring sound of an alarm.

But nothing rang. Or even buzzed.

She glanced back at the door, sure a goon would bust in.

When nothing happened, she smiled at the closest camera. Raised a brow and raised the window another few inches.

Nothing happened inside. The call of a mountain fowl echoed from the distant rocks outside.

Shouldn't be this easy.

Isa inspected the windows further. There were screens, but it wouldn't take much to push them out.

Fifteen feet would be a tough jump resulting in a broken ankle or worse, if she were desperate enough to chance it. She wasn't all that desperate, yet. Had something to do first.

Looking back to the camera, Isa made her demand. "I want to see Awena."

CHAPTER 21

A couple of hours later, the veil of darkness arrived. But not Awena. Isa had resumed pacing and counting the dots in the Aztec pattern of her bed's comforter.

Do-rag delivered a box of files and a new pair of flip-flops to her desk. When she asked him if he'd seen the old woman around, he'd grunted, picked up her dinner plate, and latched the door behind him.

Muffled laughter told her there were other goons outside her door at the moment. Neither of which sounded like Coyote. Then again, with a face as battered as his, he wouldn't be laughing it up for some time. Maybe he stood by, silent and brooding.

Restless, she riffled through the storage box which contained the Drake's Horn's tax returns for the last three years. The returns looked standard, but she knew trumped up numbers had to fill the expense boxes. Bottom line on all three years, they'd lost money. No surprise there. The bar, she knew, operated as a front and wasn't intended for profit. If she dug around, she knew she'd find inflated expenses that wouldn't get past an IRS audit. But expense gouging was a minimal offense. The IRS would respond with a charge, and big interest on the deficit, but not much more than that. El Padrino could settle his federal misdemeanor with a check from his coffers.

She'd seen bigger, slicker fraud than this. Had investigated books from big-time bankers, wall-street investment firms, and Houston's finest legal corporations.

She'd uncovered most financial tricks and loopholes out there. When it came to financial crime, Isa unraveled the knots expert criminals tied up. She could fix any fake business's books to look legit if she wanted.

She raked her fingers through her pony tail.

Maybe she should want to.

She dropped back in the desk chair. Rubbed her chin with that thought. Gaining El Padrino's trust might grant her access to other files, other business dealings.

She lifted to her feet. Started making the rounds in front of the bed.

The unfortunate position she'd been forced into today might be a door to solving the mystery around Mac. It could be a small portal, but worth looking into. She might even find something big enough to bring the drug runners down.

She stopped in front of the desk.

Undercover investigators would kill for opportunities like this. She'd been smuggled inside a Mexican cartel hideout because they needed her, which meant they'd let her live as long as she delivered what they wanted. And she could insist they keep Awena safe. Maybe she'd turn the tables and blackmail the drug lord.

She made a mental list of the risks. The dangers were numerous. Bottom line was, if she screwed this up, no backup squad or SWAT team waited in the wings to pull her out. Geez, who even knew she was in New Mexico? She'd kept her move to Albuquerque on the hush-hush to keep it undercover. Only the sergeant and Claire knew anything about the relocation, and she'd shared minimal info with them. She'd even gone so far as to offend her two friends to keep them at a distance.

Yes, she'd created her own solo suicide mission.

She looked toward the moon-lit window. A fifteen-foot escape jump didn't look near as frightening as snitching on cartel killers.

This wasn't mission impossible. This was real life. Real guns. Real, evil people.

Isa dropped her head back to stare at the ceiling.

Forget this death wish.

But she already had the pros and cons columns lined up in her brain.

Years ago, she'd enrolled in a special training class where she learned about Stockholm syndrome. The students reviewed several documented cases where kidnapped victims strongly identified with their captors. Some had gone so far as to refuse rescue, which had been the case in Stockholm, Sweden, when six hostages sympathized with their captors so deeply they refused to press charges once released.

She gazed around the luxurious room. El Padrino counted on a similar connection, it appeared, betting his over-the-top provisions made him out to be a generous caretaker.

She could play along.

Which was a ludicrous idea.

Isa started pacing again.

At forty-three steps, she stopped. The number one priority, she decided, would be locating Awena and making sure she was safe. Number two would be getting dirt, forensic dirt, on the cartel. Three—well, that would go back to the original plan, and she would investigate Mac's death or ... *Did she want to admit it?* The thought had never been far from the surface of her brain. Now that she knew that Mac co owned an abandoned restaurant with a drug lord, she wouldn't be unraveling the mystery of his death, but she would be unraveling the mystery of his demise.

Gathering the files, she stacked them in date order and placed them back into the box. The 8 x 10 plain manila envelope sticking out the side of one of the tax return folders caught on the side of the box. She drew the envelope out.

There was nothing written across the front.

Opening it, she pulled out a thick stack of real estate papers.

A deed. 126 Lancelot Lane. Kingwood, Texas.

Isa knew people who lived in upscale Kingwood, Texas, a community on the northern edge of Houston. Two jumped to mind immediately. Both worked at the HPD.

She filed that thought for later use. Fell across the bed. Let all the information she'd categorized sink in for spell.

CALCULATED RISK

The day had been long, and she was running low on mental fuel.

She yawned. Rolled to her side. Counted the swirls in the plastered walls.

Isa had no idea how long she'd been sleeping when the bedroom door creaked open. The eerie sound yanked her from a bad dream that involved Coyote, the spy cameras, and her falling two stories from the bedroom window. Glad to be out of the dream, but disturbed to wake to an intruder, she imagined a worst-case scenario.

After all the over-the-top hospitality, she figured, someone had showed up for payment.

She eased to a sitting position. The lamp seemed a decent weapon. If she could get it unplugged before that someone coming through the door attacked.

The door eased shut.

Isa ripped off the covers and sprang to her feet, glad she'd gone to bed fully clothed.

Moonlight through the window fell across a silhouette near the desk.

"I'm a martial arts specialist," Isa said. "Don't come closer."

CHAPTER 22

Isa slipped into a jiujitsu defense stance beside her bed. But considering the shadowy form that entered her room seemed short, she straightened, reached for the lamp on the nightstand. Flipped the toggle at the base.

The lights blinked on.

"Daughter."

The taut muscles in Isa's body let go their tight grips. "Awena." She rushed to the woman and wrapped her arms around her shoulders and pulled her in close. Awena's head came right under Isa's nose and her hair smelled of cedarwood and sage. Isa breathed in the comforting aroma, thinking this was exactly how a home should smell. Nothing like the cigarette and stale beer odors she'd grown up with.

Awena reciprocated the squeeze. Patted Isa's back.

Isa closed her eyes, grateful. "I'm so sorry I got you into this."

Awena's pat slowed.

"Please forgive me—"

"I can't breathe."

"Oh," Isa pulled away. "I'm sorry, I ... I guess I'm relieved to see you."

Awena straightened her braids. "Isa Padilla." She smiled wide. "Now, I know your name."

Okay, the name thing was going to open a gargantuan can of worms. Isa let it lie.

"How, did you get in here?" she asked as Awena examined the ceiling. Nothing at all unusual about Awena's obsession with ceilings, even at—Isa glanced at her watch—2:30 a.m.

"I walked in."

Oh, brother, here it went. "Yes, I see that, but how did you get past the guards?"

Awena's eyes dropped to study Isa's face. "What guards?"

"What guards? The men at the door." Isa stepped over to the door. Opened it. A guy covered in solid green ink tattoos sat in a straight-back wooden chair. He scrambled to his feet and jerked the door closed, pulling the knob out of Isa's hand. "That guard," Isa thumbed over her shoulder, a little surprised there was only one.

"Oh, him. He was sleeping. I see your room is clean. Like mine."

Isa walked back and sat on her bed. Scratched at the back of her head where a wadded-up sleep-nest had formed above her ponytail. "Okay," Her brain needed to awake enough to take on quirky Awena. "How are you doing? Have they treated you okay?"

"Oh, I am very good." Awena clasped her hands together.

"I've been worried about you." Isa shook her head. "It's hard to believe this is happening. I feel responsible."

Awena walked to the end of the bed and using her cane, she worked her way down to the floor. When she got there, she crossed her legs and pulled her skirt down over her knees. Laid the cane across her lap.

Isa scooted to the end of the bed and looked down at her.

"Isa Padilla," Awena said, her voice taking a serious tone. "I have been brought here for a purpose."

Isa appreciated Awena not blaming her, but in truth she was one hundred percent responsible for getting Awena kidnapped. "I'm going to get us out of here. I only need some time to figure out how."

"I have work to do, and now I have been told by the Mr. Padrino that you have work, too."

"Work to do?" Isa pulled down on her cheeks. "What are you talking about?" She needed coffee. Or a therapist. "We're held against our will here. I am going to try to figure some things out with their finances, but we need to get *you* back to your home. Don't you have family that will be missing you?"

"My family is everywhere."

"Do you live with anyone?"

She shook her head. "But the Spirit is always with me."

Isa glanced up at the camera, wondering if it was rolling. "Still, someone will miss you, and we don't want people worrying, right?" Maybe the old gal would respond to other people's concerns.

Awena turned her head to look up at Isa. "They took my bag with my Bible."

"Well, they're going to take more than that if we don't figure a way to get you out." Isa got off the bed started her walk about. "We have to work together." The pistons in her brain revved up a little. "Synchronize bathroom visits to communicate. Unless you have your own bath." When she passed Awena, she asked, "Have you seen the whole house yet? Are there guards at your door?"

Awena watched Isa's trek.

Isa planned on. "Have you ever scaled a wall? Wait, that's crazy. You have to be, what late seventies, early eighties?"

"You make me dizzy."

Isa stopped, the full realization dawning that Awena had found her room in the middle of the night alone. "Awena, how did you find this room?"

"A woman woke me. Told me where to go."

"Who?"

"She didn't say her name. But she knew you would be happy to see me. Very kind gesture."

"You have no idea who she was?" Before she let Awena confirm, she asked. "Why would someone do this?"

"Oh, she said that one day, you would return the favor and help her."

Maybe there were other hostages on the premises. "I have to figure out what's happening on all fronts." Isa pulled in a breath. "I've been so worried about you, and *voila*, someone sends you here. This has been one strange coincidence after another."

Awena shook her head. "There are no coincidences."

Isa tried to suppress a groan. "Awena, you have to cooperate with me. Don't you understand the danger you're in?"

"Do you have a Bible?"

Isa wanted to yank her ponytail to her nose and add up split ends. "I don't carry a Bible. God and I haven't exactly been on speaking terms."

Of course, Awena's face clouded with compassion. Deep sympathetic lines ran across her brow.

Isa wanted to grab the wisecrack back.

Awena closed her eyes. Was she praying?

"The past is a ghost that clings to you," Awena said, opening her eyes.

Isa's shoulders slumped.

"You sure you don't have you a Bible?" Awena crossed her arms like a stubborn old chief.

"Have I a Bible?" Did she not hear Isa's dark confession two seconds ago? "No, like I said, and I'm guessing no one around here does either." She stepped wide to the nightstand to make a point. "I know it is confusing, but this isn't a hotel. It's a prison, see? There's no Gideon in the drawer ..." She yanked open the nightstand drawer. There was a note pad, pen, and—if she hadn't seen it with her own eyes, she wouldn't have believed it—a Bible. Like new. Hard cover and all. "There's ... there's a Bible in here."

"Bring it to me."

Isa pulled her jaw out of her chest. Why fight the woman at this hour? Why fight the knowing sage at all? She extracted the Bible from the drawer and dropped to the floor beside Awena. Handed the holy book over.

Awena ran her palm across the top. "Perfect." The bright eyes beneath Awena's creped lids defied her age. Defying the natural order of things, they radiated such vitality. Beneath the down-and-out clothing and disregard for proper conversation etiquette, Awena had hold of something mysterious that lifted her far above her circumstances.

Isa let a heavy sigh carry away the angst bubbling up inside. "You seem to know something I don't."

"Ah, Daughter," Awena patted the floor beside her. "You seek wisely." She cleared her throat. "Finally."

Isa put her head against the bed. "Tell me then. What am I missing here?"

"Many things." She clasped her hands together. "Would you like to know one of them?"

"Tell me, please."

Awena's head bobbed in assurance. "In my beautiful journey beneath the sun, I have been granted a dream."

"What dream is that?"

"To be a missionary."

"A missionary like feeding hungry children in Africa missionary?"

"Like setting captives free missionary."

Isa pointed at Awena then herself. "Setting you and me free? Thank goodness, we need a plan."

"No." Awena chuckled. "Not you and me. Our captivity is an illusion. I speak of unseen prisons."

"Spirit stuff, again?" To her own ears, Isa's tone sounded half-hearted. But deep, deep in her heart, she knew she needed some of what Awena was trying to share.

Awena nodded. "Do not run so far ahead you lose sight of what's before you now."

"Hmm." Sometimes, it did feel like she ran way ahead of everyone else. Kicked down doors not meant to be opened.

Awena edged her cane against the floor and inched her way to a standing position. "You have been chosen, Isa Padilla."

"Chosen?" she drew the word out. "By ..."

"God almighty and the Spirit, and the Son. The Son has showed this to me."

The proverbial light bulb snapped on. When Awena talked of the sun, she actually meant *the Son*. As in Jesus. That slow realization didn't say much for her investigation prowess.

"That's incredible, Awena, but what would I be chosen for?"

"To reveal—uncover mysteries and make known the truth."

CALCULATED RISK

That sounded familiar. Isa pushed her palms to her forehead to try and remember, something ... Another light bulb. She got up and walked to her purse. The envelope with the note was still there, though it was obvious by the ripped side that someone had tampered with it. Probably read her note, then shoved it back in her purse when they took her wallet and phone. She carefully opened the envelope and unfolded the paper. Handed it to Awena.

Nothing is covered that will not be revealed, or hidden that will not be made known.

Awena leaned her cane against the bed, read the note, then looked up at Isa. "Ah, you carry the words of your calling with you."

"Someone left that in my car," Isa pointed at the paper. "After my husband died."

Awena's mouth opened slightly. "You have lost a husband?"

"There's a lot ... too much to tell right now."

Awena flipped through the Bible, found what she was looking for. She placed the note in between the pages and lifted the book to Isa. "Read there." She pointed. "Verses two and three."

Isa read. The words on her note were the exact same words in the book of Luke, chapter 12. "Someone left me a Bible verse?" she asked looking up.

"How was it that your husband found death?"

The compassionate expression on Awena's face reminded Isa of a cloud—the wisps that get between you and the scorching sun bringing a moment of shade on a hot August day.

"It is a long story, but he was murdered during his work. He was an undercover investigator in the drug scene." Isa handed the Bible back to Awena. "But I can't tell you more than that. The less you know, the safer you will be."

Awena laid the Bible on the bed, took her cane, and walked past Isa, heading for the door. "I shall see you again soon."

Isa frowned. "Where are you going?"

"It is almost the fourth watch—the hours of battle."

"But—"

Without turning, Awena said, "Prayer, Daughter. Get with the program."

Isa's jaw slipped a little at that one.

"But wait, you forgot the Bible." Isa turned toward the bed to retrieve the book.

Awena stopped and looked back at Isa. "The Bible is for you, my child."

CHAPTER 23

Two boxes stuffed with wrinkled and faded receipts arrived with the onset of the next day.

Oso carried the cartons in when the first rays of light filtered through her room. Isa was at a window, studying the size of the ponderosa pine's branches that looked to be close, but out of reach. Allergic to pine and cedar and all sorts of evergreens, her skin itched just thinking about the possibility of an escape via tree descension.

Right after he dropped off the boxes, Oso returned with plate of eggs and hash browns, offering her no communication except a loathsome glance.

But that was it. Not another visit with Awena. No Coyote. No El Padrino. Only Do-rag escorting her to necessity breaks. She spent at least an hour pacing and another reading the random receipts.

Once she plopped on the bed and picked up the Bible, opened in the middle and ran her finger down the page, counting to ten. She landed on a verse and read it.

> Thus says the Lord God of Israel, I made a covenant with
> your forefathers in the day I brought them out of the land
> of Egypt from the house of bondage.

Covenant. Bondage. There was no way she'd understand the cryptic messages in Jeremiah. She flipped to where she guessed the New Testament would be located. Opened again and scanned until she got to verses six and seven in the book of ... she glanced at the top of the page ... in the book of 2 Thessalonians.

> since it is a righteous thing with God to repay with tribulation
> those who trouble you, and to give you who are troubled rest
> with us when the Lord Jesus is revealed from heaven with His
> mighty angels ...

Three words caught her eye: *just, affliction, revealed.*

Two questions hit her brain: *Did these words mean a just God would repay her stepfather for the afflictions he forced upon her? And was "when the Lord Jesus shall be revealed" that time?*

Isa shut the book and tossed it back into the nightstand drawer. This wasn't the time to be analyzing the whys and why nots of her childhood. Or, diving into a book she had no idea how to read.

She got up and went back to the receipt box at the end of the bed.

Before noon, she'd also managed two trips to the bathroom without seeing anyone except her less-than chatty escort, Do-Rag.

Her coincidence luck must have hit a wall.

A sandwich arrived, and she spent the next two hours poring over bogus receipts. A half-box still needed sorting. Then she'd start creating categories, documenting, adding, and cross-referencing those receipts to the tax returns. All easy, fill-in-the-blank accounting basics someone in a lessor position would have handled at HPD. If this is what Coyote thought El Padrino needed a pro for, then Coyote wasn't the financial shark he pretended to be.

She dumped the last of the receipts on the bed, sifted through them. At the bottom of the box she found another real estate deed. This one wasn't in an envelope but folded several times and clearly hidden beneath the loose receipts. So strange how deeds—not misplaced lists of supplies, not someone's personal receipts, not worthless fast-food slips, but bona fide real estate deeds—just happen to be filed away with a bunch of bar purchases.

This title was for a motel on Houston's rougher side. The property belonged to a Juan Velasquez.

Buried-in-the-desert Juan?

She glanced at both cameras. Isa piled the receipts on top of the deed and carried the whole stack to the desk. Moving papers around and rearranging stacks, she stretched across the desk, shielding the papers from camera view. With the property titles positioned out of sight, she flipped each open and checked ownership. Juan owned the motel. Sicily Walters owned the house.

Isa grabbed her purse and pulled out the tattered envelope.

She reread the note for the fortieth time.

Nothing is covered up that will not be revealed, or hidden that will not be made known.

Right here. Right in a drug lord's hideaway and only two days into her by chance undercover work, something hidden was being made known. She tapped her pencil on the desk eight times. And if mystic Awena was right about Isa's calling, then someone wanted Isa to be the one to solve this mystery.

But why?

Maybe someone knew who she really was? Wanted to feed her clues?

She dared not write anything down, but mentally reviewed a few facts.

Mac owned a property she knew nothing about. Houston deeds were showing up. A pattern? A money trail? She bit her lip. What if Awena was insightful and not simply quirky? What if she'd landed where she needed to be to get answers about Mac? If she'd had access to the outside world, she could research names, addresses, public real estate records. Discover how long these people had owned the properties and who they bought them from.

The thrill of her bloodhound instincts kicked in.

Isa left the desk and stood beneath the camera nearest the windows. "I need to talk about a computer." She gestured toward the piles of receipts. "I can't make rows and rows of figures by hand. Don't you people know Quick Books?" She walked to the bed but made a U-turn back to the camera. "Seriously. How do you expect me to verify these returns with limited information?" She threw her hands in the air. "Plus, I'm understaffed."

That last smart remark made her proud.

Nine minutes later, Coyote burst through the door.

He didn't look so good.

Besides the puffy eye and swollen nose, he had the number "96" tattooed on the side of his neck with a big red ring of irritated skin encircling it.

"Making progress?" He sounded as gruff as he looked, all the wit and charm and self-assurance of the day before gone.

She leaned back from her desk chair and eyed him. "Yes, some." Pointed to his neck. "What does '96' stand for?"

"It stands for don't push me with demands. You just add up those expenses."

"I'm supposed to add hundreds of receipts up in my head?"

"Yes, and make sure those expense margins are provable."

The idea that Coyote could be the one who slipped those deeds into her boxes slammed her brain from out of the blue. But hunches were something she liked to verify. In her line of work, numbers proved the facts, not intuitions or gut feelings. She'd heard violent crimes and sex crimes detectives say they had gut feelings without forensic evidence to back it up thousands of times, and she'd seen them walk into plenty of dead ends. Not Isa. She used data and provable numbers once she'd caught scent on the trail.

"So, you're the one who decides what I see and don't see? Right?"

He gave her an impatient nod. "You've already been told I'm in charge."

Isa tapped her finger at her lip. Wanted a bigger reaction. "So, when I accomplish this mathematical feat of addition you've assigned—what do you plan for me to do then?"

"Then you're done and out of here."

Isa frowned. "I leave? You sure have gone to a lot of extremes to have me add up a few figures."

"A few? I thought there were too many to sum up in your little head."

She pulled in a cool breath to dowse the spark his insult started. "Can I see the IRS notification? It might help me—"

"Details are available on an as needed basis."

Isa raised her right brow. This guy wasn't budging. But if Coyote was the one who hid the real estate deeds in the two boxes for her to see, then why didn't he go along with her requests? She tried another angle. "You're not using me to capacity."

He U-turned for the door. "I'm not getting you a computer. Add those receipts."

"If there's no software in place now, I could set all that up." Isa stood.

But Jay kept walking.

"I want to do my part." There. She said it. Willingly put herself in a position to help a cartel leader in order to squeal on a cartel leader.

Coyote stopped. Straightened his broad back. Looked like his *aha* moment had finally arrived.

Isa made sure her next statement was in camera view. "I could take care of so much more than three years' tax returns." The words felt awkward, and she was painfully aware she looked unnatural. But could she spell it out any clearer? "El Padrino has been more than fair to me with the nice accommodations and by taking such good care of Awena."

Coyote whirled around, narrowed his good eye. "What are you doing?" he growled.

If the camera wouldn't nail her doing it, she would have mouthed the words *helping your rear, moron.* But that's not what she did, and what she said came out louder than necessary. "Looking for a piece of the action."

His brows dropped low over his mismatched eyes, and his hands fisted.

She'd jostled a nerve.

Taking a sideways glimpse toward the camera, he turned away from it and lowered his voice. "That's some bad acting you got there. Let's not forget I know you're not who you claim to be. So, cool the ambitions, Tiger. This isn't corporate America."

CALCULATED RISK

"I don't get it," she said, frowning. "I'm trying to help you."

In two strides, he had the door open.

She started to rush him from behind. Wrestle him to the floor and wrangle good sense or a computer out of him. Someone wanted her to know things and without access to outside and additional information, she would be stuck in perpetual question mode. Which is where she'd spent the last three miserable months and what put her in this mess in the first place.

Be it resolution or purpose or some other force of will, she felt pushed to dig deeper. To see where this trail led.

But Coyote was a big man—over six feet and madder than a pestered hornet protecting a nest. Too much for Isa physically. "Coyote. Wait."

Her demand bounced right off his back.

He opened the door. "Name's Jay Hernandez," he said over his shoulder. "And that's what you will call me."

CHAPTER 24

A slammed door in the middle of Isa's plea felt like running into an invisible concrete wall at full stride. An unexpected impact that left Isa stunned.

And despising Jay Hernandez.

Without hesitation, he'd dismissed her requests for technology support and offers to help build a better bookkeeping system. Whoever gave him the black eye and smashed nose earlier must have relocated what little gray matter he possessed in that arrogant head of his.

Caged like an animal—albeit a comfortable cage—she had limited access to her captors, and her one connection had proved himself uncooperative. To keep moving forward with the tip-offs, she'd have to get around this wall called Coyote. She huffed. Or Jay Stupid Hernandez. Or whatever the heck he was supposed to be in this neurotic world behind designer walls.

Of course, her memory safe opened and out popped her stepfather. That masked man had appeared harmless enough at first. Getting a distraction to keep her mother home nights sounded like a good idea, and for a couple of months, she did give up bar cruising. Angel beamed pure light the first time their stepfather mentioned fishing. Just the two of them, out for some male bonding. When they returned from the boys' get-away, though, Angel withdrew from her. She couldn't understand why. Those had been some of the hardest days.

Of course, her stepfather eventually made his way up the stairs to Isa's bedroom. Always after dark and always after beer. That's when Isa hid herself and learned to count up into the tens of thousands.

She glared at the backside of the bedroom door, then looked between the cameras. Slammed doors were really invitations for smarter tactics. Positioning herself beneath the camera near the window, she addressed it as if it were El Padrino himself. "Like I tried to tell your financial mastermind, I need technical support. If you don't want to alarm an IRS auditor with manually inserted figures, and yellow-pad sheets of notes, we're going to need some software." She looked sideways at the desk. "At the very least, I need a calculator. Mine disappeared when you took my phone."

Based on her camera-request experience, it shouldn't take long before someone came through that door. The countdown started.

She figured twelve minutes gave whoever watched on the other side of the lenses plenty of time to respond, so she counted backwards from 720.

When she reached zero, she revved up again and counted back from 180.

At 265, she gave up. "Forget it," she huffed and headed to the desk. But stopped next to the bed and thought about having to crawl into the sheets in the same jeans and tunic she'd had on for two days. Ugh.

New angle coming up. "Pajamas and a change of clothes would be nice." She pulled at her tunic, showed it to a camera. But if a need for fresh clothes wouldn't prick a hardened killer's heart, she had another idea. Isa twisted to face the other camera. "Have I mentioned that I have a cat at home? He is probably starving."

Exactly seven minutes later, an oversized bald goon with the chubby face of a toddler came through the door with a set of car keys in his hand. "We're going to get the cat."

CHAPTER 25

From the leather back seat of the Range Rover reserved for his travels, El Padrino opened his laptop and replayed the video footage of Isa requesting resources. Still a few miles away from his anticipated encounter, he had ample time to watch the fiery girl again. Twice more he backed up the footage and replayed it. The last time through, he chuckled.

Looked like she might position herself as a servant of value after all. How quickly she'd adapted. He closed the computer and studied the trees outside the window. He would need to test Isa Padilla's budding allegiance.

A blur of city lights raced by as the car picked up speed on the two-lane highway, and his thoughts moved ahead to the meeting. In Mexico, he'd lost nine girls to La Liga, the largest cartel south of the Texas border. Nine missing prostitutes meant nine income streams had vanished. The La Liga gang made a habit of raiding his brothels. This common exchange between rival cartels meant girls were passed back and forth frequently. But nine? That was a number too high to be business as usual. La Liga was sending him a warning.

He smiled inside. Warnings meant he'd successfully intimidated La Liga and their notorious leader, Miguel Lopez.

Under Lopez's leadership, La Liga had wiped out several of their rival gangs through violent tactics El Padrino once found disturbing. But since the empire he'd named

CALCULATED RISK

"96" had grown, he'd adjusted to the blood and mangled bodies—got accustomed to cruelty. Killing, after all, proved to be as effective as any well-planned advertising scheme.

Warm pride swept across his chest. Though today, he would meet with only the commander of La Liga.

He leaned forward and peered through the front window between Carlos and Raton. He'd left Oso in charge of the compound and bar while he pursued deals and solutions in Mexico.

"Should we align, a partnership between myself and Lopez would mean domination of the US southern border. Together, we can rule drug trades. Maybe more, heh?"

Carlos looked up into the rearview mirror, his narrow dark eyes bright. "After we get our chicas back?"

"If we don't get these girls, we'll get more."

Carlos nodded. "Yes, El Padrino. That is an easy fix."

El Padrino patted Carlos's shoulder. "Women are an endless commodity."

Carlos laughed. Reached over and slapped at Raton's arm. "Commodity. That's what women are. Something to consume so you can go get more."

Raton exited the highway, nodding, as if he knew what a commodity was. The men El Padrino recruited from the streets weren't the most intelligent, but they were certainly eager to make the cash. The car wound through an old industrial area with potted roads. At the end of a gravel street, they entered the back of a residential neighborhood. The homes got bigger and the walls around yards higher. Two more blocks, and they would be at Oso's family compound. El Padrino twisted around and looked out the back window at the car behind them. "Is the old woman comfortable?"

Carlos pulled a phone from the dashboard and made a call. A few Spanish words were exchanged then he nodded at his boss. "Sí, El Padrino, she is sleeping in the back seat."

"Are we near Las Misiones?"

"Sí."

"Have you spoken with Oso's sister about leaving the old woman with her?"

Carlos gave him a thumbs up.

El Padrino smiled, imagining Isa stomping around in front of the cameras once she learned of Awena's departure.

To Mexico.

CHAPTER 26

The oversized toddler's name turned out to be Nick, and he had the standard issue "96" tattooed on his sleeveless upper arm. He explained he was to take her home, retrieve the cat, and get anything else she might need. Even her computer ... and she could have it after some of the technical guys had a chance to look it over. Plus, they could swing by and pick up her car. El Padrino said an abandoned car might draw attention from the downtown parking attendants. One of the other guys would drive it back to the compound, of course. She didn't respond to any of Nick's enlightenments but let him make all kinds of promises.

Operation abandoned cat in the house successful.

But inside her head, warning flags fluttered. It all sounded a bit too generous. She might be new at this game of deception but was catching on quick. This action would cost her something, and she dreaded discovering that fee.

She would have to figure a way to stall and get alone time with her computer once she got there. Once cartel techies had hold of it, they'd make all kinds of discoveries about Isa and then wipe the device Hillary Clinton clean.

While Nick waited, Isa slipped the real estate papers back into one of the boxes, committing the addresses to memory. She placed the sorted receipts on top and hoped like heck no one would search her room while she was gone.

Placing the lid on the box, Isa peered over at Nick. "I'd like for Awena, the woman who came with me, to join us. She can help me pack a few things."

"Uh." Nick eyed one of the cameras. "What woman?"

Isa smiled. This might not be a hard sell. "The woman who came with me. Send for her, and you'll see she's a harmless old lady."

Nick looked lost. He glanced at the door, back to Isa, and then up to the camera.

Isa smiled at the thought of Awena flummoxing Nick in her apartment while she stole some time for quick research. "Go ahead. See if she would like to come along."

Nick mumbled something beneath his breath, opened the door, left the room for less than a minute, and then came back in with his chest a little higher. "No woman. Just the three of us."

But of course El Padrino wouldn't let Awena out of the house. Awena played the role of hostage held for ransom. And Isa? Her work was the ransom.

Fumbling her way through her apartment with two guards watching her every move wouldn't work. She needed a plan here. "Who, then, is coming with us?" she asked, her tone casual, as if interacting with an oversized lethal gang member were an everyday occurrence.

Nick didn't answer but gestured that it was time to go. His gullibility factor diminished a little.

She followed him out.

When they got into the garage, Isa saw an older model Jeep sitting out in the drive and a man in the front seat.

Jay Hernandez.

Nick made for a double-door refrigerator in the corner. Opened it.

Heart and enthusiasm sinking, Isa crawled in the back seat of the Jeep. Glanced around the empty back seat for the hood they'd probably put over her head. Didn't see anything.

"You're proving to be resourceful," Jay said.

Man, she hated his arrogant tone. "I have a couple of friends who help me," she shot back, buckling her seat belt.

"Yeah?"

"Cameras One and Two. They are good listeners."

Jay didn't respond but leaned toward Nick, who was positioning his extensive mass into the driver's seat and his Dr. Pepper in the cup holder. Jay said, "The boss called. Wants you to check on the American Indian woman before we go."

"What the—"

"That's what he said."

"But—"

"Look," Jay thrust his phone at Nick's face. "He texted, too. Said it would make her," he thumbed back at Isa, "more agreeable if she knows her friend is in safe hands while we're gone." Jay looked over his shoulder at Isa. "El Padrino is hospitable that way."

Isa curled her upper lip.

"That doesn't line up," Nick objected. "The old woman isn't—"

"Isn't in any danger," Jay interjected. "I know. But an order is an order. You want me to tell boss man you're questioning this?"

"All right." Nick frowned at Jay. He opened the car door then heaved and hoed his way out. En route to the garage, he kept glancing back at the car as if he expected Isa to bolt. She wasn't going to. Not without Awena and not this close to uncovering a cartel's money schemes.

With Nick in the house, Jay flapped down the visor and found Isa's eyes in the mirror. "Here's how this is going to go. The boss wants you to get your car, but you don't have a car, so you don't have keys. If my boy Nick or anyone asks, you've been using public transportation."

"What?"

"Need to take notes or have you got this?"

Isa narrowed her eyes.

"Your computer's in the shop and you recently had your phone stolen. First time ever you've been without technology." He glanced at the door to the house. "You need to sell this story."

Clearly, Jay didn't want El Padrino or anyone else to know he'd taken her stuff. Even more, he didn't want them finding her car. "Why are you doing this?" she asked.

"I need you out of the picture."

CALCULATED RISK

That didn't gel, either. Why didn't Jay tell El Padrino he knew her real name? That he had all her identification? That'd be a sure-fire way to get rid of her. Permanently.

"Then why not tell your boss the truth? What are you hiding?" she demanded.

"What are *you* hiding?" he retorted.

Isa studied the floorboard for a second, organizing the incoming data. "You already know my real name. What else do *you* know?" She lifted her gaze to meet his in the mirror.

Silent, he stared.

She stared right back.

Having her identification for more than twenty-four hours now, there wasn't much he couldn't know about her. Public records were as accessible as a phone screen. Besides knowing her real name, where she worked a week ago, and that her husband had died in Albuquerque as a cop, he probably knew she didn't have a cat.

"Confession is good for the soul." Conceit teased at his puffed-up lips. He seemed to think he had her backed into a corner.

Well, not yet, he didn't. She exhaled for effect. "I'm not a cop anymore." She tried to blink in an innocent-looking manner. "I was tired and needed a change of pace. I planned to open a coffee shop but when I got this opportunity ... I mean, working for a man like El Padrino could change things for me, you know? It's an opportunity to make some money." Isa shrugged. "Being a cop doesn't pay. Killed my husband and nobody cares."

Jay's head started shaking just as Isa saw Nick coming back into the garage.

She scooted to the edge of her seat and shot her words out fast. "Why are you covering for me? That's what you're doing, right?"

The shaking head stopped. "You're not right for the job I have to do." He twisted around to look back at her, his face close and hard as a rock. "I have someone else in mind."

"To count expense receipts?" She scoffed. "That's child's play."

He faced forward again. "What I have to do is big, and I have a partner waiting."

Nick was at the refrigerator again.

"Then why not rat me out?" Isa watched the big guy open the door, rifle through a drawer. "Let me suffer the consequences?"

"I should," Jay said, his voice tightening. "But I don't want to see your bloodied shirt on a platter. I'm not going to be responsible for another death."

Isa did a double take in the visor's mirror. *Would someone get a heater? Hell was about to freeze over.* Jay Hernandez exposed an ounce of compassion by saying he didn't want to get people killed.

Nick opened the door. Shot Jay a questionable look and wrangled his way back into the Jeep. "She's going to show us where she lives, right?" he thumbed back at Isa. "But shouldn't we cover her eyes?"

Jay let out a gust of exasperated air. "Yes, Nick, she'll show us where she lives. And no, Nick, she's no longer a threat. Isn't anyone briefing you, Nick? You seem out of touch."

Nick grumbled and started the car.

Easing back in her seat, Isa watched Jay dismiss Nick's insolence. Something in the ounce of vulnerability Jay had expressed made her think she could persuade this guy she was the one for his big job, whatever "big job" meant. She was in for the sake of the greater good, which was solving her husband's murder, getting Awena back to safety, and now maybe uncovering a court-admissible laundering scheme. Then she'd figure out if brewing up coffee would be in her future.

"How's the old woman?" Jay asked, reaching over and shaking Nick's shoulder."

"Fine." Nick glanced back at Isa. "She's fine, I guess." He backed the Jeep away from the house.

That's when Isa got a look at El Padrino's substantial compound. She guessed it to be at least six bedrooms, probably more. When they turned to ease down the steep drive, she saw three casitas nestled in the hills that butted up to the house. The rest of the driveway wound through rocky terrain until they passed through a gate flanked by two wiry guards, automatic weapons strapped across their chests.

A layer of the hospitable façade crumbled.

CHAPTER 27

When the trio pulled into her apartment parking lot, Isa dumped the miniscule contents of her purse on the car seat beside her. "I can't get in my apartment." She tried drilling a hole through the back of Jay's thick head with an icy stare. "I don't have my keys. Hmm, wonder who does."

As if he was a magician, Jay lifted one single key for her to see. Never mind that somewhere she had a jumble of keys on a ring. Who knew who had that gold mine?

"Let's go." He motioned at Nick. "You stay here. We won't be long."

Nick opened his mouth to protest, but Jay cut him off. "Rules, Nick. The three of us go trapesing around a place like this, the neighbors might get antsy. With only Isa and me, we won't look suspicious. They'll think she's got a new boyfriend." He ran his fingers through that mess of blond hair. As if that would help.

"I could be the boyfriend," Nick protested.

Isa's throat constricted.

"Get real," Jay said. He opened his car door, slipped on a pair of aviators, and shoved the gun he pulled from the glove box into the back of his pants. "You." He pointed at Isa. "Hurry up."

Oh, brother.

Following her across the apartment lawn, Jay stayed close enough that she could feel his breath on her neck. His twitching nerves told her he wasn't just pretending to be her lover. He operated more like a guard, his attention all over the place—glancing behind trees, eyeing corners, grabbing the back of her tunic when he wanted her to stop. Their short visit to her apartment wasn't a dangerous venture, so why did Jay survey the grounds like Secret Service on presidential detail? Maybe cartel members anticipated danger at every turn. Maybe, like bats, they got overexcited at twilight. Maybe he needed a therapist in the worst way. She wanted him to ease up on the James Bond nonsense so she could have his full attention. Convincing Jay that she was the right person for *big job* was urgent.

But he seemed to be in another world.

Climbing her flight of stairs and putting a little distance between the two of them, she brought the subject up again. "If your plan is to get rid of me, how will you convince El Padrino to let me go? He's got collateral on me by holding Awena."

Jay stepped sideways up the steps, his back against the wall, his head doing one-eighties. "I plan to prove you're inept and not worth his time."

"That will not be easy." She crossed the landing in casual stride like she lived there. Because she did.

He peered over the railing surveying the grounds below. "It shouldn't be a problem."

"I don't like to brag," Isa countered. "But my sarge once called me a genius for detangling a particularly difficult case. If I am an expert at knowing how to uncover difficult financial fraud, then I'm an expert at knowing how to hide it." She pointed at a door. "This is my apartment."

Jay turned, studied the door, then pulled the key from his pocket. He didn't slip it into the doorknob but looked left then right.

"You're in way over your head," he said.

"I think you are."

That got his attention because he looked right at her. "Do us both a favor and make a few mistakes. Then I can get you out of my hair before you get yourself killed."

Get herself killed? Confirmed. Jay had a conscience.

Inspired by his show of integrity, she pushed harder. "Who is this person you think can do a better job than me?

Wouldn't they have the same deadly risk?" She shoved her hands on her hips. "Aren't *you* at risk?"

He put his finger in her face. "Don't."

She batted it away like a gnat. "You are setting up an inside sting on El Padrino, aren't you?"

Shaking his head, he glanced back at the door. "You need to stop."

"That's it, isn't it?" She restrained herself from putting her finger in *his* face. "I'm onto your game."

"You're not as smart as you think." He slipped the key into the doorknob.

She'd nailed it. Jay Hernandez didn't fit the typical cartel persona, and she figured him for an outsider looking to scam El Padrino. She could work with that. Like a double agent, she could get information from both sides. "Let me work with you." Her heart jumped a couple of beats at the prospect. "I'm already in place. Efficiency matters."

"You're wasting your brilliant breaths, genius."

"You know I can do this."

He turned the door knob. "No, I don't."

"That's why you planted those deeds for me to find."

"Deeds?" He eased the door open.

"You don't know?"

"What kind of deeds?" he asked, pulling the gun from behind his back. He peered into the entry hall. Frowned. Seemed over-anxious to meet the cat. The one that didn't exist.

Jay Hernandez didn't know about the title records stashed in the boxes he had sent to her? That meant someone else had set out to give Isa the clues. "Property titles. Deeds to real estate. Are you listening to me?"

He stepped into the apartment.

She kept talking. "I'll show them to you if—" She grabbed the inside of the door. Leaned in behind him.

Jay pulled off his aviators. Put them on her entry table.

"*If* you let me work this gig you think you're going to pull off." She'd never tried so hard to convince anyone of anything.

"Don't you ever stop talking?" He asked over his shoulder in a hushed voice. Jay lifted the gun.

Isa raised a brow. Yeah, she could stop talking. When she was ready to execute the silent treatment. They weren't at that point in this conversation yet. Fine, let 007 perform his apartment sweep. Then maybe he'd calm down and listen.

Following him into the short entry hall, she determined it a good time to let him know she lied about the cat. "By the way, I don't have a c—"

His empty hand shot up to silence her.

She threw both of hers up in frustration.

Jay wrapped both palms around his weapon. Like he positively expected to find someone around the corner.

She had to admit, he looked like a pro with his chin down, torso low. By some weird rule of the universe women found men in protective mode attractive. But she had to say, Jay looked ridiculous, like a gangster wishing he was a cop.

Then Jay's face froze over.

That gun aimed at something.

Isa's pulse kicked up a notch. She knew a threatened man when she saw one. She'd seen her fair share of guns leveled with purpose.

"Well, genius," he said after few tense seconds. "You've got one big cat." He shot her a frosty glance.

She stole a look around the corner. Gasped.

"Hey, Isa." Claire Washington stood there, *her* gun out and pointed at Jay. "Who's your sketchy friend?"

CHAPTER 28

He didn't get the nine girls back. Their fate ... well, that was out of his hands now.

He should have felt some remorse over the travesty, but the positive outcome of the brief meeting outweighed his financial losses.

He'd obtained what he really wanted. El Padrino would host Miguel Lopez at a meeting in Albuquerque in a matter of days. Lopez would send an associate to check out accommodations before his arrival, a common security precaution. As a rule, cartel leaders didn't walk into situations blind, but would have full knowledge of where they were going and how many exit doors were at their disposal.

His driver pulled the Range Rover into the same gated community they'd driven through earlier. Fine homes tucked behind security walls lined the street. Oso's relatives lived like kings and queens, thanks to El Padrino's grace.

Yes, he did things differently, and others were taking notice.

They pulled through an open gate and into the circular drive of a two-story home.

"She'll be right out." Raton stepped from the car to keep watch.

While he waited, El Padrino punched Sophia's cell number into his phone. When the call went to voicemail, he disconnected. Frowned. She hadn't answered a call since he'd left.

CALCULATED RISK

He waved away the encroaching dark disposition. He didn't need Sophia's approval, though she'd managed to make him crave it. He shoved the phone back into the pocket in his shirt. Tonight, he had reason to celebrate. Tomorrow, when he returned, he would dazzle his wife with the news of a future alliance with Lopez.

When a small figure came out the front door and approached the car, Carlos got out and opened the Range Rover's back door opposite El Padrino.

The American Indian peered in.

"Please, join me," he said.

Awena squinted. Searched the ceiling of the car.

"Here." He motioned for her to get in. "We shall discuss your accommodations."

The old woman tossed her cane in, then climbed in beside him. "I see that they do not ride in cars. I've always wondered about that."

This time, he wouldn't let her pull him into a pointless conversation. He gestured toward the house. "Tell me, are you content here, in this home?"

Awena looked back out the window. "It is a fine place. A fertile field."

"You would be comfortable here with Oso's family? For a week? Maybe more?"

"What of Isa Padilla?"

He expected that question. "She is of great value to me. Do not worry for her safety."

"Okay," the woman agreed. "But I will speak with her by phone."

El Padrino anticipated that response, as well. "I'm not sure that can be arranged. International calls can be a challenge."

The old woman's broad lips drooped in thought. After a moment, she said, "They have need of me here. But you must give me your word no harm will come to Isa Padilla."

"You have my word." He clasped his hands together.

"And I will need two or three Bibles."

"Of course. Whatever you wish. You can have Anna Maria send word through my associates with any concerns or needs."

"I accept your offer," she said and gave him a solemn nod.

As if she had a choice. He motioned to Carlos to open Awena's door.

Awena patted the seat beside him. "I have a question for you."

He lifted his smile back into place. "Yes, ask me anything."

"A demon guards something in the kitchen at India Magic. I'd never seen him before. What is it that you hide there in Isa Padilla's building?"

What did he hide there? If the two women had located the heroin and marijuana his men stored in the kitchen walls behind the pantry, then this woman wouldn't be asking what it was. Did Isa Padilla know something she'd neglected to confess? "We must get you a doctor, old woman. Your imagination has rusted with age."

She lowered her brows. "Is your number 96 a biblical reference?"

Clever, insightful woman. He pushed back in the seat and studied the deep lines around her eyes. Her ramblings unsettled him. His mother's spiritual pronouncements had made him ill at ease, as well. But feelings of unease had never held him back. "Where do you get these ideas, old woman?"

"My rusty discernment."

This made him chuckle.

The old woman grunted. "Keep your secrets, then. All will be revealed in time." She lowered her chin. Looked him in the eye.

"It's time to go." He gestured to the open door.

The old woman scooted out of his car.

Leaning across the seat, he watched her, unsettled. Awena had her back to him, cane tip on the ground. "Genesis 9:6," he declared before she was out of earshot. He pulled the door shut.

Awena spun around, her eyes wide with surprise.

"For those who serve me, I *am* God's image." he whispered beneath his breath.

CHAPTER 29

Eyes locked on Claire, Isa tried to organize the incoming data. What was her friend Claire doing in her apartment when Isa hadn't been there for two days?

"Claire," she finally said. "What are you doing here?"

"Who is this?" Jay cut in.

"Drop your weapon," Claire countered. "I'm a police officer."

Isa didn't need Jay feeling threatened by the presence of cops. Cartel guys were known to be trigger-happy in tense situations.

"She's more friend than police," Isa explained. "Now let's all put our weapons away." She stepped up to Jay and put her hand on his arm. "Claire is a good friend."

Neither gun holder lowered their weapon.

All right then. "Claire, this is Jay. Jay, this is Claire. Now that we've had proper introductions, can we move to the next phase of acquaintance without blowing somebody's head off?"

"Her first," Jay said.

"No," Claire replied.

"Okay, both of you. On the count of three." Isa pulled in a breath. "One, two, get ready, here comes the final number ... three."

Jay dropped one hand. Eased to a standing position but kept the arm balancing the gun taunt.

"Oh, for goodness' sake, Claire," Isa blurted. "This is my boyfriend, Jay."

Claire eyed Jay. "You gotta boyfriend?" She lowered her gun. "Girl, what is wrong with you? Mac's only been dead, what? Three months?"

Jay stuffed his gun in the back of his pants and put his arm around Isa. Pulled her in close and jostled her shoulders. "Boyfriend, Jay, that's me."

Isa wanted to roll her eyes but gave him a slight jab to the ribs instead.

He flinched and tightened the boyfriend grip.

"Claire." Isa yanked out of Jay's embrace that felt more like a restraint. "How did you get in here?"

"I'm a cop, remember? We used to work together. We used to be friends. But friends tell each other things, Isa." She holstered her gun in the leather pouch strapped around her shoulder. "You came out here because of this guy?"

"Hey." Jay broke in. "Let's not be rude."

Claire kept going. "You said you needed to get away. That you were starting over. It ain't looking good for you to have some guy stashed in Albuquerque when your husband was killed here."

"Wait a minute." Isa thumbed at Jay. "I just met him. It's a new relationship."

Jay slipped his arm around Isa again. "Yeah, we are new but, you know ... it's serious."

Isa's internal dragon gagged.

"Something's fishy here." Claire shook her head.

"You're jumping to quick conclusions, Claire. I can explain this ... it's ... that, well, I'm in shock at finding you in my apartment."

"I've been here since yesterday, waiting on you."

"You could have called and let me know you were coming."

Claire crossed her arms. "I did. You haven't answered."

Of course, Isa didn't ... have a ... phone. *Thank you, Jay Hernandez.* Surely he'd seen she was getting calls.

"Could we nix the girl squabble, honey?" Jay gave Isa a loving smile. "We got a ride waiting outside." He nodded at Claire. "We're picking up a few things for my girl, here. Then we're off."

Isa pulled away from him again and stepped close to Claire. "Caba sent you, didn't he?"

"Okay, I'll tell ya the truth. He's wearing down the floor in front of my desk. He asked me to come check on you. But you don't answer calls, and you show up with a gun-toting thug with a gang symbol looking like a neon sign on his freaking neck." Claire crossed her arms. "What the heck? Now I'll have to either lie to Sarge or break his heart with the truth."

Isa jutted her chin forward. "I don't work for HPD anymore, remember? I'm a private citizen. I don't answer to Caba. Or you."

"You're still one of us. You need to get yourself back home where you belong."

Behind her, Isa sensed Jay relax, shifting his alliance to Claire. "I agree."

Isa cut her eyes back at him.

"Go back where you belong, baby. I'll catch up to you in a day or two."

Apparently, Claire didn't like him butting in because she shoved her hands on her hips. "What's a white boy like him doing in the Mexican cartel anyway?"

"Who said I was with a Mexican cartel?" He touched his neck. "I like the number 96. It's like a 69, you know—Yin, Yang."

"This would go smoother if you'd keep out of it," Isa snapped at Jay.

Claire pointed at his neck. "Ninety-six is major cartel signage. Isa, what is his last name?"

Jay and Isa exchanged a glance. Of course, Claire would go back to Houston, look Jay up and start to unravel Isa's plans.

"It is Jay ... Jay ... Jay White." She faced Claire. "As much as I'd like to chat, we have plans, so, you need to leave."

"Leave? Just like that? You want me to go without telling me what's going on here?"

Isa bit the side of her bottom lip. Nodded.

"All right, then." Claire adjusted the gun at her ribs. Flipped her curls. "I'll call you. When Mr., uh, White isn't around."

CALCULATED RISK

"No." Isa's eyes met Claire's again. "I lost my phone." Isa glanced back at Jay, who looked like he wasn't sure this was going the way he wanted. "Right, Jay? I haven't had a chance to replace it."

Jay was shaking his head. She feared he might blow the whole ruse and force her to go with Claire. But he played along. "Yeah, she loses everything."

"I'll text you my new number when I get one," Isa said.

"Right." Claire stepped past Isa and pulled right up into Jay's face. "Just so you know I know, Mr. White." She put her finger at the tip of his nose. "Isa doesn't lose anything. She's got a gigantic case of OCD and organization is her obsession." She clicked her tongue a couple times. "You two don't fool me."

CHAPTER 30

Claire, head high, pulled the door closed behind her.

Isa rushed to it. Twisted the deadbolt. Wrapped her hands around her ponytail and stared at it, trying to digest what had happened.

A lot had happened. First, she lied to a good friend. Second, the jabbing knife at her conscience told her the lies where coming too quick and easy. Third, Claire practically accused her of having her husband murdered by a gang member. And fourth? The fragile case she was constructing to convince Jay of his need for her would crumble within a matter of days, maybe hours, once Claire investigated a few things. Isa could imagine the HPD hounds gathering in the office bullpen and debating foolish Isa, who'd joined a cartel. There would be a call for action.

"You're an okay liar," Jay said from somewhere behind her.

She twisted around.

"But Jay White? You couldn't come up with something better than Jay ... *White*?"

The problem with Jay Hernandez was ... he was no street swindler looking for a win. This guy had training in some official capacity, be it military or police or—she brushed past him and dropped into the chair opposite the sofa. "Claire will dig around and figure out who you are and where I'm staying. They'll either stage a rescue or bring me in on suspicion of my husband's murder."

"Yup, you've made one heck of a mess. It's time for you to exit my life." He moved to the sofa and looked behind the blinds. "She's backing out." He pulled his phone from his pocket and started tapping on the screen.

"What are you doing?"

"Getting her license."

Problems piled up like the garbage in HPD trash bins. He'd probably have some thug run Claire off the road to keep her silent.

"Don't send anyone after her. I'll handle it," she said.

Without looking up he responded. "I'm not putting a hit on her, I'm investigating her." He finished tapping at the screen. "And figuring out how I'm going to make her go away. You don't have a way to communicate, remember. You're supposed to be a hostage. What the heck do you think you're doing in the middle of this cartel, woman?" He didn't give her time to answer that question. "You are one big headache." He eased down on the arm of the sofa, still punching at his phone screen. "I didn't know your husband was murdered here in Albuquerque." He thrust his hands into the air. "How did I miss that glaring detail?"

"You're a cop," Isa whispered, rubbing her face. "Playing both sides."

He looked up at her, eyes on fire. "You think so? You don't know the half of it, and you need to stay out of all of it." He started punching at his phone again. Then he shoved it to his ear.

She sucked in a breath, half expecting him to snitch her secrets to El Padrino.

But he put on a friendly voice. "Nick ... yeah, I know ... I need a little time with the lady, if you know what I mean. Go get a beer and be back in an hour ... No, man, it's all good ... I'll take the heat, but there won't be any ... No man, I'm not letting her out of my sight, if you know what I mean ... No, Nick, I am not a fool like you. The accountant and I have a little" ... he snickered ... "personal business to attend to."

"Oh my gosh," Isa said when he disconnected. "*That* is all men think about. Do you seriously think I would—"

"Relax, genius. I'm buying a little time." He pulled the gun from behind his back and slid off his perch on the sofa's arm. "I need a second to figure out how to get rid of you. Tonight."

CHAPTER 31

Isa glanced at the gun beside Jay. He wouldn't shoot her. He'd been much too concerned about her getting killed by gang members and too repulsed at the news of Juan's death to be an executioner. "You're a dirty cop."

"Okay." Jay flung his hands in the air. "Congratulations. You get the prize for top-notch detective work. I am indeed with a drug squad." He looked like he might laugh and scream at the same time.

She blinked a couple of times. "So, I'm right?"

"You guessed it." Jay dropped his head on the back of the sofa and stared at the ceiling.

"What kind of bribes are you getting?"

He lifted his head again, eyes glazed with frustration. "You don't get it. I'm not driving down both sides of the road. I'm a special agent with the Federal Bureau of Investigation." His head fell back again. "Heard of that agency, genius?"

Isa crossed, then uncrossed her arms. "You're FBI?" She crossed them again. "As in undercover FBI?"

"On semi-permanent loan to the Albuquerque field office from headquarters in Dallas. Once I infiltrated El Loco Padrino's operation, we staged an IRS audit to get a deeper look at his books. But our appointed accountant and my supposed partner, well, her sister had her baby early. She took two days off, and I've been stalling until she could get here." A groan emitted from his chest. "When my sister had a kid, I didn't take any time off. Women agents. Always something. Now I've got you to contend with."

Isa felt as if she'd stepped into bad dream where one person morphed into another without warning—one of those nightmarish nights where she lost track of who was who. Including herself. "This has gotten complicated."

"You are a smart one."

The sarcastic remarks never stopped coming with this guy. "What are you looking for?"

"For a way to get you out of the picture."

She waved him off. What an amazing scenario they had on their hands. He had an experienced accountant sitting right in front of him. He didn't realize the convenience.

"No, really," she said, thoughts running way past convincing him of anything and how she could begin to tie some suspicions together. "What are you looking for inside his books?"

He shrugged his shoulders. "The usual. Money laundering, drug smuggling, human trafficking, accounts of dead bodies." He sounded like he read from a dictionary. "All in a day's work." Sitting upright again, he lifted his brows. "Oh wait, it's not a day's work. It's six months hard labor getting into El Padrino's inner circle, and you are about to expose my cover after being here, what, forty-eight hours? Tell me something. Are you blowing up my operation because you really want to join a cartel, or is this about your husband's murder?"

Isa pulled at her cheeks. She couldn't get the word *unbelievable* out of her head. If she wrote a summary of this case, no one would believe her. The number of coincidences, which was eight, were unreal. Maybe this started as an informal look into circumstances surrounding Mac, but now? Now she had the opportunity to help bring down an evil and despicable drug cartel leader.

"Yes, okay," she conceded, hands moving from her face to her ponytail. "This started with my husband's murder."

"I knew it."

"Look, I didn't come here expecting to be kidnapped into a drug smuggling operation. I came to open a coffee shop, in a building I rightfully own, by the way. I did plan to dig around Albuquerque's drug scene a little. So what? No one can explain to me what my husband was doing in Albuquerque when he died. He was supposed to be working in Houston on a drug sting that night. I'm looking for answers." She dropped her hands to her lap. "Can you blame me?"

"You should let the law do its work."

That statement hit a nerve. A sensitive one that was sick of hearing about the law working. It wasn't working. Period. "Well, you've been on the ..." she formed quote signs with her fingers. "*Inside* for six months. You tell me. Was Mac Phillips a part of your big, secret operation?"

"Don't know the name."

She wanted to knock the blasé look off his face but restrained her clenched fist against the arm of the chair. "What about Johnny Morris? That was an alias he'd used before. That name ring a bell?"

"Nope."

He was awful quick to answer. She didn't believe him. "I don't think you're trying to remember."

"You've jumped on the wrong track," Jay said. "Your late husband had nothing to do with me or the cartel I'm working." He wiped his hands together like he'd hatched a magnificent idea. "Let's get you back to Houston and your accounting job."

That wasn't an option. She was not giving up this opportunity. "Listen to me," she said and counted off her fingers. "Number one. Someone in El Padrino's house wants me to see properties in Houston because they've planted this information in the books. Two. Someone left me a cryptic note in my car about revealing hidden things. Three. My husband secretly owned the building I was in when *you* took me against my will. That's a heck of a pile of facts that put me ahead of you in uncovering dirt on El Padrino. I'm not leaving."

"Wait a minute." He scratched at his mass of blond hair.

Finally. It seemed she had gotten through Jay Hernandez's single-focus brain.

"Someone in El Padrino's house wants you to see what?"

"Properties, deeds, titles. All in Houston. If you'd been listening to me—"

CALCULATED RISK

"The India Magic building is a drug storehouse. Did you know that?" His brows smacked together in concern. "*Your* husband owned that? I thought you were lying about that building."

Her arms flew into the air. "That's what I've been trying to tell you."

Jay eyes shot back and forth. Looked like he had trouble getting the facts where they belonged.

"So, you're saying someone has been baiting you with information and your husband was a traitor cop?"

The *traitor cop* words said aloud stung harder than expected. She'd loved, or at least thought she'd loved, a man who, if this were true, would be considered the lowest of the low of humanity? She thought she might tear up but decided she wouldn't give Jay the opportunity to gloat. She steadied her wobbling heart. "Welcome to the bigger picture." She got up and headed to her bedroom to retrieve what she'd come for.

"We need to work on your exit strategy," he called after her. "I'll see to it the old lady you brought with you gets out of there. Springing her will be quick and easy."

Her laptop wasn't on the nightstand where she'd left it. She glanced across the bed, then over to the dresser. Walked around to look at the floor on the other side.

No laptop.

Isa went back into the living room. Started tossing pillows then fell to her knees to look under the sofa.

Tapping on his phone, Jay said, "What's your exit plan?"

"My computer's gone."

He glanced up momentarily. "Really?" Then his eyes went back to his screen. "Plan, Isa. We need to get you out of here."

"It's not here." She peered under the chair. "Each night I go through the same routine. Research cartels, plug in the laptop at my nightstand, turn out the light. I don't misplace anything. Ever."

"Your friend with the gun mentioned OCD."

Isa pulled up to her knees. "That's it." She should have known. "Claire took my computer. She's going to look at my research history. But ..."

"But what?" He finished with his phone and shoved it in his pocket.

"Why would Claire ..." Thoughts she didn't really want to think about her friend creeped around in her head. "It looks like Claire made the decision to confiscate my computer before we got here." Isa got to her feet. "She must have stashed it in her car earlier. If her being here was supposed to be an innocent check-on-my-friend visit, why would she steal my computer?"

"Maybe your former department thinks you've gone batty. Seems a reasonable conclusion. I can understand them sending in a friend to check your status and snoop around. They have a brotherhood to look after." He pushed off the sofa and put his gun in the back of his pants. "I'm having some guys look for her. Bring her in for a brief so she'll stay away."

"Okay. Once she knows you're a cop, things might make sense to her."

"You need to write down the property addresses in Houston, and I'll have the office look them up. We need to stage your escape. I'll convince Nick you outsmarted me and got away." Jay shook his shoulders like he dreaded the thought. "That won't be an easy sell."

Isa bit her lip. "No."

Jay raised his brows.

"Number one, I can't remember the addresses off hand. And number two, I'm going back to El Padrino's to dig around and find out who's interested in me getting those property titles. I'm not changing my mind as long as Awena is a captive in El Padrino's house. I'm your inside partner now, and you're going to have to accept it ... Mr. White."

CHAPTER 32

On highway 25, north of El Paso, El Padrino eased his head against the back seat, a small ache beginning in his temples. Twice he'd called her. Twice she did not answer. Though he'd knocked around his fair share of women, never had he taken a fist to Sophia. On the day they married, he made a vow that she would receive everything she deserved—his admiration, his respect, and an equal share in his wealth.

Everything she deserved.

"El Padrino." Oso twisted to face him from the front seat. "A text." He held up his phone. "The accountant and Jay are not yet back to the compound, and the outside security camera picked up someone walking across the lawn towards your living quarters."

The throb in his forehead pulsed harder. "Who was it?"

Oso shrugged. "They did not get a clear picture, Señor. This could be one of our men, but they have been told to stay away from your quarters when you're not there."

"Sophia is in the house, yes?"

"I'll check." Oso started typing into his phone.

"Have Snake check with Nick and let me know where Coyote and the accountant are." El Padrino pulled his laptop from the seat beside him and opened the camera app.

Sophia never allowed cameras in their bedroom, but she'd agreed to let him place a couple around the exterior of the patio of their private area as a security precaution.

CALCULATED RISK

Scrolling through screens, he opened the footage of their uncovered patio overlooking a rocky drop into a canyon. The flood lights were turned on, but the patio empty.

Except.

Something on the ground.

He took a screen shot. Widened the photo with his fingers.

On the tile, next to the white wrought-iron table where he and Sophia had shared many meals, was half of a snuffed-out cigarette.

Except, Sophia didn't smoke.

"She's there." Oso said, looking back again. "In your room."

El Padrino slammed the computer lid shut.

CHAPTER 33

Jay Hernandez didn't get it. Someone had fed Isa possible incriminating evidence. Someone wanted Isa to uncover the truth.

"You heard me, right? I'm going back to the compound." She did an about face and walked back into her bedroom. Jay followed but stopped at the door when his phone dinged with a text.

She pulled underwear and Polo shirts from her drawers and khakis and jeans from her closet. She marched into her bathroom for the toiletries.

From her vanity in the bathroom, she heard Jay say, "Great. Nick's back already. You are really messing things up here."

Miniature bottles filled with shampoo and conditioner went into the travel tote.

"Not happening," Jay stated. His phone dinged again. Pounding the screen with his thumbs, he said, "And Nick's a little too impatient."

Isa squeezed past him to get her suitcase in from the entry hall closet.

"You're killing me here."

She packed it all, then she pushed past him again, the suitcase in hand.

"Come back here."

She stepped into her entry hall. Glanced at her apartment key on the table. Jay moved in behind her and she thought he might try to physically force her to stay put.

But he talked instead. "I outrank you, and I'm ordering you to stop this advance."

She stole a glance at him over her shoulder. His face radiated a deep shade of maroon and a trail of smoke almost lifted from his ears.

"I'm a civilian and don't take orders anymore." Daring him to do something about her resolve, she unlocked the deadbolt.

"Isa." His tone rose with the last syllable.

She pulled the door open. She wasn't changing her mind. "Cover your butt if you need to, Jay. Tell the FBI and the HPD and whoever else you're afraid of that I'm your inside snitch because, tonight, I'm joining this cartel."

A summer gust hit her face when she stepped outside, and for a millisecond, she had the urge to grab her key and run.

She stood motionless for a second. Didn't hear Jay. He and his arrogant self must have waited for her to come rushing back in like a rookie, anxious to follow his orders. He didn't know her. Didn't know she'd survived a sicko stepfather, her brother's overdose, and Mac's lies.

Isa scurried down the steps.

From behind the steering wheel of the car, Nick looked relieved to see her. She opened the backseat door, threw her suitcase in. But she didn't take the subservient position of hostage and crawl in the back beside her stuff. She pulled the front passenger door open and took what Jay would consider his assigned seat. Clicked her seat belt. Nodded at Nick.

"Uh, where's Jay?"

"Giving the cat to my neighbor." She smiled. "He'll be right here."

CHAPTER 34

Isa pulled the visor down, pretending to check her lips. In the back seat, Jay wore a scowl that made his bruised face look menacing. When he caught her looking, he curled up one side of his puffed-up lip.

Their partnership was off to a rocky start.

"Hey, where you going, Nick?" he huffed from the back seat.

Isa assumed Nick drove them back to the mountains and El Padrino's home.

"The bar," Nick answered. "Picking up Oso."

She could feel Jay's body tense from the back seat. Heard him swear under his breath.

The rest of the ride was silent, though Jay shot her plenty of messages through the knee he kept jabbing into the back of her seat.

When they pulled into the Drake's Horn's parking lot in back, Isa settled into her space, eyes searching the alley that ran between the bar and India Magic. Jay had stated that India Magic served as a drug storehouse. She could see how easy it would be to move drugs back and forth down the secure, walled alleyway.

Nick lumbered out of the car then leaned back in. "You comin'?" he asked Jay.

"No."

"Oso is meeting us here. Could be a while." Nick glanced over at Isa. "Don't lose her."

"Who are you giving me orders?" Jay spouted.

Nick slammed the door. Sauntered off towards the bar.

Isa heard Jay thrash around in the back seat then open his door.

Good. She wouldn't have to listen to his tirade, since he'd obviously decided to go on into the bar.

But that's not where he went. He put his bruised face in her car window.

She humored him. Rolled down the glass with the hand crank.

"We're going in," he growled.

"I don't trust you yet." She started the hand crank in the other direction.

Jay put his hand on the top of the glass and pushed.

"You're going to break this," she said trying to get the window up.

Jay opened her door, reached across, and had her seat belt unlocked before she could react.

"Out," he said, his good eye narrowing at her.

"Fine." Isa got out. Threw her purse over her shoulder.

He walked, she stomped to the side door.

The Drake's Horn had transformed. When she'd been ushered in two days earlier, the bar stools and chairs had been haphazardly turned upside down on counters and tables and the place had reeked of stale cigarettes and shoddiness. But tonight, the air teemed with chaos. She practically had to swim through the fog of cigarette and marijuana smoke.

She asked Jay for a gas mask.

He grabbed her wrist and pulled her to a booth in the corner.

Three bikers and one scantily dressed young female occupied the cluttered table next to them. *Free Bird* blasted from nearby speakers.

Before Jay scooted into his side of the booth, a middle-aged woman with red hair at the ends of long gray and brown roots slipped up beside him, her arm reaching for his shirt. "Oh my, who gave you that nasty black eye?"

"My mama!" Jay laughed.

"Are you drinking tonight, Jay Boy?" The waitress must have had an eye for Jay because her hands on his chest went way past what Isa considered personal boundaries. Guess it made sense for the gals to go for Jay. Among the fine selection of eligible bachelors in the Drake's Horn, Jay had all his teeth.

"You know what I like," he told her. "Juice me up."

The red ... er ... red, gray, and brown head must be the waitress. She never acknowledged Isa's presence.

"I'll have a water," Isa called as the woman disappeared into the haze.

Jay slipped into the booth seat opposite her. "That's the door," he said, nodding to the front of the bar. His voice volume hovered just above Lynyrd Skynyrd's guitar licks. "Go now and I'll make sure you make it out. I can have a Fed car pick you up in ten minutes."

"Nope, but my car's been in a parking lot down the street for two days. Can your guys drop by and put some money in the meter?"

His face turned maroon again. "You like to count, right?"

Odd question, but she answered. "Yes, why?"

"I'm going to give you three reasons you need to get up and walk out of here. You're not employed by any agency that can cover your reckless and spontaneous decisions. That makes you a liability, not an asset, not to mention an uninsured nightmare." He shot two fingers in the air. "I'm not free to run your errands. I've been sequestered by El Padrino just like you." A third finger shot into the air. "I don't trust your ..."

Nick walked up, his eyes dazed and looking like he'd inhaled more than the lingering secondhand smoke. He pulled a chair up to the end of their table as if invited. She found it odd how quickly the lowly thugs like Nick cozied up to newcomers like her. Always it was the undesirables that welcomed in the new kid. Nick sat down, took a swig of the beer in his hand. "Three what?" *Free Bird* faded, and the moaning sax intro to Bob Seger's *Turn the Page* started up.

That Jay was fast on his feet.

"Three times I've asked the lady to dance with me, and three times she's declined," he fibbed.

Clever. At least he's pretending that I somewhat belong.

"Maybe she'll dance with you, Nick."

Isa's heart stopped for a second, then she narrowed her eyes at Jay.

Nick's eyes, on the other hand, lit up like the Fourth of July.

Isa glanced over at the dance floor. One couple propped each other up there, swaying in and out of the single beam of light spotlighting the center.

"Okay, Jay." Isa said as the partial redhead returned with his drink. "You're on. Let's dance."

"Hold that juice for me, Nick," Jay said sliding out of the booth and patting Nick on the head. "Maybe she'll give you the second dance."

Nick's fireworks fizzled. "Why don't you kiss my—"

Jay pulled her onto the floor so fast she didn't catch the last of Nick's invitation. The FBI agent yanked her up close, both arms tight around her waist.

"Hey," she warned. "If you keep up the rough stuff, I'll show you how I take down an opponent."

"You're the one who wants to play cartel games." He looked around. Nodded at someone wandering aimlessly across the dance floor. "I'm making you look legit."

"Whatever," Isa retorted. She clumsily moved her hands around his shoulders, looking for a platonic place. "I think you like being a macho guy in El Padrino's cartel."

He raised his hand up to the middle of her back. Commenced the swaying—offbeat of course.

"You like the action, the guns, the girls, and playing a big shot to El Padrino's brow-beaten indigents, don't you?" she asked, looking over his shoulder.

"Oh, I see what you're doing," he said. "You'll feel better about this foolishness if you convince yourself that I'm a creep. Makes you feel like the hero. Well, you're off base. Big time. There are a lot of other things I'd rather being doing right now. I'm not here because I love undercover work. I'm here because ..." He paused. Looked down into her face, then back up to the patrons beyond the dancefloor. "Because cartel members have killed agents who were like brothers to me. Because I've seen girls as young as eleven kidnapped and forced into prostitution. Because drugs are ruining our society. I do what I do as a sense of duty."

"Shall I get your shield, Captain America?" She might regret that remark if she let herself think about it.

Jay smirked.

She thought about it. Wished she hadn't blurted out the Captain America comment. Most people drawn to law enforcement careers felt a true dutiful calling.

"I lost a brother," she said, deciding to try and relate to her new partner. "Overdose."

He pulled her in closer, almost like a hug.

"Let's get you out of here." He almost sounded like a friend. Maybe this guy wasn't a robocop, but a human with a heart of flesh. "Before you screw important stuff up."

Isa's body went rigid. "What makes you any better than me?" She pushed away from him.

He caught her by the wrist.

Isa tried to jerk her hand away without making a scene, but he pulled her into him again.

Before she could wrestle out of his hold, he had one hand around her face and his lips covering hers.

Jay kissed her.

Unbelievable. She jumped back and crouched, ready to take him down on the dance floor.

He chuckled and motioned for her to come close again. "Come here, babe."

"What do you think you're doing?" The dragon pawed at her gut, looking to take control.

His eyes narrowed above an insulting grin. "Claiming you."

She looked around. No one seemed to notice that the two of them had almost come to blows.

"Claiming?" Here came the dragon's fire. "I'm not property."

Jay stepped closer. "If you're going to play this game, then these people ..." He nodded around the room. "These criminals and thugs need to think you're my property. I can't watch you 24–7. But if they believe you belong to me, that might deter a few unwanted advances in the future. In other words, I am covering your hide."

"Oh, spare me the super-hero arrogance." She straightened. "I can take care of myself."

"Oh, really?" He got close enough to tower over her—a lame display of dominance. "You can't. You proved that when you got yourself kidnapped."

"How do you know I didn't plan that?" she retorted.

A bar patron in a Harley jacket walked across the dance floor close enough to hear the heated exchange.

Again, Jay covered. He reached over and tenderly moved a strand of her hair from her forehead while nodding at the biker. He smiled lovingly, but his words were border-line hostile. "You're on my turf now. Play my way or go find another playground."

CHAPTER 35

Not long after sunrise, El Padrino made his way to the office to take care of a few details. Then he wandered into the kitchen where their cook, Maria, prepared his and Sophia's coffee. Always they had their coffee together, discussing the day's agenda. Sophia had insisted they start the ritual when they married. Kept her close to him and the business's progress.

But today, Sophia didn't show.

He finished his coffee on their patio where someone had removed the cigarette butt. Afterward, he found her in the living area of their private quarters.

"You missed our morning coffee." El Padrino came up behind her and ran his hand down the back of his wife's shoulder-length hair.

"Luca is not feeling well," Sophia feebly offered, her gaze lifting from the papers in hand. "I wanted to stay close."

He walked around to the front of the sofa to face her head on. "Should I not know when my son is ill?"

She shrugged. Placed the paper beside her. "It is nothing serious. Only a child's cold."

"I can have a doctor brought up to see him."

"No." Her answer came quick. "He will be fine."

Watching her close, he waited to catch a hint of betrayal in her eyes.

But Sophia didn't flinch.

"What are you reading, mi amor?" he asked, redirecting himself more than her.

"A list of my mother's assets." She exhaled dramatically. "Antonio mailed it from Italy. He's requested I come to help sell her house. He has chastised me again for missing her funeral."

"You know how I feel about your leaving the country." He'd put this issue to rest weeks ago. "It's not safe for you to even leave this compound. So how can I let you fly halfway around the world?"

"You are a good man, José," Sophia said, insincerity barely detectable, but there. She unfolded her long legs and stood. Tipped her head and then, as only Sophia could do, she eased the tension between them with her luminous dark eyes. She came to him, wrapped her arms around his neck. "I want for nothing because of your care. But my family needs me."

He slipped his arms around her waist, felt the curve of her hip. "You must forget about Italy."

She dropped her chin, and he kissed her forehead.

"You can stay busy by planning me a fiesta, love. I have news."

She lifted her gaze. "News?"

"Miguel Lopez will come here." He tapped his chest. "To meet with El Padrino."

Her lips parted in a sly smile. "José, I am proud for you."

"He's sending an associate ahead, to inspect our security. I want to impress him." He ran his forefinger down her cheek, questioning the sincerity of her words. "As well, a fiesta will show the family we are celebrating the new union. That our alliance is a good thing."

"Does *our family* include that woman you've brought into my home?"

He pulled her hair back, lifting her face to his. "What is this? You knew an auditor was coming."

"I didn't know it would be an attractive female."

"No?" He enjoyed the igniting spark of jealousy. Made suspecting her of ill intensions less formidable.

"She is not what I expected."

"Sophia," he reasoned. "You are the queen of my home and my heart. The accountant is nothing more than a tool.

As we discussed, I cannot let financial records leave the compound, and so the bookkeeper needs to work here."

If the little accountant kept Sophia vying for his attention, then he could certainly find more than an IRS audit to keep Isa busy and close. "Besides," he soothed, "I've been told Jay Hernandez chases after her. It will be entertaining to watch the accountant rebuff that untamed dog."

Her expression went flat again. "You see, instead of listening to your wife, you watch these games from your cameras." She dropped her arms and made an abrupt turn.

He let go and let her walk away.

Fiery Sophia. He might have to douse her flames soon.

CHAPTER 36

In the bathroom, Isa rubbed a towel at her wet hair, wondering if Jay would ever really cooperate with her. If last night was any indication, then she could guess he would be a constant challenge. After the kiss on the dance floor, he'd all but ignored her. Except to slap an arm around her when Oso arrived. Once she, Jay, Oso, and Nick returned to the compound, Jay and Oso disappeared behind double doors off a side veranda. Nick had been the one to escort her back to her bedroom. Locked her in, of course.

But thank goodness for a new day. For the shower and fresh clothes. She threw the three-days-worn tunic in the corner trash can. The navy T-shirt and khakis felt like home. Something needed to, because she was about to become one of El Padrino's family members.

That thought made her heart dip.

She wiped her towel across the fogged-up mirror. Studied her damp face and wet hair. By way of miracle or those eight coincidences she'd tallied up last night, she found herself in the unique position to make a difference.

But here she stood, all soggy and untrained, unprepared, and under qualified. In the mirror, she looked more like a skinny rat drowning than a poised undercover agent.

She bit her lip. Could she really do this? Feeling brave in her own apartment last night, all this seemed so doable. But the morning had arrived with realities. Hard ones. Like guys with guns, locked doors, and cameras creeping on her 24-7.

She leaned closer to the mirror. Didn't see anything exceptional there.

Who on earth did she think she was, anyway?

The scrutiny session moved to her hands—the small and bony things that pushed pencils up and down columnar pads. These were the hands of a bookkeeper, not a fighter.

She curled her fingers into a fist. Studied her knuckles. She'd never hit much of anything except the books. Well, there was the time she'd tackled a purse thief running out of the grocery store. And another incident when she stopped a perp high on meth from escaping the HPD. That one had earned her a black eye. But the truth was, her jiujitsu and gun experience were mere training wheels on a bike she wasn't confident she could ride.

What did she think she was doing?

She looked back into the mirror at her wet face. Frowned. "I'm an idiot," she murmured. "Should have gotten out of Jay's way last night when I had the chance."

But that would disappoint Awena. Her new friend believed they were both there for a reason. She shouldn't allow past fears and failures to dictate her actions now or in the future.

What if God really did choose her for this mission?

She could do this. Would do this. Didn't matter what skills she didn't have, or what weaknesses she did.

Isa lifted her fists to the mirror. Took a boxer's stance. She would do this for a whole lot of good and moral reasons starting with vindicating her brother's death and ending with things she knew she had yet to discover. It would all come out in a future spreadsheet. But for now, she was in— one hundred percent in.

The door to the adjoining bedroom creaked opened, and Jay stuck his head in.

"Hey, Mohammed Ali."

Isa whirled to face him. "Are you some kind of creep? I could have been naked. How did you get that door unlocked?"

He put his finger to his lips to shush her then reminded her, "I'm a cop."

"A perverted one."

He stepped in. Gently pushed the door shut behind him.

"I waited 'til the water stopped, gave you to time to get dressed." He visually checked both doors and scooted closer.

The guy had no respect for personal boundaries. She had worked hard to get hers nice and wide. No coworker cop had ever gotten through her walls—except for Claire on the occasional girl's night out. Well, and Mac. He'd bounced right over her barricade, and the day Sergeant Caba told her Mac was dead, she'd vowed to never let anyone scale her walls again. She stepped back. But Jay got closer.

"What are you doing in the bathroom while I'm still in it?"

He gave her a look that said he didn't have time for explanations.

"I hope you have intel on Awena. I haven't laid eyes on her in more than twenty-four."

"We can't find Claire—"

"What about Awena?"

"I'm working on it. But right now, we need to find Claire."

"Your FBI guys probably didn't perform an accurate search. I hear they get their nails done while real cops are doing all the hard labor."

He ignored her. "My people are watching for her. May make a call to your sarge to inform him so no one else comes looking for you. But no one, I repeat, no one is happy about you being here." He put on a scowl then eyed both doors again. "Here's today's plan." He leaned in too close again. Last time he'd gotten in her face, he'd kissed her. Isa pulled her chin into her chest as far as she could tuck it in.

Speaking softly into her ear, he laid out a scene he wanted the two of them to construct.

"Ew," she said as he whispered on. "That's the best you got?"

CHAPTER 37

Back in her room, Isa spent a couple of hours manually tabulating receipts and contemplating how Jay lived in a dream world. But she followed his lead, hoping a bit of compliance would buy her some loyalty. Across her desk and the top of the bed were hundreds of different-sized and various colored receipts from the Drake's Horn, setting the stage as she'd been instructed. She ripped page five of her calculations from the yellow pad.

Jay would show up any minute. She slipped the page in her hand on top of the other five.

On cue, Jay walked through the door.

The swelling in his face had gone down considerably, and he looked to have spruced up a bit. He even wore a pocketed polo instead of his standard T-shirt. "Hey, gorgeous." He played the role of slime ball well. Amazingly fitting.

She went back to her figures because even though they were acting for the cameras, she couldn't make herself feel flirty. "Hey."

He ambled over to the end of the bed, looked over her piles. "How's the work coming?"

"Just double-checking. I'll get you a list of the needed receipts to fill in the gaps by the end of today." She could hear her own awkwardness.

"Good job," he said, moving in behind her chair.

Isa was focused on the painting above her desk when his hands gripped her shoulders. She bit into her bottom lip, glad neither camera could see her face.

CALCULATED RISK

Jay commenced to massaging her shoulders, cameras watching. The exaggerated motion of his hands hurt. He had no clue how to tenderly touch a woman and would be single the rest of his adult life. Putting her hand on one of his to slow down the vigorous rubdown, she adjusted her shoulders.

He didn't get the signal and kept digging into her shoulders.

Moving ahead with the plan, she pushed her chair back, but accidently knocked it into his knees. He grunted but kept his hands in place as she managed to get to a standing position.

Even from the camera's remote point of view, this had to look ridiculous.

Isa pulled half the room's air into her lungs and twisted around, nose to nose with Jay.

Awkward.

His hands went to her hair—not pulling the hair tie from her ponytail and raking his fingers through her locks, but clumsily pulling at the loose strands around her face. She wanted to screech *ouch, stop that*, but she smiled and tilted her head and hoped like heck that this replicated an amorous expression.

He leaned in for the kiss they'd discussed—the almost-kiss that was to convince whomever watched the footage that they were officially together. She closed one eye, the other watching for him to do as he promised in the bathroom. Interrupt the moment.

He stopped right before their lips met. "Oh, my phone. Someone's texting."

He patted his shirt pocket and lifted out his cell. Began tapping like he was responding to a message. Still facing the camera, she reached behind her and scooted the yellow pages off the deeds beneath them. Jay, faster and smoother than his romantic moves, clicked several pictures of the documents hiding beneath her piles while he bent over the desk, pretending to text.

"Everything okay?" she asked, shielding the view of the real estate titles he had photographed.

"Yeah," he said returning the phone to his pocket. "Now where were we?" He put his hands on the desk, either side of her.

At the end of this charade, she hoped.

"I think we were here." He leaned in riskily close and off script.

She improvised to save them both. "Jay," she said his name as sweetly as her lurking dragon would let her. "I really need some help. Can't you convince *our* boss to get me an iPad or Notebook, at least?"

The cameras couldn't see his face. But he grimaced. She'd drifted off script, too.

"Okay. I get it. You need to get your work done." The laugh that followed sounded convincingly warm and sincere, his FBI acting skills finally showing up. He started to turn, but Isa, playing her role as his whatever, reached out to stop him, get another try at a computer. But as he turned, her hand missed his shoulder and landed on his chest.

He flinched but gripped her hand with his, and pressed in.

Jay had hard pecs.

She pulled out of his clasp fast. That brief touch made her head go somewhere it didn't need to go.

The confusion that flashed across his eyes was quick but there. They stared at each other, the characters they were supposed to be playing dissipating into the uneasy air.

In the middle of their first cooperative effort, a bizarre chemistry developed.

Isa looked away first.

He'd snapped the pictures they needed. She should forget the computer for now and let him leave.

Jay didn't move, for some reason. There were some blurry lines wiggling between them, and she cleared her throat, attempting to straighten those lines out.

Finally, he broke out of their trance. Stepped back, looking like the real FBI agent he was—a pompous stiff. Moving toward the door, he said, "Later," and was gone.

CALCULATED RISK

No. This was the absolute wrong direction for things to be going. She barely liked him and didn't need opposite-gender tension showing up just when they started to work together. Isa turned to face the desk.

The deeds needed to go back into their boxes before someone spied them from a camera.

But she couldn't make her hands work.

A fluke. A misreading. A moment that had come and gone so quickly, neither would remember it, and that moment was affecting her ability to get her job done.

Isa plopped down into the desk chair. Got a fresh paper. Picked up a pen.

Started a new list.

Reason number one she should never remember the way Jay looked when she touched his chest.

Mac.

CHAPTER 38

The shadows long with the late afternoon sun, El Padrino pulled up the day's recorded video footage on his laptop. He watched Coyote Jay paw at his new accountant.

Put a new toy in a cage with a feral dog and he would tear it up every time.

Jay and Isa's initial clashes indicated the two would be incompatible and therefore competitive. Which meant each would vie for El Padrino's favor. But his top financial consultant and new accountant sharing intimacy instead of hostility? That scenario unsettled him.

Watching Jay stroke Isa's hair, El Padrino clenched his jaw.

He'd yet to determine the legitimacy of Isa's outrageous claim that she owned the India Magic building. So he'd sent for Sicily. She would come, and she would explain to him why the title wasn't in his inventory of real estate yet, even though he paid cash for the building months ago. And while she was at it, she could give him an update of a couple of other property titles—the ones his wife indicated were missing.

Instinct told him to get rid of the brewing problems named Jay and Isa and bring in another accountant to handle the audit. But the IRS auditor would arrive at the Drake's Horn within two weeks.

He twirled a pencil between his fingers. Predicaments never slowed him down before. He created opportunity out of dilemmas, and this problem would be no different.

CALCULATED RISK

He dropped his pencil to the desk and shut down the camera app. Isa Padilla—flirting with Jay, yet making demands of El Padrino—might be a little too ambitious. Or, she might be playing Jay. She might—and he grinned at this thought—be playing them all.

Getting to know the real Isa would become a higher priority.

His phone buzzed with a text message from Oso.

My sister is requesting the Bibles the old woman wants. Now she wants eight instead of two. And she asks for them to be dual languages—Spanish and English. My sister also asks how long the old woman will be staying. They have grown fond of her, lol.

So the little Native American had converted Oso's family. His mother would have done the same thing. Better Awena spread her prophetic nonsense in Mexico. The thought of her filling his workers' heads with visions of demons made him uneasy.

He'd think about sending along the Bibles. Last year, he'd allowed his cook, Maria, to place her Holy Books in the guest bedrooms, after all. He chuckled. His cook crossed herself every time someone cursed, but also before she turned the stove burners on.

Women—so tied to the nonsensical.

Including his sophisticated Sophia.

He laid his phone aside and closed the laptop, his gaze drifting to his bookshelf—another thing he possessed that thug-heavy Mexican cartels did not. The accumulation of knowledge. Philosophic, intellectual academia. Even though he'd read less than half the books on his shelves, their presence represented who he really was.

He couldn't wait to show Miguel Lopez his collection.

His phone buzzed and he glanced at it. Another text from Oso.

Bibles, El Señor?

He answered.

If your sister wants the Bibles, we will send them. I have not yet decided what we will do with the old woman.

He would contemplate that later.

After he determined what Isa Padilla was made of.

CHAPTER 39

Up with the morning sun, and staring again at the stack of receipts, Isa tapped the edge of the invitation on her desk.

Someone had scooted a three-by-five card beneath her door during the night. The hand-written note invited her to a fiesta that would be held that evening.

Luck, coincidence, or providence, it looked like she was being accepted into El Padrino's inner circle.

The thought of attending a Mexican cartel's social event horrified her. But the opportunity to get an insider's look at El Padrino's network was something she couldn't pass up.

CHAPTER 40

At precisely 6:00 p.m., Do-Rag knocked at her bedroom door, which was much nicer than his usual custom of barging in her room. He explained the fiesta was on the main verandah and she should take the stairs, turn right, then left, then right again at the bar. From there, she could figure it out.

Butterflies fluttering around the dragon, she nodded and asked, for the first time, "What's your name?"

"Mike," he said.

"Mike," she asked, "do you know if my friend Awena will be at the party?"

He shook his head.

She didn't press him.

Making her way and noting the house layout, she encountered a guard holding up a wall, half asleep. An automatic rifle leaned against his hip. He ignored Isa as if her wandering around El Padrino's house was a common sight.

Something in the cartel castle had changed.

Do-Rag's ... er ... Mike's instructions weren't dead on, but she managed to find her way through the Saltillo-tile halls and common areas. The hand-woven baskets and Georgia O'Keefe art gracing the walls created an enchanted feel she shouldn't be embracing. But the house, she had to admit, radiated warmth and welcome.

How had an evil man created such a beckoning façade?

Isa entered a hall with windows cascading the length of it on one side and got her first look at a fiesta, El Padrino style.

CALCULATED RISK

This was no HPD Bar-B-Que.

Around a series of graduated hot tubs, hot pink, yellow, and turquoise umbrellas topped heavy wrought-iron tables. Silver chafing dishes and layers of breads, cheeses, and fruits graced a buffet that stretched the length of an eighteen-wheeler. A mariachi band tuned up on a grassy knoll.

Like figurine cake toppers that did not adequately depict the real-life bride and groom, fine-looking people milled about beneath the umbrellas of the cartel's gathering.

Isa tightened her ponytail.

She recognized a couple of El Padrino's family members. The oversized snake guy she'd confronted in India Magic at the beginning of this charade was there, as were Oso and Nick. On the other side of the hot tubs, she spotted Jay all cozied up to a Latino version of Hollywood's former famous couple, Angelina and Brad.

But no Awena.

She tugged at the collar of her polo. Self-conscious was not a good enough phrase to describe her response to the fashion fluttering about the lawns.

She quickly pulled her shirttail out, pulled the hair tie from her ponytail to let her hair down, and opened the double-glass doors, giving her flip-flops a scornful look. Why hadn't she remembered to get her tennis shoes from the apartment closet when she had the chance?

Scanning for Jay, she spied him headed her way. He lifted his glass to acknowledge guests as he passed them, looking like he belonged.

His facial swelling seemed to be on the decline.

"I haven't seen Awena in two days," she gushed when he reached her. "Have you?"

"Settle down. You don't want to look nervous."

"I am responsible for her."

"Yeah, well, neither of you should be here."

Washed with relief that Jay was back to his obstinate self, she appreciated his ignoring the voltage that had passed between them the previous evening. She needed to forget about it.

"It's too late to revisit that conversation," she said. "I'm here. Can we move on?"

He adjusted his shoulders and glanced around. "I heard they sent your friend over to stay with Oso's family. His sister's like the best cook ever. Almost as good as Maria—"

"Where is Oso's sister's family?"

"Can I get you a drink?" he asked, nodding at another party attendee. "Or change the subject? I can't be overheard feeding you information."

"I need to lay eyes on her."

"You're telling the wrong person."

"Your closer to our Lord of the Drugs than me. Surely you can extract a little info on a helpless elderly woman."

Jay rotated his neck as if she were already a pain in it. "We have our eyes on her, okay? She's safer where she is than here. That's all I can say. Now let's get you something to drink and find a more private spot."

Isa didn't like it one bit that she didn't have access to Awena. But as long as the FBI had her friend under surveillance, she'd try and convince her dragon to settle down.

He guided her toward a temporary bar set up on the other side of the hot tubs. They passed a circle of men. In the middle of the machoism stood El Padrino, sporting dark sunglasses and a tropical shirt open at the neck. His gold chain glittered in the setting sun.

Her new boss's gaze followed her across the lawn. She felt it with each step.

Isa ordered a water with lime and got down to business. "Anything on the real estate deeds yet?"

Jay tugged at her elbow, pulling her out of the bartender's earshot. "The work you did before, sitting at a desk and maneuvering a little math around to present to a jury, that might have gone fast. But my work is first-line infiltration, and that takes skill and time."

She frowned.

He shrugged off her facial cue and then, benevolently, offered her a few info nuggets. "My guys are surveilling those properties to determine who or what stays there.

Could be storage for cocaine and pot, could be used as housing for his guys coming and going across the border. Or, could be these locations serve as brothels."

"But these properties are in other people's names. And that is a blazing red flag." She glanced around at the gaiety building by the minute. "So where did Padrino come up with this chic crowd?"

"From business dealings." Jay said it as if that should be obvious. "Our boss has two sides. There is the José Ventura monarch who trades in precious metals. His nobleness also owns an avocado farm in Michoacan so that he can keep locals employed." He took a sip of his drink which looked to be orange juice. "Then there's his other side, the power-hungry cartel leader."

"Who takes care of but also kills employees." She added, remembering Juan's bloodied shirt.

"He flips Mexican real estate, too, but I haven't been able to find anything he owns here in the States. He rents the Drake's Horn building downtown."

"Not likely," she said her glass at her lips. "He's hiding money. No cartel rents anything." Then Isa squinted, the setting sun's rays in her face. "Do the party guests know he's a drug thug?"

"Oh, they all know. They all want a piece of big money action and right now, the drug industry is among the biggest. La Liga cartel's annual revenue is near $3 billion. And speaking of La Liga, I heard Miguel Lopez was right here at the compound. I should have been here, too." He smirked. "But no, I was babysitting my newest problem."

Isa took the opportunity to scan the party goers again and ignored the slam.

Jay bent down to speak in her ear. "I'm going to put my arm around you and walk to that table over there." He slipped his hand to the small of her back, his touch light and cautious yet charged with that bizarre chemistry she wanted to get past. "We need to move around, appear like we're comfortable with the crowd."

"I *am* comfortable."

"You're tied up in knots."

He guided her to an empty table under one of the yellow umbrellas. "Keep standing. We don't need to become sitting ducks for Nick or Snake. Those two can stick like glue."

"Got it."

"There's more to El Padrino," Jay continued. "He's complex. That's what you learn in undercover work. Once you're in, you discover despicable things about your targets, but you learn normal stuff, too. José Ventura can be charitable. He recruits guys from recovery programs who can't find jobs. He sees himself as a supporter of his people, like an old-time lord or something. Uses the number 96 as a reference to being made in God's image and therefore, all he does is for the good of something." He gave a quick sideways nod. "Mostly for the good of himself."

Isa gasped. "So, he compares himself with God."

"Yeah." He moved a lost lock of hair from his forehead. "That's why it takes skill to do undercover. You can't get attached or pulled into their worlds."

Isa checked out her flip-flops. *Mac.* He had shown all the signs of getting pulled into a cartel's fantasy world.

This wasn't the time to think about her and Mac and how they'd gone wrong. She needed to stay on task. "So how are you going to bring our boss down?" Isa stood on flip-flop tiptoe to eye El Padrino still in the center of the macho circle. Seeing her, he dipped his head in a greeting. She sank back to her heels.

"Easy on the big vision." Jay smiled at her.

She wished her heart hadn't warmed when he did.

"El Padrino is only getting started. He's small potatoes in comparison to the La Liga gang, but still bringing heavy loads of heroin and cocaine across the border." Jay's smile flattened. He took a pull of the orange liquid in his tumbler, then said, "La Liga. That's our real target, and I'm assigned here for now because our boss wants an alliance, and I want an introduction."

She kept quiet, letting Jay spill all the information he wanted.

"Evidently I missed it a couple nights ago while babysitting you." He glanced over her head and did a survey of the party.

Isa started to initiate her own verbal jab, but Jay redeemed himself with his next statement.

"So, maybe we'll pull El Padrino in on laundering to get him out of the way and me into La Liga."

He said *we*.

She gestured at the "96" tattoo on his neck. "What did you do to deserve that?"

"Just part of the job." Jay touched the tattoo, but jerked his head sideways, seeing something or someone coming close. "Lean in and kiss me."

That command sent a jolt of apprehension through her. "Surely we don't have to make out to be convincing."

He grabbed her hand. "Hang on then. El Loco's coming over."

A cop or female thing, Isa wasn't sure, but her skin started to crawl before she saw the cartel boss, before she felt his firm touch on her shoulder. It seemed she pivoted in slow motion when, with dread, she came face-to-face with El Padrino in party mode.

He looked her up and down like a Hollywood talent scout who had found his new starlet.

What a switch. Was she seeing him in a different light here at a relaxed Mexican fiesta, or had he bought her act, believing she would be an asset to his empire?

CHAPTER 41

The games commenced.

The man who'd refused Isa possession of her own property, who'd ordered her abduction, who had a man's bloodied shirt delivered on a silver plate to prove he'd kill anyone for insubordination, took her gently by the arm.

"I have some people for you to meet."

Jay let go of her hand and Isa, in khakis and flip-flops, metamorphosed from prisoner to espionage mole. She was on.

El Padrino led her to three men—each holding a tumbler and a gawk that wandered all over Isa. The lust was palatable.

She glanced back at Jay. He raised his orange juice in a sick sort of congratulatory gesture. She was getting what she wanted—rubbing elbows with the subterranean creatures of the dark world.

"Gentleman," El Padrino announced, "this is Isa Padilla, my personal accountant." He squeezed her elbow. Heads nodded, but one of the cavalier wannabes eyed her flip-flops. In Spanish, another asked where he picked up a hot *and* smart chick.

El Padrino relocated his hand to Isa's back, his smile apologetic. He replied in English. "We met negotiating a real estate deal."

That was when the guy leering at her chest chimed in. "How come we haven't met before?" He had a ridiculously ambitious grin slathered across his pale face. She pulled at her polo's neckline instead of rearranging his smile with her fist.

El Padrino gestured to the man with his glass. "Andres here works for my real estate company. He doesn't like it when I make private deals."

The men beamed and chuckled and gushed over El Padrino. She guessed they'd fawn over every insipid comment he made to keep his eminence happy. It felt like *The Godfather* being played out in front of her.

El Padrino pulled her away. The next introductions included a second cousin with bleached-orange hair and a wine glass in each hand. El Padrino said she worked at one of his bars. Then Isa met a banker from California who wouldn't make eye contact, and he disappeared soon after introductions. Pure sketchiness.

Her new boss then insisted she eat and led her to the buffet. They passed Jay on the way. He'd taken up with Andres the realtor and pretended not to see her. Figuring out when to appear attached to Jay and when not to would be a challenge, because romance didn't come easy to her in real life. The faux version proved to be even harder.

The mariachi horns blew, El Padrino filled her plate with shrimp tacos, and the crowd livened up.

Even though it was a party where most attendees were engaged in illegal activities, the music, the evening breeze, and the warm aroma of spicy food made her feel weirdly normal. Like she wasn't a prisoner, but a guest. The gray shades of undercover work inched into her black and white box.

But to lap up the atmosphere and food would mean she wasn't much different from Mac, who'd obviously connected to an unaffordable upscale lifestyle. To keep her focus where it needed to be, she mentally repeated two pressing objectives: Deliver Awena to her home. Find the laundering scheme.

El Padrino steered her toward a table of attractive people. Like in the movies, they all laughed, looking gorgeous and gleefully delirious. But still, she could imagine Mac here, loving every minute of it.

In the beginning of this mission, which felt like years and not days ago, she'd been driven by the questions surrounding his death. But unanswered queries gave way to the realization that Mac must have succumbed to the alluring yet shallow enticements dancing like mad in front of her now.

Mac had jumped in over his head. She thought she might tear up at the revelation but kept her gaze on the couple from Brazil seated across from her. El Padrino toasted something she'd missed, and she lifted her water and laughed, following suit of those at her table while having no idea what El Padrino had said.

Then she glanced around for Jay and spotted him two tables over. He signaled for her to glance over at the hot tub area.

She didn't have to look around long before finding what he wanted her to see. The exotic woman's black hair spiraled around her shoulders. Her ivory dress hugged voluptuous curves. And her dark, hawkish eyes dissected every inch of Isa.

A cold chill coursed down Isa's back.

Those gathered around the woman must have sensed something wrong because they either backed away or made clumsy attempts to look elsewhere.

Isa shot a nervous glance at El Padrino.

He popped a shrimp into his mouth. "That's my wife," he said, clearly aware his bride was staring, her scalpels aimed for Isa.

She felt like a cadaver in a morgue with the coroner walking in the door.

Jay had his lips twisted up in an evil grin that declared she was about to get what she deserved for infringing on his undercover work. Payback wore an ivory dress.

"Let me introduce you." El Padrino bore one heck of a menacing smile.

CHAPTER 42

Isa had known the millisecond that Jay gestured towards El Padrino's spouse this woman was not someone she wanted to tick off. En route to meet the one with the hostile stare, Isa pulled her elbow away from El Padrino's grasp only to have him reach for it again. The back and forth elbow exchange happened three times before they arrived in front of his wife.

El Padrino seemed to enjoy his bride's irritation, oddly.

Hoping to defuse the threat, Isa extended her hand in an eager manner.

Sophia didn't return the gesture.

El Padrino's hands finally went for his wife and he embraced her with a kiss on the cheek. "You look lovely," he said, his flattery flagrant.

That seemed to slightly soothe the prickly wife. Her eyes shifted to Isa.

"This is Isa Padilla," El Padrino offered. "The accountant who is staying with us for a little while."

"How long?" the wife asked, skipping the customary etiquette phrases such as *nice to meet you.*

Isa held her glare, even though she'd rather grapple with a man the size of Snake than take on a jealous wife.

"As long as needed," El Padrino replied. He turned to Isa. "Isa, this is my wife. Sophia." He practically rubbed his hands together in sadistic glee.

"Hello," Isa offered, rubbing her hands down her shirt.

"You should equip her with all that she needs to do the job, José. Then maybe you won't have need of her for long."

CALCULATED RISK

Ouch. But how ... did she know Isa wanted or needed things?

With that, Sophia flipped her hair and slithered away. She disappeared into a group of females whose thick and sculptured brows were raised in indignation.

A self-satisfied leer spanned the width of El Padrino's face.

Now she had two people that wanted her out. Jay and Sophia. El Padrino, on the other hand, warmed up a little too fast to make sense.

Unlike accounting, where numbers spoke the truth, undercover work seemed to depend on nuances. El Padrino's course could turn on a dime, or on his wife's mood, evidently.

"I think Sophia wishes you to have what you ask for," he said after he'd watched her saunter away.

Isa didn't want her boss to think she'd blabbed all over the compound about her computer needs. "I, I didn't realize your wife was aware that I needed a couple of things."

"She is aware of many things," he said, an evil little cloud passing over his expression. "I shall give you the computer." He put those awful hands on both her arms. "I like you, Isa Padilla." His mouth said the words she wanted to hear but his eyes said something much more intimate. "I choose to trust you. For now."

She swallowed hard, hoping he didn't see that nervous lump drop down her throat. "Of course. I'm ready to make some money."

"My business is not only about money. You must remember this." He put his disgusting finger on her lips. "When you work for El Padrino, you are my family."

Isa hoped that meant more like a sister than a mistress because she wasn't going there. Ever. "Jay's explained it to me." She shot a loving smile in Jay's direction, hoping El Padrino understood the message.

He ignored her hint. "Welcome." He leaned forward like he wanted to consummate the new relationship with a kiss.

"I'm assuming you'll let Awena go now." She put her palms on his chest to hold him back.

"Of course not," he answered, allowing her to rebuff his physical advance. "She will stay under my generous care as long as you do. She doesn't seem to mind the finer life."

"But there's no need to keep her. I'm not going anywhere."

"I'm not a fool, Isa Padilla. I keep my guarantees close."

"I'd like to see her."

"That is impossible." His eyes took on a warm glow. "You see, she's gone to stay with our extended family in Mexico."

Isa's inner dragon sat upright. *Mexico?* Jay had neglected to say that Oso's sister lived in Mexico.

He had moved Awena outside her reach. She wanted to blow a bonfire of insults at the smug drug lord. Or show him a move or two that jiujitsu had taught her.

But somehow she controlled herself. Stood silently counting the pockmarks in his cheeks.

"Now if you'll excuse me," he said, "I see my honored guest has arrived." He nodded at two men standing near the glass doors she'd come through earlier. "Los Zetas has sent us representatives."

These guys, like her, hadn't put on their best for the party. One wore saggy jeans and the other wore a handgun in the front of his pants. Both had slicked-back hair.

"Of course." She wondered if he expected her to curtsy.

By his imperial grace, her boundaries had widened. But one step outside his margins, and she could end up like Juan. She turned to locate Jay.

Jay had escaped the clutches of the drunk cousin and met Isa halfway.

"Any progress?" His smile was smooth, every bit as confident as El Padrino's.

She had progress, alright. Acquired some infuriating information. "You didn't tell me Awena's in Mexico."

"I knew you'd find out soon enough."

"And Sophia Ventura wants me destroyed. What's the plan to fix these little challenges?"

"I—" something stopped him midsentence.

That something was tapping Isa on the shoulder.

CHAPTER 43

Jay's raised brows told Isa that whoever tapped at her shoulder was someone to dread. She inched around in trepidation.

Sophia.

Isa flinched, expecting the woman to punch her in the nose. Sophia made intense, direct eye contact, and Isa had no idea what would come next.

"I would like to talk to you," she said. "Perhaps tomorrow." Then Sophia waved at someone out in the swelling crowd, glanced at Isa again, and walked away.

Watching Sophia walk away, Jay managed to state the obvious. "It's getting dark, and it's getting weird."

Darker and crazier by the second.

He turned back to Isa. "I think it's safe to slip away for a few minutes."

She moistened her lips then said, "The boys from La Liga are here."

"I know. I'm in a meeting with them later."

He what? Oh, the things he *didn't* tell her.

"But for now," he said, "let's make our affair look legit, since there are cameras everywhere and we have an opportunity to play the role. And don't ask because I have no idea what just transpired between you and Sophia Ventura." He draped his arm across her shoulder.

They moved toward a dimly lit corner at the courtyard wall. What a night.

"Put your arm around my waist," he said.

Isa grudgingly complied and muttered, "This is all like a dream."

But Jay, apparently high on his OJ, stopped and jostled her shoulders. "Don't be dreaming about me. It's business, nothing more."

She pulled away and shoved him in the chest. "I meant Sophia, you moron."

He raised both hands in surrender pretense, a wicked little chuckle in his throat. "You're pushing around the wrong person."

"Can we talk business?"

He reached for her elbows, pulling. "Maybe."

She resisted.

"Remember. The cameras." He almost sang the warning—like it was an invitation to a romp around on his playground.

She let him take her all the way to the wall, his arm heavy on her shoulders again.

Evidently parties brought out the best in Jay.

"So, about Sophia ..." Isa said, trying *not* to be playful.

"Sophia is a lioness." He made a stupid growl sound. "Wild animals are unpredictable."

"I'll say." Isa gazed back at the partiers trying to ignore the dark shadow that fell across Jay's form. The atmosphere, his mischievous attitude, and his good looks sent her thoughts where they shouldn't go.

"She defends her husband," he shrugged. "And she watches over some of his business, though El Padrino would never admit that."

Isa crossed her arms. "What would she want to talk with me about?"

"Like I said, she's wild." He looked skyward, eyes roaming the stars. At that exact moment, Playful Jay morphed into Agent Jay, and Isa was pleased with the switch. She didn't have the emotional bandwidth to play the girlfriend tonight.

And to her great pleasure, Agent Jay started dumping important information. "I hear Sophia had an affair with some guy at the Drake's Horn a year or so ago. But I don't believe all gang-initiated rumors. I can't imagine any woman being insane enough to cheat on El Padrino. He's killed for less reason. But I've been wrong before." He pushed his hair out of his eyes as his gaze dropped to her again. "Once."

"Once wrong? You're a humble guy."

"Yeah," he shrugged as if serious. "So, to answer your question about Sophia wanting to talk with you—"

He stopped, concern in his eyes.

The next thing that happened caught her off-guard.

He reached for her face.

Oh no, he wasn't caught up in the music and the shadows and the moment, was he? Yet his hand kept coming. *Please no. Not the face.* She could feel her stepfather's hand clutching her chin, his thumb pressing into her cheek. She flinched and stumbled backwards to avoid the incoming boundary breach.

Jay's face flipped from concern to contempt. "Settle down." He demanded. "I'm getting a bug out of your hair." He extracted a giant moth from the top of her head. Tossed it over the wall.

Isa wanted to disappear.

He put his index finger back in its favorite position—in front of her face. "You've got colossal issues."

She straightened. "Okay. Okay." Pulled the hair tie from her wrist and wrapped it around her hair, getting her ponytail back in place. "Enough of the insults. I didn't read that right, so let's move on."

He exhaled pure exasperation and leaned back against the courtyard wall with arms crossed to create his own boundary. "You're some piece of work, Phillips."

"I ... never mind. Get back to your point." Isa put her hands on her hips.

He pulled in a long breath. "Well, here's my take. Sophia has either decided to trust you ... *or* Sophia is going to run a knife through your back."

CHAPTER 44

With the party still raging outside, El Padrino made his way through the silent halls of his hacienda, stopping to admire the artwork he'd purchased over the years. As he studied each piece, he considered his own creative accomplishments. Like an artist at the easel, he painted people in and out of his masterpiece. Tonight, the fiesta was his canvas. Even with alcohol swirling in their heads, he could always identify the people who would prove to be loyal. Loyal subjects kept their eyes on him, hung close. The disloyal used festive occasions for their own agendas and motives.

History proved that many great leaders gathered their loyal not only through fiery speeches, but also heart-inspiring celebrations. Tonight he had given his crew and La Liga a taste of what was to come. He'd also determined a few motives.

Sophia's jealousies looked obvious. That momentarily satisfied his building suspicion as she missed coffees, rebuffed his advances, and forgot to mention important facts—like his son feeling ill.

Next, he considered Jay Hernandez's motivations. He seemed the perfect, loyal subject, flashing his teeth and nodding at everyone—a zealous gringo enjoying El Padrino's favor.

At the fiesta, Isa had looked like a clumsy duckling flapping around a pond of swans. But her bold ambitions indicated she craved power. She would grow tired of Jay

Hernandez and his second-tier status soon enough. The accountant *would* turn her eyes to El Padrino in the future. By then, he would have her tangled-up in his web and her allegiance unquestionable.

At his office door, he stopped. Checked his watch. He didn't have much time before he would need to leave, as the men from La Liga had given him the disappointing news that their boss would be coming—but not to El Padrino's compound. Over cerveza and tacos, they had casually stated that Miguel Lopez would meet El Padrino at an undisclosed location to be announced at two-thirty in the morning. He'd heard that Lopez could be shifty like that, making plans and changing them so he never gave a rival or snitch the opportunity to set up a sting. American law enforcement had a high price on that man's head.

But El Padrino had other business to tend to first.

He had kept his next contemplation waiting for the last two hours while guests at the fiesta drank and danced and fell more in love with El Padrino's generosity.

Twisting the heavy iron knob, he pulled himself away from the musings and into the moment. With a push, his door slung open. The room dark, moonlight swept across her handsome form seated in a chair opposite his desk. Most would have driven themselves mad with worry, waiting in the dark for their judge and jury.

Not Sicily. The moonlight pouring through the windows revealed that she lifted her chin.

El Padrino took pleasure in the spirited women he surrounded himself with. Other men gravitated to the beautiful, but empty-headed. Not El Padrino. He found a woman's mind every bit as alluring as her form.

He eased through the shadows to stand inches from Sicily's knees. Propped himself against his desk.

She appropriately waited for him to speak first.

"It has been too long since you've made contact. I've missed you."

Her nonchalant answer was as predictable as the fear she would soon experience. "I've been on duty, as you know. People get suspicious when I drop everything."

"Of course, a woman of your position must take precautions."

What Sicily didn't understand though, was that a man of his position would have to respond to her carelessness. "It has been brought to my attention that I've yet to receive the titles on properties I gave you cash to buy. I dislike it when people let me down. Have I let you down, Sicily?"

There was a slight and humble shift in her tone. "No, not yet."

"Then why have you denied me the things you know belong to me?"

She uncrossed her legs. The first sign of nerves. Anxiety could be as beautiful as the art hanging on his walls, only he held the paint brush. "Perhaps you thought I wouldn't notice. But Sicily, nothing escapes my attention."

"I ... I'm working on it." Ah, there. With a few words, he had complete control. He pushed off the desk. Stood over her. "Help me understand." He found her dark eyes compelling, they swelled so. "What has happened to my properties?"

"I ran into a problem, and I'll take care of it."

He could practically see her heart pound through her chest, though she tried so hard to appear in control.

"I promoted you from a runner to real estate venture capitalist and this is how you repay me?" He slowly bent to place both hands on either side of the chair's arms.

He could smell her fear.

"I'll deliver."

Her vibrating answer wasn't convincing.

"My Sicily," he whispered, and he stroked her curls. "What am I to do should you fail me?"

She jerked her head away. "That won't happen."

"It already *has* happened." He straightened. "Have you heard that Juan is no longer with us?"

She stared, reminding him of a princess awaiting her executioner.

"It's a pity he didn't prove reliable. You'll attend a meeting with me tomorrow."

"But—" she protested.

"Yes?" he asked.

"I have to get back to Houston tonight to show up for work tomorrow. The sergeant is already asking questions."

"Call in sick. Or tell him the truth. I don't care. You'll be with me for a few days until you get this problem solved."

"The deeds were taken," she blurted. "By a partner I recruited."

"Who is this partner?"

Her eyes darted back in forth in search of some sellable answer. "That's the problem. I recruited his help and he ripped me off. Stole the deeds. But now, he's dead."

"Dead, you say? Who is he?"

"He was another cop but got ... well ... involved with another gang."

"This is not sounding good, Sicily."

"But I know where the deeds are." Her chest lifted with a tight breath. "Give me some time, and I'll get everything back and in the right name."

El Padrino's phone buzzed. He pulled it from his shirt pocket and checked the text. Oso would be ready to go soon.

"I'm giving you twenty-four hours to either produce my property titles or tell me where I go to find them. Until then, you'll be with me." He returned Oso's text, telling his faithful worker to escort Sicily out.

He'd get the truth out of her.

He left Sicily sweating it out in the chair and headed for his bedroom on the opposite side of the house. Locating Sophia and telling her goodnight was next on his list. She'd earned his attention tonight and he wished to grant her his favor.

CHAPTER 45

Way before sunrise, Isa pulled open the nightstand drawer. Coincidence, or not, someone had left a Bible in her room, and since sleep came only intermittently, it seemed a good idea to investigate a couple of spiritual concepts that were materializing in her brain.

She remembered a Sunday school teacher saying the Bible lived.

Isa's parents hadn't bothered with spiritual things except when her mother on the rare occasion used God as a convenient excuse to inflict guilt. It had been a neighbor who came by on Sunday mornings and picked Isa up for church. Relieved to get out of the house on tumultuous weekends, she'd waited eagerly at the curb for her ride. No one noticed Isa slipping in and out of the house on those Sunday mornings as her mother and stepfather slept off Saturday night's charades.

She had always known about Jesus. Didn't everybody? You couldn't get through a Christmas season without seeing him in multiple plastic mangers beneath glaring yard lights dotted around neighborhoods. But at that tiny Baptist church, she'd learned Jesus was more than a babe in a manager. There, she discovered he was one with God, and had come to reconcile all sinners to God. And she had been told if she would believe that, accepting him as her Savior, then she would be guaranteed the joy of a heavenly afterlife. Isa remembered how the concept resonated and how her ears were attentive, same as in math class, to the Bible teacher. The idea that God wanted to bring love and order out of the fear and chaos in her life gave her something concrete to hold onto. At least for a little while. But her strong yet naïve belief never ushered in the love she craved from her mother, nor stopped the roaming hands of her stepfather.

She picked up the Bible and went to the concordance in back, scanning for the word *called*. Several Scripture references fell beneath the word, and she flipped through pages and read a couple of passages. When she opened to Romans 8:28, she read the Scripture several times then circled it with the pen from the drawer.

> And we know that all things work together for good to those who love God, to those who are the called according to His purpose.

When her neighbors had moved on to other charitable projects, Isa continued to think about Jesus and even sensed his love. But with constant family failures, she'd eventually given up on the miraculous fairy-tale rescue she desired, and determined she'd find ways to make herself invisible until she could move out of that house of horrors. She waited six long years.

Her senior year, Angel died of an overdose, and she moved in with a friend.

Looking back, Isa didn't know how she'd survived those days, those weekends of cat-and-mouse and drunken wars. Except that maybe God had protected her from things that could have been so much worse.

He'd been there with her. Perhaps she had given up on him, but he never gave up on her. Now, could he use those horrible days to accomplish something good?

She sat higher in bed and circled the Scripture a second time, writing the number 3 beside it. She had three reasons to believe what she'd just read.

1. She wanted to.
2. Something good needed to come from the turmoil and deception in her life. And ...

3. God saw to it that two people went to the trouble to remind her he still cared. Those two people were Awena and the unknown note writer.

Maybe she'd gotten a miracle after all.

Isa straightened her shoulders and closed the book. Starting now, she should try and see events not as mere coincidences or luck, or out-of-the-blue flukes, but as sovereign encounters.

Including Mac's short stint in her life and the cryptic note she found in her car. Also counting the building she knew nothing about, but which supposedly hosted a resident demon. Moving forward, she would consider that getting kidnapped by drug cartel to discover one of the cartel members to be an undercover FBI agent on assignment was not an accident but providence. God surely had purpose in El Padrino flipping from threatening to enamored with her, even though that had drawn heavy contempt from his wife.

And God must have a purpose—on this fiesta morning-after—in the person knocking on the door at that very moment.

Feeling an ounce of triumph, Isa threw back the covers, and because she always slept in her clothes, she marched to the door.

CHAPTER 46

God might have purpose in this early morning encounter, but the family member knocking at Isa's bedroom door wasn't cheerful about it.

In a gruff voice, he said, "Let's go."

Slipping on her flip-flops, she asked, "Where am I going?"

Apparently hurting from the previous night's indulgences, he didn't answer, but headed in the same direction she'd gone the evening before.

They eventually ventured down an unfamiliar and long hall draped with expensive-looking art, and she got dumped on a small, topless patio overlooking the lower half of the jagged rock mountain.

A white wrought-iron table with place-settings for two seemed out of place atop the wilderness mountain sloping away. A pair of French doors guarded a spacious bedroom with a king-size bed, a wall-sized mirror, and a large, white kiva fireplace. Flames pranced in the hearth. Considering the late summer and the early hour, the fire seemed out of place.

The bedroom. The flames. The lovely little breakfast table. From all appearances, she might well be on his breakfast menu. She hoped *this* was not God's plan, because she wasn't up to fighting off El Padrino and any romantic notions he might have in mind.

Her stomach went queasy. Like seasick on the deck of a ship instead of the side of a mountain. *Of course* there would be a price to pay for El Padrino's sudden friendship and security. A woman working for a cartel leader should expect that.

She'd rather hurl herself off the edge of that patio than accept his advances.

How did female undercover investigators deal with men used to having their way with women? What would God want from this sick situation?

Tracing the roofline, she scanned for cameras. The silent minions hung guard there, ready to report her every move. If she made a run for it, they'd watch her route, they'd reveal her fears, they'd expose her developing cover. Stupid cameras.

She tried to appear nonchalant and meandered to the edge of the patio. Pretended to study the view, looking for a pathway down ... should El Padrino come through those doors with expectations she wasn't willing to meet.

Behind her, the door opened. Isa bit down into her lip so hard, she felt a blood vessel swell.

She whirled around to face him, ready to argue her way out of the situation, or go down in flames.

It wasn't El Padrino that stepped through those doors, but Sophia Ventura.

Thank you, Lord. I think.

Dazzling in the morning sun in her oversized top and tight leggings, she wore her hair swept to one side, like she'd crawled out of bed beautiful. Sophia looked inhumanly confident and at ease. A woman in charge.

Isa straightened her navy polo shirt, feeling relieved but very UPS delivery girl.

"Good morning," Sophia chimed, her voice mesmerizing. What was a woman like this doing married to a cartel leader?

"Morning," Isa choked, hating the sound of her southern drawl.

Sophia gestured to the table. "Please, join me for breakfast." She pulled out a chair and eased her charm and beauty down into it. This woman made everything look luscious. Even sitting. "I've looked forward to this," she added, as if she and Isa were besties.

But they were not. Isa knew the hypnotic Sophia had her own agenda for the friendly breakfast.

"Okay," Isa said and with her hand pulled her chair out from beneath the table. The arm caught the edge of the table, rattling the flatware and carafe full of OJ.

Sophia reached out and steadied the wobbling bottle. "This table is uneven. I must get it leveled."

On a charisma scale, Sophia ranked a ten. Isa barely made the chart. She slid down into her chair, wishing she could interrogate a nervous white-collar crime suspect instead of playing cat and mouse with the smooth operator opposite her. Who played cat and who played mouse hadn't yet been established, but Isa planned to bring her A-game to the unsteady table.

"I'm so glad you're here," Sophia cooed. "Please relax." Her soft smile beckoned Isa to give her a chance. "The cameras are off, and my husband left for a business meeting early this morning. You are safe."

Hating that Sophia could read her so well, Isa fidgeted with her fork.

"You probably think it bizarre that I'm reaching out to you." Sophia poured the juice into a small cut-glass wine goblet. "I'm guessing you were coerced into working for my husband against your will, and last night I treated you badly." She stopped. Angled her head forward. "I'm sorry about my behavior."

Isa lifted her fancy glass to Sophia. "I'll take some of that."

Sophia nodded knowingly, as if Isa's gesture for juice was somehow a truce. "Begin again?" she asked, eyes round with innocence. She poured Isa some OJ and set the carafe back on the table.

An older Latina stepped onto the patio. She carried two plates of some delicious-smelling morning foods in her hands.

"Maria!" Sophia clapped her hands together. "I'm starving." Bobbing her head at Isa, she exclaimed, "I hope you like *juevos rancheros*."

CALCULATED RISK

The aroma of roasted chilies wafting from the plates, the alpine mountain setting, the hostess reaching out in friendship—all seemed a bit surreal. For a moment, she thought she might be dreaming. So she pulled Mac, and Awena, and El Padrino's faces into her mind, and told herself to keep it real.

Sophia took a plate from Maria. Handed it to Isa, "I'm curious to know how you first met my husband."

That query popped out unexpectedly. Isa eyed Maria as she passed the second plate to Sophia. Evidently, Maria could be trusted with sensitive conversation.

"We actually met over a rental dispute." Isa looked from Maria to Sophia "Your husband says he has a rental contract on an empty building I inherited."

Maria stood at the table in anticipation of something. To either join in the chat or get a response on her eggs. So Isa scooped up a bite. "Oh, wow," she murmured before she got the whole bite down. Euphoric was not a good enough word for the flavors bursting across her tongue.

Apparently satisfied with Isa's reaction, Maria shot Sophia a smug don't-doubt-my-eggs smirk and turned for the door.

"She takes pride in her work." Sophia laughed quietly. "Doesn't appreciate my suggestions or critiques."

Isa watched the aging chef waddle back to the door, wondering if she, too had initially been forced here, only to become comfortable with the situation. How ironic that in the middle of an evil empire, luxury could trump morals.

Isa shook off the thoughts and looked back to her hostess.

That's when the mood hit a big curve in the road.

Tears spilled down Sophia's face.

CHAPTER 47

Sometime around two-thirty in the morning, El Padrino had received a text to meet Miguel Lopez in Las Cruces, New Mexico, not Albuquerque. He was encouraged to get rooms at the Red Roof Inn. He did not do as encouraged. Instead, two cars carrying both Sicily and guards drove the three hours to Las Cruces, and the entourage checked into the Radisson Hotel at the edge of town. At precisely 6:00 a.m. and as expected, the incoming text gave him the location for the meeting to be held in two hours. Lopez played a chess-like game where pieces moved around a board, vying for dominance. These changes were not surprising, however, and he'd play along to meet face-to-face with this elusive cartel leader.

El Padrino's Range Rover pulled into the parking lot of Rosita's Mexican Grille. Sicily and two guards stayed back at the Radisson because Sicily would be making frantic calls. He wanted those property titles in hand by the end of the day. By his best recollection, three deeds were missing. One, a building in Houston and another, a home in Albuquerque. The third deed, Isa Padilla claimed to have in her possession. Sicily had better have answers. He'd entrusted her and Juan with too much freedom. A mistake that would not happen again.

He'd have his new accountant uncover the transactions and stay on top of his buyers from this point on. Once he proved to her that the India Magic property was, in truth, his.

But that would be tomorrow. Today, Miguel Lopez sat waiting inside Rosita's Mexican Grille.

CALCULATED RISK

El Padrino opened his own door. Stepped out into the humid morning air. Rain would be coming with the onset of fall, along with many other changes.

He'd never seen Miguel Lopez face to face. The notorious leader kept a low physical profile and let his reputation do the brandishing that shook lesser men's hearts. Not El Padrino's heart, though. He anticipated the meeting with pleasure. Saw it like two empires, two business minds, coming together.

The satisfaction of victory already tapped at his chest.

Rosita's neon signs were dark, the shades on the windows pulled down. Most likely, Lopez owned the place. Not in name, but in asset as something he controlled away from the government's prying eyes. It was how cartels spread their money around but also gained community respect. They created jobs and gave disadvantaged men dignity again.

Per the instructions, El Padrino was to enter from the rear kitchen door. Not out of disrespect, but for security. He and Oso walked around to the back of the building to an alley. A member of La Liga, AK-47 cradled in his arms, waited by the back door.

El Padrino nodded at the low-level personnel. No words were necessary.

The guard motioned them in.

Inside, he recognized the two La Liga members who had attended his fiesta. They patted him and Oso down after accepting Oso's Smith and Wesson 40 and El Padrino's Hi-Point 9mm. Then he and Oso were ushered into a private dining area. Three additional guards stood at strategic points near shade-drawn windows.

In the middle of the room—at dining table covered by a red vinyl table cloth—sat the man.

Miguel Lopez, the most infamous cartel leader to date. *To date*, El Padrino reminded himself. That was about to change with the weather.

Lopez stood. Offered his hand. His shake felt firm, although he was not a man of great stature. Hooded eyes and a broad mouth gave him a boyish look. Not one El

Padrino expected. But the tell-tale forming gut spoke of his middle age and his lack of discipline.

El Padrino's lips curled up in a satisfied smile. The great Lopez would be no match for him.

Oso stayed at the door. The two cartel leaders took their seats, one across from the other.

El Padrino, as the superior negotiator, naturally took the lead. "So, I meet the leader of the La Liga at long last. I have looked forward to this day."

Lopez cast his eyes on the table as if he needed to think about that statement.

El Padrino kept his eyes on the man. Didn't intend to take his eyes off him from this point on.

After a moment of silence, and with El Padrino about to burst with words and plans, Lopez looked up. "You want your prostitutes back? But your business ventures have slipped into La Liga territory. What is in La Liga territory belongs to La Liga."

El Padrino grimaced. "These issues were settled when I met with your associates. I have not come for the meager income of young girls." El Padrino steepled his fingers. "I have come to form an alliance, a partnership that will be greater than any single cartel."

Again Lopez dropped his gaze and hands to the table. His index finger tapped as if he had all the time in the world. "So I have heard. What do you offer La Liga that we do not have?"

With the meeting back on track, El Padrino relaxed a little. "I bring you a large portfolio of real estate that spreads from Arizona to Texas."

Those words got Lopez's attention, because he looked up at El Padrino.

"Worth more than ten million," El Padrino continued, the words like honey on his tongue. "But equally important ..." He paused for effect. Let that statement sink in. "I will bring high-ranking people who will protect your interests and mine."

"And who are these promised people?" Lopez asked, his thick brows high in anticipation.

"Enforcers from the Houston Police Department."

CHAPTER 48

At the sight of Sophia's tears, Isa near dropped her fork in Maria's huevos rancheros.

Sophia looked like she'd seen the ending of a heart-wrenching movie, the waterworks on and she, wiping at the deluge with her petite napkin.

What the heck?

Sophia waved her napkin at Isa. "I'm sorry," she sputtered. "Please forgive me."

"It's okay—"

"No. I wanted to have a pleasant meal with you. Get to know you." She swiped at her nose. "I am going about this all wrong."

"Wh ... what's all wrong?" Accounting entries were so much easier to analyze.

Sophia tilted her head back and searched the sky for something. Words, maybe. She sucked in a quivering breath. "I didn't realize the scope, you know?"

No, Isa didn't know. She shook her head, unable to unearth her inner actor.

"I thought I married a man." Sophia spread her arms wide. "Not an entire drug industry." Dropping her hands in her lap, she lowered her gaze. "Somehow I missed the fact that I'd be part of this brutal game."

"I'm not sure I'm following you." Isa fibbed. Truth was, she did sense where Sophia headed with the tearful homily—and by no means was Isa prepared to respond to a cartel wife's confessions. Talk about boundaries. Isa needed hers out front and intact, coincidences or not.

"You'll be part, too. You can't let him suck you in."

"Well ..." Isa shifted around in the increasingly uncomfortable wrought-iron chair. "I'm here getting the books in order for an audit."

"It won't end there."

"I know that I am ..." Isa leaned in to whisper, "breaking the law. But reviewing expenses is all I've been asked to do. I want my building back and some compensation and I'll move on out of everybody's way."

"You don't understand. José doesn't lose. Anything or anybody. I'm not only warning you." Sophia leaned across the table. "I'm looking for you to help me out of this trap."

Bingo.

Isa straightened. Could feel her heart start its descent to the caverns of dread next door to her dragon's lair.

"I have a son." Sophia sniffed. "I must do what is right for him. I need to get as far away as possible." Her big brown eyes blinked away more tears. "I have family in Italy."

"So you need a plane ticket?" Isa knew the answer couldn't, wouldn't be that simple. "You want to disappear in Europe?"

"He would find me. He knows no geographical boundaries. Did you know that a man from India owned the India Magic building before you?"

Isa nodded. Funny, she didn't remember mentioning to Sophia what building she and El Padrino were negotiating over.

"My husband had that man killed. India has the world's largest population. If José can find a man he barely knew in India, he will find me in Italy. He knows where my family lives. He would hurt them to get to me."

"Raj Khatri is dead?" Why would El Padrino have Raj killed? Did it have something to do with her owning the building now? Her heart stopped its descent and raced back up, bypassing her chest and landing in her throat.

"Yes," Sophia answered, her hands twisting her napkin. "Do you not understand that the drug industry is built on violence?"

Oh, Isa understood that fine. She'd never get Juan's bloodied shirt on a platter out of her mind. But getting involved in a cartel marriage going wrong seemed like a very bad idea. "Okay, slow down." Isa ran her fingers through her hair. Tightened her pony tail. Needed to go back to the beginning. "Why me? You've got to have better connections than me out there." She gestured to nowhere in particular but very much wanted Sophia to come up with some other options.

Sophia pummeled right through Isa's hints. "This isn't only about me," she said, a dark shadow inching across her face. "He has his eyes on you. I tried to save you."

Isa must have missed something. She didn't recall telling Sophia she needed saving. "Again, I'm only the acc—"

Sophia waved Isa's weak objection away. "I pretended to be jealous of you at the party last night in hopes my husband would agree to let you go. But I couldn't convince him." She stopped, blinked. Seemed to contemplate the boulders. "I can tell you from experience, once he decides you're his, no one else will ever have you."

"I'm so sorry you're in this situation." Isa fought the sudden urge to get up and give Sophia a hug. She reached out and grabbed the distraught woman's hand, instead. "I don't know that I can be of help."

Sophia shook her head. "I know why you are here."

Isa let go of her hand. She couldn't really know. Could she? Unless Jay told her. But Jay wouldn't do that. Unless he was a fake undercover agent and ... she stopped her mind from going down that hazardous trail. Pulled herself out of the empathy role and put herself firmly back in the acting undercover agent role. "I'm here to fix your husband's taxes." She flattened her expression. "Nothing more. I am sorry."

No way she could have been prepared for what would come out of Sophia's mouth next.

When she said it, Isa's head spun so fast, everything went blurry. She laced her fingers through the wrought-iron seat on the chair to keep from spinning into orbit. Wondered if she'd heard it wrong.

CALCULATED RISK

But she hadn't. Sophia's seven words changed everything.

"I met your husband before he died."

CHAPTER 49

The Range Rover pulled into the back-parking lot of the Radisson Hotel. El Padrino and Oso exited the vehicle and walked silently across the lot. But El Padrino wanted to burst out with plans taking shape in his mind already.

Now a potential partner to one of the most infamous and powerful cartel leaders, he'd need to be more elusive, unpredictable. He saw more back doors and alleyways in the future. And increasing his fleet of automobiles that kept threats guessing about his locations.

The thought of pending fame made his chest warm, and at the side door of the Radisson, he slapped Oso on the shoulder. "We have done it, my friend."

It had been nearly six years since the last time he'd consumed alcohol, with the exception of a toast at special occasions. None of those, save his last wedding night, compared to this. Perhaps he'd indulge with champagne, or he and Oso would share a steak dinner instead. Estimating the financial increase, he also imagined the real estate he'd own.

Among the many considerations racing through his head, notions about Sophia pestered him still—her unpredictable mood, then the jealousy. The thing that bothered him the most though, was the physical distance she put between them.

"We're on the sixth floor," Oso said, pointing to an elevator. His initial agreement with Lopez included exchanging top men for transparency and good-will purposes. Oso would be joining Lopez for a few weeks while one of the top men from La Liga would join El Padrino in his home and offices for the same. The next three days must go exactly as planned, with meetings, territorial establishments, and property exchanges.

Maybe these plans should not include Sophia. Perhaps she didn't belong in the new kingdom.

But of course she belonged. Sophia's mind held mysteries yet to explore.

He rotated his shoulders, waiting at the elevator. Never mind that now. Tomorrow or the day after, he would deal with Sophia.

In the elevator, El Padrino pulled a little more pride into his lungs. Oso noticed. "You are a great negotiator," he said, staring at the backside of the elevator door. "I am proud to work for you, El Padrino."

Moments like this made the challenging times worth it. Nothing came without cost. El Padrino would rise higher.

He entered the suite, told one of his guards to order him a macchiato. Oso nodded his head knowingly. His number one man, Oso knew El Padrino well.

El Padrino took a seat in the wing-back chair. Felt like a throne with his loyal subjects surrounding him. Called for his prisoner to be brought before him.

Within seconds, his men escorted her in.

Sicily did not look well. The dark circles beneath her chocolate eyes testified of her lack of sleep. Good. Neither had he nor any of the accompanying guards.

She opened her mouth, and out came the excuses. "If you'd let me go back to Houston, I can follow the trail of mistakes. Find the deeds. Otherwise, I don't see how we'll get them back into your inventory."

El Padrino cocked his head. Drummed his fingers on his leg, giving her more time to spout noise.

"The partner I recruited was killed. All I need to do is get into his bank box. I can figure it out because I'm friends with his wife. I need a few more days and—"

El Padrino held up his hand to stop her. "Oso? Do we have a car available?"

At the door behind him, he heard Oso reply. "Yes, El Padrino. Of course."

Sicily stuttered. "You mean ... um ... you'll let me drive to Houston?"

"No." El Padrino let go a labored sigh. "That door has closed."

Her eyes bulged. Surprised. Shocked. Speechless. Some of his favorite responses.

"Oso." El Padrino looked over his shoulder. "Where is my macchiato?"

"It's coming, El Padrino."

"How far will you take Sicily, Oso, before I get to take my first sip?"

"Where am I going?" Sicily looked between the men, a beautiful confusion covering her face.

Of course she didn't get her answer. She didn't deserve one.

But Oso answered El Padrino. "Twelve or so miles, Jefe. Ten, fifteen minutes."

El Padrino smiled at Sicily. Enjoyed looking at her one last time. "You may leave."

"What's going on here?" She looked like she might really know.

"We're tying up loose ends," he said.

Sicily no longer mattered. The loss of two or three properties paled in comparison to what he'd gained through his alliance with Lopez today. In her position, she had the opportunity to complicate matters. Her mistakes weren't worth the effort it would take to correct them.

A guard guided a wiggling Sicily out the door. She looked back at El Padrino, a pleading look in her eyes.

She knew. She was too smart not to.

He watched Oso leave the room. Sophia wouldn't leave his mind.

A knock at the door and room service delivered his macchiato. The cream mixed with coffee created a beautiful blond color. For the most part, brunettes had been his go-to for women. Maybe that would change.

He took in the stylish first-class hotel room. Everything he did from here on would be first class, too. He balanced the saucer and cup on his knee. Watched the clock on the wall tick away another ten minutes.

When his phone dinged with a text, he glanced at it. Oso had written one simple, perfect word.

Done.

El Padrino grinned. Took a sip of his coffee.

CHAPTER 50

I met your husband before he died. The words echoed off the numbing walls of her brain. A thousand more words formed and joined the ricocheting chaos. *Lies, murders, schemes.*

So her husband *had* succumbed to the shallow luxuries El Padrino offered.

She hated El Padrino.

Now, Sophia reached for Isa's hand, her touch feather soft and her lips moving. But Isa couldn't hear her words because Isa wasn't at the table having breakfast. She was in her living room nine months ago reliving that first hunch that Mac hid secrets.

"Oh dear." Sophia squeezed hard enough to pull Isa back into the moment. "I did not mean to shock you."

Isa blinked, still riveted, still stunned that she was blind to all that had happened right under her nose.

"Let me explain," Sophia said.

Was this happening? Had the answer she'd put her life at risk for slipped out of that woman's mouth so unexpectedly?

"Please do," Isa murmured.

Sophia's eyes searched Isa's. "You had no idea, did you?"

Isa shook her head. "No." Releasing that word into the air, Isa imagined herself blowing out a candle. The last bit of hope that he'd loved her enough to be honest. That she had married a good cop, and more importantly, a faithful man.

CALCULATED RISK

"When you came here ..." Sophia's thumb made little circles on top of Isa's hand. "When I first saw you on the cameras, I knew."

Isa's pulse pounded in her ears. Sophia knew things she didn't. Mac knew things she didn't. Probably Jay, too. What a fool she'd been.

"I put it all together. I knew you weren't a criminal looking to get involved in this awful industry. Look at you. You look like the ROTC recruiting poster."

Isa stared, unblinking.

"Why my husband hasn't figured all this out, I'll never know."

"How did you know him?" Isa asked, her voice small compared to the Jumanji drums banging in her head.

"I met your husband briefly at the Drake's Horn. I believe he used another name then. I'm not outside these walls much, but I was there with José one day while he took care of some business in the back. I saw Mac. He didn't fit the cartel profile just like you don't fit the cartel profile. I asked one of the guys about him and they brought him over. Introduced him as one of the mules from Houston. A cop mule."

Isa's chest caved. A runner. *Mac—transporting drugs.*

"So when did you discover that I'm his wife?" she asked, fighting off a queasy feeling.

Sophia scrunched her face. Looked uncomfortable with that question. "Let's say I have a friend with discreet connections in the drug world. It wasn't hard to discover Mac was married to someone inside the Houston force." Sophia tilted her head. "You've come seeking retribution, haven't you?"

Isa couldn't answer that. Not because she needed to keep at least a portion of her cover intact, but because she'd never thought of her quest in that term. Retribution—a word implying damage. Had this been about revenge and not a fact-finding mission?

Somehow, in between the self-reflection and banging drums, Isa found a lucid thought, an important question. "Your husband doesn't know *any*thing about me?"

Sophia's eyes formed circles of innocence. "No," she declared. "I have kept this from him. I am ashamed to tell you, but, there was a time I had my husband's back. José came to depend upon me and my sources. I have a person who can unearth facts no one else can find. She's an amazing sleuth."

Sophia glanced upward, her eyes red and on the verge of tears again. "But it has to stop. I'm trying to make things right." The chuckle from her chest sounded self-deprecating. "My pretending to be jealous of you makes you look legitimate in my husband's eyes. He knows I would have vetted you and if I found anything, would have ratted you out immediately." She put her hands in her lap. Leaned over the table, closer to Isa. "My husband believes I don't want you here. We need him to continue in this fantasy."

Isa squeezed her eyes shut. Wasn't ready to think about what they should and shouldn't be doing. "Who shot Mac?"

Limbs rattled overhead. Was there a breeze? Or was that a demon mocking her? She wished Awena to be by her side.

Sophia studied her plate.

Isa watched her, waiting.

Finally, Sophia answered. "José ordered his murder."

The truth hurt worse than Isa thought it might. Felt like a sharp blade to the gut that set her dragon on fire.

"Mac stole some property that belonged to José," Sophia said. "José had him killed for it."

Isa's back went rigid. "India Magic?"

"Possibly. I'm unsure of the extent of Mac's offenses. Some things, José did not share with me."

"So somehow, as a mule, Mac got hold of a property El Padrino wanted." But how?

Sophia kept talking. "It will not be long before my husband puts all of these facts together. Fortunately, he is temporarily distracted with an alliance he forms with La Liga. But that won't last for long. We must move fast."

Move fast? Was she insane? Isa had just been informed that her husband was a criminal killed by a criminal. "What do you want from *me*?" Isa asked.

"I want you to get my husband arrested."

CALCULATED RISK

How ironic. Isa wanted that too. But she couldn't find the right slot in her brain to drop that thought into. If she let Sophia in on what was already underway, she would expose Jay. As of now, it appeared Sophia thought Isa a lone-wolf vigilante. She needed to get her head clear. Talk with Jay and figure a few things out. "That's not why I'm here." Isa lied to buy some time. "I came to get answers. You've given them to me."

She started to stand but Sophia reached out and grabbed Isa's wrist with both hands. "Please don't leave me yet." Tears filled her lower lids again. "I will help."

Was this madness an open door? Did anything make sense here? "What can I do? Like you said, it won't be long before this whole compound knows who I am."

"I can lead you to incriminating evidence."

Why would she need Isa to find evidence? Being his wife, she had more proof of crime than anyone. "Why don't you expose him yourself? You could get into a witness protection program."

"I know nothing of money laundering or real estate trades. But I hear things. We need hard evidence that will stick. I don't know all the nuances and laws of your government."

Isa thought of the deeds someone had slipped into the receipt boxes she'd gone through. "You've already slipped me some evidence, haven't you?"

Sophia face scrunched in question. "What? No."

"Forget it," Isa said. "Things are too complicated. I'm having a hard time keeping up with who is who." She lowered her gaze to Maria's cold and stiff eggs, sprinkled with blood-red chilis. "I wasn't even sure Mac had been here. I landed here by accident. I don't think I can—"

"But," Sophia interrupted. "You are the angel God has sent to find facts that will put José in jail for life."

Isa almost snorted. Awena would love this—the cartel's wife thinking Isa an angel. She snapped her wrist from Sophia's grasp and eased against the back of the chair. An idea began formulating, which was miraculous. That she could even sit across from her husband's murderer's wife was unreal, and here the two collaborated. "Okay, Sophia. If you can get me access to all the bookkeeping and real estate information, I'll find any court-admissible evidence that's there. But first, I want you to get Awena back here."

Sophia lifted one side of her mouth in a grin that made her look a little too proud of herself for winning the breakfast battle of wills.

But what the heck. The drums in Isa's head were beating again. Except this time, their rhythm felt like a war cry instead of a death march.

"I can do that," Sophia cooed.

CHAPTER 51

Isa flipped over the twelfth page of her yellow legal pad. The information she'd pulled from the miles and miles of documents—some, no more than a cell phone snapshot of a hand-written real estate receipt—so far, was not as much as she wanted. But way more than she expected.

Out of habit, she glanced at a camera. But Sophia had assured her they'd been disabled for a couple of days.

That Sophia, she moved fast. She expected quick results, too, explaining that her husband would be home from his business trip in three or four days. Before his return, she would need to retrieve the laptop she'd given Isa, and have it wiped clean. Dispose of the multiple flash drives she snuck in, too. The one important thing Sophia didn't give Isa was the password to the internet connection, which made research impossible.

Sophia seemed to have all the details covered before Isa had even gotten back to her room.

But for hours now, Isa had inched her way through documents, hand-recording transactions.

Once she confirmed her suspicions about the money scheme, she'd have Jay take pictures with his cell. Then cover her trail by disposing of her handwritten notes.

If Jay would show up already.

He hadn't been by her room all day, and that created an uneasy feeling for several reasons. In this ever-changing environment, who knew who to trust? Perhaps she felt uneasy about his absence because maybe he'd decided to stop collaborating with her. Not that he ever really started. He'd made it clear he found her burdensome, and it wouldn't surprise her if he was leaving her out of his loop.

Dang that Jay Hernandez and his macho, independent methods.

The familiar swoosh of her bedroom door opening made her think he'd finally shown up. Ready to let the guy have it for not being around, Isa jumped to her feet.

But the person who'd stepped through the door wasn't Jay.

Maria entered, Isa's dinner in her hand.

Isa blew out a long stream of disappointed air. "Oh." She fell back into her chair. "I thought you were ... never mind. Leave the dinner there." Isa pointed to a side table by the chair.

Maria did as requested.

Isa got back to the laptop and legal pad.

Without warning, Maria—maybe an inch taller than petite Awena—peered over Isa's shoulder.

That stopped Isa in her documenting tracks.

Reflexes kicking in, she flipped the legal pad over with her right hand and shot her left up in front of the Laptop screen. Which hid nothing. Maria could see right through her silly spread-eagle fingers.

Isa peered back at the little woman. "Can I help you?"

Maria's gaze moved to Isa's face. Her Spanish eyes held a no-nonsense, factual air. "You take El Padrino down with this?" Her crooked finger pointed at the screen.

Isa gulped.

"You take me out with you." She flicked Isa on the side of the head. Then the little Mexican lady made for the door. "Bueno," she stated before shutting the door.

Isa blinked at the empty space Maria had left. Evidently, this cartel cook had eavesdropped on her breakfast conversation with Sophia, and who knew what other conversations that took place around the compound.

That head flick left an impression. Guess now she'd be grabbing Awena and Sophia *and* Maria on her way out. Isa pulled at her cheeks with the realization. All the women in

El Padrino's compound were captive in one way or another. Made Isa out to be a female liberator. Perhaps this was her grand, God-given purpose.

Encouraged, Isa went back to her work.

El Padrino not only owned the Drake's Horn bar in Albuquerque, but from what she could decipher, he possessed a car wash, a car dealership, and an avocado farm in Mexico, with an independent real estate agency in Houston. All in his real name, José Ventura.

As well, she saw multiple deeds to residential properties in and around Phoenix, Houston and Albuquerque, but these titles held different names, most in either Sicily's or Juan's names. Several residential homes belonged to Sophia, then there were a few in random names she didn't recognize.

Looked like Juan and this Sicily—the person Snake mistook her for on her first day inside India Magic—were stacking up the housing market. A notion formulated in Isa's mind. She hadn't seen this particular laundering scheme before, but realized it was a loophole in the real estate system.

Isa pushed her chair back. Got up and paced, her go-to method for mental sorting.

At the bedroom door, she stopped. Tapped her finger on her lip. The paper trail was all over a real estate map with little connecting to El Padrino. Why? Because El Padrino didn't want a paper trail.

She needed access to public records to prove the idea taking shape.

One person could get that for her.

Isa pulled the door open. No guard.

She stepped into the hall and looked both ways. Nice and empty.

She had no way of knowing if Sophia disengaged all cameras, or specific sections. She made for the bathroom, executing a perfectly relaxed stroll in case the hall cameras were rolling.

Inside the bath, she turned on the sink faucet and slipped to the side, bedroom door.

CALCULATED RISK

Tapped.

With no response, she knocked a little louder, then laid her ear against the door. Nothing.

Isa turned the knob, pushed the door open a few inches. Jay lay across the end of his bed.

He wasn't moving.

CHAPTER 52

But was Jay breathing? Stretched across the end of his bed, an arm twisted unnaturally above his head, it didn't look like it.

She pulled the bathroom door open. "Jay." She tiptoed in. Stopped a few feet from the end of the bed, eyes watching for movement.

He lay still as a corpse.

Her hands shot to her mouth.

Could ... he ... be dead?

She wasn't a crime-scene investigator, but training taught her to never tamper with evidence.

Jay looked strangely peaceful. She'd heard that about the dead.

His body wasn't twisted or contorted. One arm hung over his head, the other tucked beneath him. His face was turned away from her and his wild hair shot in a million different directions. But there was no visible sign of blood from a gunshot or knife wound.

Maybe he was just unconscious.

"Jay," she said in a hushed, but desperate tone.

He didn't move.

What had happened here?

Her thoughts reeled with scenarios. Remembered Mac talking about an HPD case a couple years back. A Mexican cartel known for their potent home-made meth had conducted experiments with poisonous chemicals on their own members. Wiped out a tenth of the cartel.

"Hey, Jay," she said, tempted to rush at him and shake his body.

But she should never touch a body involved in a crime. One more time. "Jay."

Nothing.

They'd poisoned him.

Now her hands went to her head, palms pressing into her pulsating temples.

She glanced around the room. Noticed his cell phone on the nightstand.

Jay's cover must have been blown. A cartel goon poisoning him while El Padrino was off the property made sense. El Padrino didn't seem to embrace the messy parts of cartel life.

Isa had but one option. Get his phone, call in his FBI team. Making a wide arc around the end of the bed, she got to the night stand without looking at his face. This wasn't the way she wanted to remember Jay.

Heart sinking, she picked up his phone. Knelt next to the bed.

Silently, she begged God to please not let this be her purpose—her fault. She hadn't meant to blow his cover. If she was the one who'd blown his cover. Jay was a lot of things hard and annoying, but he was a good man serving his country.

Hands wobbling, she punched his phone screen.

Phone locked. And she, of course, had no code to punch in. Isa needed a technical epiphany.

"What are you doing?" Jay's voice sounded like he'd swallowed gravel.

She sprang to her feet. *Well, well, he's alive.* She rolled her eyes in his direction.

One bleary eyeball stared back at her.

"What do you think you are doing?"

She smelled his morning breath.

He was *sleeping*? Isa grabbed the pillow beside her and swung it at him so hard, she knocked him off the end of the bed.

A muffled *ouch* sounded from the floor.

"I thought you were dead," she said and flopped down on the bed. "Geez, Jay, you scared me to death."

His head popped up from the end of the bed. "You thought I was what?" He worked his way up and sat back down, scratching at his head. "I met with some of the guys. He pulled at the shirt riding up his flat abs. "Didn't get much sleep. So I crashed ... like what?" He glanced at his watch. "an hour ago."

Isa didn't care that he'd had a rough night. They had work to discuss. "Where have you been all day?"

"Why are you in my room?" Jay's aggression was awake, even if he wasn't. He ran his hands around in his hair. As if that would help.

"Aren't we supposed to be working together?"

He cocked his head. "What are you doing with my phone?"

"Are you kidding me? Can I get a word with you, please?"

Rubbing his eyes, he looked above the window opposite them. "Well. We can't talk here."

Isa followed his gaze to the lone camera above the window.

"I need to go to town for a meeting." He scratched at his hair again. "You can come with me." He held his hand out. "Can I have my phone now?"

She pulled the phone closer to her chest. "If you brush your teeth."

CHAPTER 53

The unexpected call from Sophia had left El Padrino pleased, but also perplexed. "I don't understand this request."

Why would she have a sudden interest in the American Indian woman he'd placed at Oso's sister's home?

"I am trying to explain it to you, José. She could be of use to me here. I need a gentle woman to keep an eye on Luca. It recently occurred to me that she would be perfect for him."

He rubbed his forehead.

"It is a wonderful idea," Sophia reiterated.

Angry as he was with her, she could be convincing. "You know, I am the one who makes decisions about what each of our workers does and does not do. We've had this discussion."

"I know. But she's ... she's perfect. Like a gift that landed in our laps."

El Padrino fixed his eyes on the window of his hotel room. His wife's mood had changed again, her tone easy and smooth. Why not grant her this request, if this wish was the true motive? "I'll bring her back with me. But you must not let her spend time with the accountant. The American Indian is my security policy that the accountant will stay put for the time being."

Through the phone, her silence spoke loudly.

"Sophia?"

"Oh. The accountant. I was having such a good evening until you mentioned her."

He smiled inside. "Do we agree?"

She waited several seconds to reply. "I'll be happy to keep the old woman with me and Luca only." A heavy sigh reached through the phone. "I prefer to pretend that sleezy little accountant isn't in my home."

He chuckled, but something seemed off. A hunch. But hunches had helped him maneuver the elusive corners of success.

Disconnecting from Sophia, unease grew in his chest.

"Oso," he called.

Oso appeared from the sitting area of the suite.

"Have the old woman at your sister's brought here tonight."

"Okay, Jefe."

"And Oso, let's prepare to return to the compound early. Right after my next meeting with Lopez."

CHAPTER 54

Isa waited in the hall while Jay brushed his teeth. She followed him to the car where the dynamic cartel duo of Nick and Snake awaited in a Prius. A Prius. As if that wasn't the funniest sight she'd ever seen. Two gargantuan-sized gang members filling the insides of a little economy car. Somehow laughing didn't seem appropriate. But needed. Very needed.

Isa realized she drew dangerously close to that thin line between punch-happy and bloodthirsty. Sometimes her dragon couldn't tell the difference.

But before they backed out of the drive, the two in front said or did something that put Jay into alert mode. She didn't know what, because they were speaking Spanish too fast for her to follow, but Jay went rigid beside her in the backseat and stopped contributing to the conversation.

Isa thought of the note still in her purse warning her that things hidden would be revealed. When, then, would she need to reveal the truth of her agreement with Sophia to Jay?

She didn't dare ask where they were going or what they were going to do. But still in her navy polo and khaki pants, she raised a brow when Nick pulled into the parking lot of the Drake's Horn. The last place she wanted to be. Especially in her UPS delivery-girl uni. Talk about sticking out in a crowd.

There, all three men exited the car, Jay faster than the other two. But Isa crossed her arms.

CALCULATED RISK

When she didn't get out, Jay bent down and looked in. "Let's go."

Nick and Snake Face headed for the bar.

"You're not telling me something. We're supposed to be working together."

"Come on, Isa." Jay sounded impatient.

"I told you I needed to talk to you. I thought you had a meeting. Why are we here?"

He crawled back into the back seat. Faced forward. The little veins in his temples started to show beneath his skin. "If you want to do this, then do it. If you don't, then let's get you out of here. Take off running now. I'll cover for you."

She glared at him. "You still want me out of your hair."

At this, Jay moaned. "Okay, yes, I want you out of my hair. Out of the picture. But you got yourself into it, so ..." His shrug was over-the-top exaggerated. So animated and smug, she could not only see, but taste and smell the sarcasm. "You're in. All right?"

Her dragon blew out a puff of smoke. "What's wrong with you? I'm trying to get a moment with you to share some information." She rolled her eyes. "You see, I've been working while you've been ... let's see. What were you doing all day? Oh yeah, that's right. napping."

That was the wrong thing to say.

He rolled his head around to look at her like she had three heads of her own. "In the last thirty hours, I've gotten one solid hour of sleep. Don't preach to me about working. You have no idea." He stopped. Looked forward again. "I'm gonna stop there.' He squared his shoulders. "Get out of the car and walk with me into the bar. We do not need to look like we are doing what we're doing."

She flipped the door handle and got out. Filled her lungs with fresh air. Marched around to his side of the Prius. Looked in. "I'm here. Let's go."

He crawled out and went straight for the Drake's Horn's side door.

At least he opened it for her.

When she walked through, he slung his arm over her shoulder and waved at the bouncer at the desk. Oscar-worthy Jay showed up. The bouncer nodded them through.

Sliding into the oblivion of the biker bar, he put his lips near her ear. "We have to look like we belong in El Padrino's community. We'll talk here."

People were already looking at her like she was a kid escaped from prep school, though it was hard to believe anyone could see her through the haze of smoke. She nonchalantly covered her mouth and nose while Jay pulled her through the crowd.

Some freak grabbed her backside. Right on the khaki's pocket.

She turned, ready to slap at the jerk. But Jay yanked her on.

She wished she'd donned the dollar store tunic she'd thrown away. Showed less of her minimal curves.

At the back, he settled on a sticky round bistro table without stools. Pulled her in close, a little too frantic and a lot too rough. "Talk fast. I have to meet someone over there." He gestured across the room. "Picking something up tonight."

She yanked out of his arm. "Picking what up?" He hadn't mentioned that before they got in the car. Where was the Jay she'd knocked off the end of the bed? Who'd willingly brought her along for his meeting?

"Come on, Isa, tell me what is so important that you broke into my room, tried to read through my phone, and insisted we talk tonight?"

"I'm sorry." She used her most sarcastic voice. Which was also, her most natural one. "I'm not sure why the sudden anger issue, but I'm trying to be helpful. I suppose I could call and inform the FBI myself."

The slight smile he put on looked ironically amused. "You might have that chance. Something's going down. I hope it's not you or me."

Wait. Isa caught her breath. "What? What are you talking about?"

Glancing over her head, Jay flexed his jaw.

She'd never seen him so ... so edgy. "Jay, what's happened to you from the time we left the compound to the time we got here? What did you hear?"

CALCULATED RISK

His eyes narrowed as he seemed to read the crowd. "Something Snake said to Nick. They were talking in code and I don't know if that's because they don't trust you, or don't trust either of us. But it's not a good sign."

"I didn't hear anything unusual."

"That's the difference between me and you. I'm the professional."

Isa threw her hands up. "Okay, so you speak better Spanish than I do, but please, let's not do this." She sliced at the air between then with her index finger. "We are supposed to be a team. Just tell me what they said to each other."

He turned, his face hard, his lips set. Something terrible, horrible, had a grip on him. She could see it in those ice-blue eyes.

"Tell me," she whispered, shocked by his intense gaze.

"El Padrino ordered a kill today." A slow blink and he moved his unsettling scrutiny back across the dancefloor. "On a cop."

Her heart came to a screeching halt. She gasped.

"So, I need you to stay here while I meet my connection. There's things I need to know."

"But ..." wasn't out of her mouth before he pulled away and walked into the haze.

Her polo clung to her sweaty back as she tried to keep him in sight. But the crowd swallowed him up. He'd left her alone—a cocker spaniel in a room full of coyotes. Her dragon stirred, uneasy with the situation and the startling information. If Jay was right, then that would be two cops killed. Mac and now another, both by El Padrino's command. Did Jay have a partner and not tell her? Or had another cop, like Mac, gone bad? The questions whirled around in her head like the smoke in the room.

Until she saw a slime ball headed her way. He was big, not as big as Snake or Nick, but at least six foot and packing more than a few extra pounds. Tattoos didn't cover his entire body, but he clearly hosted gangster markings on the arms and the one single tear beneath the eye—a sign someone close to him had been killed in a gang war. He ran his hand through his slicked-back, ducktail hair.

Her dragon blew up more hot air.

This could well be the grabber who had his hand on her earlier. She was in no mood to conduct an animal behavior study with this ape. Neither was the dragon.

He slid into the spot Jay had vacated. Had probably watched Jay walk off.

"Pretty young thing." He oozed raunchy and the smell of beer. Set his can on the table. "Where you been all my life?"

The pathetic pick-up line ripped at her last patient nerve. Isa cocked her head. "All your *useless* life?" She tossed her pony tail. "I've been at school learning, at a job getting experience, and at a life that doesn't include drugs, alcohol, or slobs."

Ducktail frowned at first. Then one side of his mouth lifted like he found her insult amusing. "I like over-achievers." He slid his hand up her arm, and when she jerked it away, he tightened his grip. "Where ya going, Little Girl?"

Wrong move on his part.

Before her thoughts fully processed what she was doing, her little bit of jiujitsu training responded. She twisted her wrist up and out of Ducktail's grasp, her arm making a full circle to wrap beneath his. Then she yanked that tatted-up arm upwards, sending his beer, like a rocket, into the wall behind them. Isa shoved the palm of her left hand up his nose. Hard.

Stumbling backward, Ducktail's nose spurted blood and a whole flock of foul words flew from his mouth.

Isa snapped to defense position, ready to kick and trying hard not to compare the man's bulk to her last jiujitsu opponent's size. Which was a girl.

"Why, you little ..." Ducktail growled.

CHAPTER 55

Sophia stepped into Isa's empty bedroom. An open computer and piles of paperwork on the desk told Sophia that the accountant had made headway into her husband's records.

She rubbed at the back of her neck, studying the columns without disturbing the paperwork. Isa would be one of those who could walk into a room and know if a hairbrush was out of place.

Three whistle-blower flash drives lay side-by-side on Isa's desk. The red drive was the one she'd loaded with the copies of hand-written notes she'd made on property purchases José made long before she decided to keep records. The other two held incriminating bank records and the real estate docs she'd taken control of.

Isa's yellow pad of notes lay on the other side of her computer. Running her index finger down the page, Sophia saw that Isa categorized the real estate by the initial buyer. The owners were Juan, Sicily, and Gabriel Martinez, aka Oso. But there was one property in a name she didn't recognize, which was strange. She thought she had her husband's trust and complete account of all properties.

It didn't matter now.

Sophia tapped her chin. Smiled. She knew it would take an expert to figure this real estate web out. But it would not take this woman much longer to detangle her husband's key laundering scheme.

Sophia's father had taught her well when he said, *Lay a few breadcrumbs and the mice will follow.*

CALCULATED RISK

She closed her eyes and visualized the future—one where El Padrino wore an orange jump suit in a federal prison and she donned a bikini on the Isle of Capri. But first, she would make a detour in Mexico, sell her lover the properties that were still in her name—six middle class homes near Katy, Texas, and four modest rentals in Belen, New Mexico. And there was the commercial building just south in Socorro, the one she'd convinced José to purchase recently. None of these, of course, would show up in the files of real estate she had fed to Isa.

Isa Phillips had not been in the original plan, but it had been easy to pivot and pull her in. The fact that she was Mac the cop's wife was troublesome, however. Isa's motivations centered on vendetta rather than greed, and that meant Isa couldn't be bought.

It had been so easy to flip Mac and his partner Sicily from José's loyalties to hers. Since she had methodically taken control of the records, Mac and Sicily bought properties in her name instead of their own, with the promise that they would each end up with real estate of their own. She'd already given Mac the India Magic deed and that's what had, ironically, brought Isa to her door.

Mac—what a disappointment he turned out to be. As soon as she had handed him her good-faith gift of the building in downtown Albuquerque, he'd begun to waffle, wanting out. Said Sicily was dealing with major remorse and going to blow not only her cover, but a couple of other mules from the force. Mac didn't want to be anywhere near Houston police or El Padrino's operations when she did. He couldn't trust Sicily anymore, and Sophia decided she couldn't trust *him*.

So she had Mac taken care of. Her husband hardly noticed the absence of the C-level runner. But had she ordered Sicily's execution, José would have certainly noticed her absence. That woman had become his key real estate buyer. So, Sophia planted a few insinuating seeds of distrust.

Sicily had gotten in over her head—a cop, working on the inside with a cartel leader, and then betraying him by working on the side with his wife.

Inside, the butterflies of anticipation fluttered, and she knew it to be an amateurish sensation. One day, planning complex maneuvers using people and their motivations would become second nature.

Within a few days now, her husband's aspirations would prove his end, and she'd have a real estate portfolio she could offload to the man who ran a real empire across the span of the Americas.

Nor would she let Isa be a problem. After they put José away in the prison system where his little kingdom would slowly deteriorate, she'd have Isa taken care of.

CHAPTER 56

At first, no one noticed the altercation in the corner, but when Ducktail loudly called Isa a not-so-nice name, heads turned.

Now her dragon spewed fire.

This wasn't how she'd hoped the night would go. All she wanted was a quiet information exchange with Jay. Let him know she had found money laundering that could prove the size of El Padrino's ill-gotten empire. And she'd wanted to tell him about Sophia.

The adrenalin speeding through her veins smothered the apprehension she should have been experiencing. She wanted to beat this drunk to China and back. Teach him a lesson.

Looking to make himself intimidating, Ducktail's spread his feet apart, all prepared to rumble.

No matter. Isa set her jaw, pushed her leg back, shot her hands forward, and readied her knee to do serious damage to his lower gut.

The man let out a guttural war cry and charged. Head down. Which was the dumbest thing anyone in a fight should do. Every self-defense student knows you never ever take your eyes off your target. She side-stepped out of the charging bull's path, allowing him to make head-first contact with the bistro table. Both Ducktail and the table crashed against the wall.

Which only made him madder. Which only drew a crowd.

CALCULATED RISK

Great.

Someone yelled, "Take her, Eddie."

She turned, ready to give whoever had the big mouth a piece of her mind. Which was stupid because, everyone knows you never take your eyes off your target.

But that's exactly what she'd done.

Ducktail must have gotten to his feet. He rushed her from behind. Got Isa in a headlock. Squeezed tight to cut off her air flow. Isa pounded her foot at his ankle. He grunted but kept dragging her backwards, toward a dark corner.

In defense class, she'd learned that most people will pull at the outside of the attacker's arm, trying to create space around their windpipes. But the right move is to shove your hands and forearms between your neck and the attacker's arm, creating more width than the bad guy can keep his grip on. She squeezed her eyes shut, trying to cram her hand between his nasty-smelling arm and her esophagus.

"Let her go, Freakazoid," some female supporter from the growing mob hollered.

Isa's eyes popped open to identify her lone ally, and that's when she saw Jay, face hard and eyes narrowed, pushing his way through the horde.

What happened next passed in a blur.

She felt Jay's body smash into her. His hand went beneath Ducktail's chin and all three were back against the wall.

Ducktail let go of Isa to fight off Jay, but sandwiched between the two men now, she couldn't free herself. She made good use of the situation and elbowed Ducktail in the stomach as the men's arms flew around her. Finally tossed to the side, Isa whirled around to see Jay pulverizing the drunk's face with one hard hit after another.

Ducktail slid down the wall and made a heap of blue jeans and greasy hair on the floor.

Jay finished him off with a rib-cracking kick to the chest.

The music stopped, the crowd backed up, and one of the big mouths said, "Man, you coulda killed him."

Wiping the back of his hand across his mouth, Jay turned. Put his eyes on Isa.

A knowing look passed between them. But she wasn't sure if he knew what her knowing look meant which was, *we got him.* Was that intense fire and heavy concern in his eyes real? Or an act for those who watched the action?

She gave him a sideways smile.

All manner of concern in his face dissipated when he said, "Can't you stay out of trouble?"

Before she could open her mouth to offer a deserved insult, something at Jay's feet buzzed.

Simultaneous, their heads, and the heads of the blood-thirsty Drake's Horn's patrons close by dropped to look at the floor.

A phone. It buzzed again.

The whole bar seemed to quick freeze.

Nick stepped through the ice. He got into the space between Isa and Jay. "Hey, is that yours?" He picked up the buzzing phone. Looked at Jay. "I thought you had a droid, Man."

Jay grabbed the phone out of Nick's hand before Nick had a decent grip on it. "Yeah." Jay flipped the phone open and disconnected the call.

"Why'd ya beat Eddie like that?" Nick looked between Jay and the pile of Eddie. "What's up, man?"

"Nothing's wrong," Jay shot back, shoving the phone in his pocket. "He had it comin'."

The smart-aleck DJ started the tunes back up with Cindy Lauper's *Girls Just Wanna Have Fun*, and the crowd drifted back to their respective dark corners.

Except Nick. He stepped closer to Jay. "What's up with the burner phone?"

CHAPTER 57

El Padrino shifted around in the suite's wing-back chair, unsure what to make of the tardy Miguel Lopez. They'd scheduled this meeting for the evening, the exchange of top leaders planned at nine o'clock sharp. Lopez was to come to his hotel room.

Yet, here he and Oso sat at half-past the hour. Though he'd often left men waiting on his own whims, he did not like being on the receiving end of such demeaning implications.

Finally, his phone buzzed with a text from Lopez.

I have been delayed. Meet tomorrow. Same place. Same hour.

Tossing his phone on the table beside him, he cursed. Lopez played one unfortunate game, testing El Padrino's patience and commitment. "Tomorrow," he said, looking at Oso. "I'll give him one more day and if he postpones again, we'll have to send our own message."

Oso nodded. "What kind of message, Jefe?"

"A deadly one."

"Maybe his troubles are legit." Oso shrugged.

El Padrino turned that thought over. Didn't like it. No, men like Lopez had other people take care of their troubles. He should have shown up.

Getting up and moving to the window, El Padrino looked down at the parking lot six stories below him. He had associates down there, watching, waiting.

"Oso, tell the men we will wait twenty-four hours, then I shall decide if this La Liga alliance will stall. Should it stall indefinitely, death shall become Lopez's prophecy." He turned and smiled at Oso. "Now, bring the woman up to me. I wish to be entertained."

CHAPTER 58

Nick's face was all scrunched up in a question mark, and this made Isa think that his brain might not be so wee-little after all. Isa hadn't seen Jay defend himself to a gang brother before, and she anticipated what this would, exactly, look like.

"Nick ..." Jay stepped closer to Nick. Puffed out his chest. "My business is *my* business.

Nick lowered his forehead. "I think your business is El Padrino's business."

The two—standing chest to chest—brought a picture of *Clash of the Titans* to mind, the Drake's Horn the perfect setting for a C-grade movie re-enactment.

Jay tapped Nick on the chest. "Maybe there are things you and her don't need to know." He tossed his head toward Isa but kept his face nose-to-nose with Nick.

Isa pulled an indignant chin to her chest. She wasn't the one asking questions.

"Maybe a man's got more than one gata," Jay was snarling now.

Isa opened her mouth. "Gata?"

"That's right, woman," Jay answered her louder than necessary. "The alley's full of kitties."

Was Jay comparing her to a cat? Really?

Nick's pursed lips twisted up in an evil grin, letting a couple of tense seconds pass. "Maybe you should share some of your litter with the boys." He started to chuckle.

Jay's snarl eased into a half grin, his head nodding.

CALCULATED RISK

Isa got up on her feet, brushing off her khakis at the knees. Even though she knew Jay was covering for the burner phone, the idea that he used women—multiple lovers—as a reason to hide his secret phone, was disgusting. Barbarians—she stood in the middle of a bar full of them.

Nick threw his head back and laughed.

Jay offered Nick a high-five. "Sí? Comprende?"

Isa fixed a rock-hard stare on Jay.

"See what you've done, Nick? You've gotten me in more trouble with my woman. Now, you're going to have to give me the car keys, so I can drive her around the block and straighten her out." He held out his hand.

Without hesitation, Nick pulled the keys from his pocket and dropped them in Jay's palm. Evidently, male code dictated that one macho man didn't question another about the size of his harem. But Nick was making catcalls at Isa as Jay pulled her away by the arm. Maybe Nick thought she would be available, seeing as her man kept several kittens around. Or maybe Nick thought she was crazy, which would have made Nick really close to being right.

They reached the parking lot in seventy-nine seconds. She'd counted. Kept counting until they'd driven two blocks away and Jay pulled into an alley, stopping the car.

"A cat? You called me a cat?"

"You stay here." Jay opened the car door.

"Where are you going?"

Ignoring her, he crawled out of the Prius.

She leaned across the console. "Hello. What are we doing?"

He slammed the door shut. Started down the alley, extracting the burner from his jeans.

Incredible. The arrogant, secretive, self-sufficient Jay was never going to see her as more than a problem. She opened the car door. Got one leg and her head out and yelled, "Hey, what are we doing here?"

He spun around, the phone almost to his ear. "Stay in the car. That's an order."

Her lungs exhaled fire. She got everything back in and pulled the car door shut as Jay disappeared into the shadows. Isa pounded the Prius dashboard a couple of times, the adrenalin rush from the bar brawl still in her veins. She added a few foot stomps then leaned back in her seat, muttering *how could he* beneath her breath.

Thunder rolled in the distance.

A few tears might relieve the immense frustration, but she hated to admit he'd pushed her to that point.

Then she got honest with herself. Jay's behavior shouldn't be driving her mad, considering another cop had been killed. Working at HPD, she'd experienced the deeply personal phenomenon, too. Of course she'd grieved over Mac. Would continue to, even though she'd now uncovered his sins. But the men and women in law enforcement bonded in unique ways. They were soldiers managing the war zones of life and protecting civilians as well as each other. Jay's mood was tied to the news he'd received.

Isa pulled at her cheeks. Let the seriousness of the situation take hold. Another warrior lost to the border cartels. Another brother gone. How long before the industry would be crushed? How many more victims, like her brother, would be pulled into the drug vortex before the storm ended?

Would she or Jay be its next casualties?

CHAPTER 59

As she went through her husband's desk drawers, Sophia's laptop rang three quick signals, the alarm for the outside camera at the drive. A car approached the house. Probably the group that took Isa out for the night.

Though she'd told Isa she had disabled the household cameras, that hadn't been the entire truth. She had disabled the little spies for a few hours when she'd given Isa the computer and flash drives containing José's real estate purchases. Made sure her husband would never see footage of her giving Isa evidence. But having the cameras off for a full day would incriminate her. So, with the cameras rolling, she'd watched Isa at work on the computer. Obedient Isa.

Sophia had also watched Isa slip from Jay's bedroom, Jay at her heels like a love-smitten teen.

But Isa had better not let Jay in on Sophia's secrets. Not yet. The time would come when all the family would know what she'd done. By then, she'd be long gone and the next phase of her plan underway.

The camera app dinged again, and Sophia refreshed the screen, expecting to see that little crew returning, but a new Lexus drove up the drive. She strained to get a look at the driver. Who was this and how had they gotten past the guards?

Sophia tensed, mentally running through different, possible scenarios. What if José had discovered her scheme and sent an assassin? That fear lived in her constantly. This car could also be carrying the American Indian she'd requested be returned.

Or ... it could be ...

She shut El Padrino's desk drawers, closed her laptop, and made her way through the house to the garage, realizing there could be one fascinating person who could fool guards into letting him through the gate.

When she opened the garage door, she saw the car had parked to the side of the drive. The headlights blinked.

She smiled. This was exactly who she hoped it was.

The driver's side door opened. Stepping out, the driver shut the door and stood there.

Her heart skipped a beat.

"Mi querida." He called her his favorite name—his desired one.

Hips swaying, she put one foot in front of the other as she walked toward him. "You don't surprise me," she stated, getting close enough to make out his face. "I should have known you would come."

He didn't smile. Didn't flinch. Waited for her to react.

Pushing herself against him, she pressed her lips onto his in a kiss meant to leave an impression.

CHAPTER 60

Back from the alley, Jay got in and slammed the car door. Started the motor without saying a word. Pulled the gear shift into reverse.

A thunderclap rattled the car and Isa flinched. Desert storms could pop up quick.

Jay didn't make it easy for her to extend the grace she'd found for him moments earlier. Quite the opposite. Jay Hernandez had a bolted shut, double-chained, no-entrance-allowed personal door. And he wasn't letting anybody in tonight.

Trying to get things back on track, she spoke up. "I was thinking, why don't you give me the burner phone, if you're done with it. I'll snap some pictures of the evidence I've been trying to tell you about when we're back at the compound."

"The phone's destroyed. Gone." He said it with zero reflection in his voice.

"You already disposed of it?" He was hard-core agent material. "Then I need you to let me take your phone and snap some evidence photos. I've uncovered something. I think it will prove what you need without faking your way through an IRS audit."

"I'm listening." He turned the wheel and pressed on the gas so hard, the Prius managed a lunge backwards, throwing Isa's head forward.

"Jay, what is it? What happened in the alley?"

He ignored her of course.

Without bringing the car to a full stop, he shoved the gear into drive. "Tell me what you got on El Padrino."

The car's motor juddered. She pressed her palm into the dashboard.

"I've got something that may stick to him."

Going the opposite direction of the Darke's Horn, Jay picked up speed.

"Don't we need to go back for Snake and Nick?"

"Those guys can find their own way."

"Won't that make them mad?"

"Talk, Isa. Tell me what you got." He lowered his forehead, eyes glued ahead. "Then tell me it's enough."

Enough? The shadows on Jay's face were dark, backlit by the streetlights flashing by. Another clap of thunder and she knew. This was her moment. *Talk Isa*, she told herself. *Give it all to him.*

"It will be enough. Quitclaim deeds."

"What?" Jay's hands turned the wheel, taking a corner so fast, she slammed the passenger door again.

"Quitclaim. It's a simple process." She gripped the seat belt across her chest. "First time I've seen it used for money laundering, but it looks like a quick way to hide assets. Though it's not bullet proof. Could we slow down?"

"Is there a bullet-proof money-laundering scheme out there?"

"This one is clever."

His foot retreated from the gas pedal. "So you do have something, then?"

"Yes."

"How did you get the information on this ... what did you call it?"

"Quitclaim deed."

"Never heard of it." Jay executed the next turn at normal speed.

"I've seen some files. Made hand-written notes that we can snap photos of. I'll destroy the notes once we get them documented."

"Files? You saw files?"

"That ..." She pulled in a breath. "Is another part of the story, and it involves Sophia."

He shot her a stunned glance. "Who did you say?"

"Sophia."

He muttered a bad word under his breath then said, "Let's get back to the claim thing. We will deal with Sophia in a minute. What is this procedure and how does it work?"

"Quitclaim deeds are used to transfer properties between people and usually within a family. For example, when a parent transfers a home or land to a child. Or in cases of divorce when one spouse is removed from the deed." She paused to check his understanding.

"Keep going," he said.

"It's an easy way to grant property to someone without involving legal action. The person transferring ..." She nodded him on though he never glanced her way. "Well, that person is called a grantor and he or she remises, releases, and quitclaims his or her interest in the property to a grantee, which is the recipient of the property."

"I'm going to need you to speak English."

She exhaled. Finally, she had something to offer this case and something to offer Jay Hernandez. For unestablished reasons, that mattered. "To hide big cash, El Padrino has been buying property."

"But our guys haven't found evidence of that in court records."

"Exactly. He pays cash and has the properties put in ..." She made quote marks with her fingers. "Family members' names. Even though that's a risky move. Whoever has their name on the quitclaim deed could make a maneuver to keep the property. So El Padrino has these temporary property holders quitclaim the deed back to him. Except the quitclaim is not being filed in the county records, so when searching for properties, you'll find nothing in his name."

They pulled up to an intersection. "Why is that?"

Isa used the simplest of terms. "His real estate is still listed under the name of the original cash buyers he's funded. But he's got the quitclaim deeds in his own personal files, and in a court of law, this is still a binding contract. You see, he owns the property, but it's registered under someone else's name. So if, and when, he wants to sell these properties off, he first gets a buyer. After he's secured a purchase agreement, he submits his quitclaim to the county, showing he's the real owner. He can sell that property the same day. It's a fast maneuver that leaves his name out of search engines in case anyone, such as FBI undercover agents like yourself, are looking for properties in his name." Isa let that germinate in Jay's brain for a second. "In other words, he owns properties in Houston, Albuquerque, and spaces in between the two cities, all in other people's names while he holds the deeds. Looks like he rents some, then flips others."

"This sounds complicated."

"It's not. Listen," she said, angling her shoulders toward him. "It's the easy things that get overlooked. While most forensic accountants would be looking for offshore investments and money transfers to Swiss bank accounts, he's moving real estate around under our noses."

He seemed to be turning that over when his face clouded at the recollection of something not good.

"It's Claire," he said.

That was an unexpected comment.

"What's Claire?"

"The real estate deeds I took pictures of in your room—Houston. She must have been buying real estate on El Padrino's behalf."

"What?" Isa's brows dropped deep over her eyes. "No way. Claire doesn't have anything to do with any of this."

"She's the buyer using a different name to purchase properties for El Padrino."

"She's a detective with HPD, not a 96 cartel member," she retorted. Jay was speaking crazy now, but Isa's chest was tightening up just the same.

"It's Claire," he said, his voice flat.

He was headed down a trail she didn't want to follow.

"It's not Claire," she scoffed. "I know her. She sips Chardonnay and browses Ikea catalogs." Within the walls of her narrowing chest, her heart ached. *Not Claire.* She couldn't be bought. Could she?

Isa pressed her hand to her neck. "She wouldn't do this. Like I said, I know her,"

"Like you knew your husband?" His soft tone didn't disguise the cutting words. Their sharp edges sent an electric bolt through her. "There's no shame in being duped, Isa. You were played."

Her response came quick. "You don't know anything about me, my husband, or any of my relationships. You couldn't know. You've perfected the art of acting so well, you wouldn't know a real relationship if it ran over you like a freight train."

She knew he didn't deserve what she suddenly dished up, but Claire. But Mac. But ...

He pulled through the intersection and over to the curb. Slipped the gear shift into park.

Isa gripped the car-door handle. "What are you doing now, Jay? Running to the shadows again?"

Jay kept his eyes on the gear shift. It wasn't anger that covered his facial features. Pity crawled across the face that had been rigid most of the night.

"Las Cruces police found Claire's body in an alley today."

What he said didn't make sense.

"That's where El Padrino is now. Las Cruces. Making deals with La Liga."

No. Claire was in Houston harassing the sergeant about Isa and her Albuquerque antics. The Las Cruces guys had it wrong. Terribly wrong.

Neither spoke, but it wasn't quiet. The sirens going off in her brain were so loud she couldn't think. Couldn't process.

Like the perfect exclamation point at the end of the stinging truth, rain drops peppered the windshield then slid down the glass.

It's not supposed to rain in the desert.

She felt Jay's heavy hand squeeze her shoulder. "On the call in the alley, my connection told me about Claire. We'd never located her after she left here three days ago. She didn't go back to Houston. She must be the cop Nick and Snake talked about in the car. Has to be the same person.

CALCULATED RISK

It can't be a coincidence she was in Las Cruces at the same time as El Padrino called for a hit on a cop. Now it makes sense why she busted into your apartment and took your laptop. She wasn't concerned, she was probing."

Coincidence. The rain hit a rhythm—a frantic tempo.

"Isa," Jay said. "Claire ... it's the truth. She was in with the cartel."

CHAPTER 61

Odd it could rain this hard in desert. And yet it poured while Isa sat in a cartel-owned Prius at a neighborhood curb discussing how Claire, her friend, her coworker, her confidant, was a turncoat. She had probably worked alongside her traitor husband, Mac.

Overhead, the thunder mockingly applauded her epiphany.

Behind the burning eyes that threatened to turn on the tears, Isa's memory banks replayed scene after scene of deception. First her stepfather faking parental love, then Mac lying, lying to the one he'd promised to cherish, and then Claire with her counterfeit concerns over Isa's move.

"Claire lived in the Woodlands," she stated, her voice void of emotion.

Jay slipped his hand back to the steering wheel.

The revelations continued to roll across her injured heart. "One of the properties you snapped a picture of? It belonged to Sicily Jackson. That house is in the Woodlands." The heavy words fell like stones into her lap and she tried to handle the weight of it all. "Claire never invited me over. Lots of lunches, after-work drinks, a time or two we had dinner at my place. But she never invited me to her place."

Jay didn't say a word.

"How did I miss that?" she asked, not wanting an answer. Or maybe she did want an honest response. Just not one couched in Jay's typical sarcasm.

He didn't respond, and so the inch of space she opened for him to step into closed back up. With all the confounding and maddening emotional turmoil roiling around her, the dragon knocked against her rib cage. He wanted out.

Predictable, stoic, and less-than slightly sympathetic Jay. Never mind him. She had a laundering scheme to expose, then she'd go back to Houston and sort out her bad relationship history.

"So Claire is Sicily. What now?" she queried, working hard to sound unaffected.

He rolled his shoulder. Jay hid something.

"Claire always told me, 'Let the law do its work.'" She gazed at him a long time. "You tell me Jay, is the law doing its work?"

He didn't have an answer, and the silence between them grew wider and took the shape of a barricade.

When the rain relented, Jay put the car in drive and pulled onto the street. Mumbled something about picking up Nick and Snake.

"So, how many, Jay?" On her side of the fortification, she'd started to figure a couple of things out. "How many Houston cops are the FBI tailing?"

"A few."

"Me?" Isa pointed at herself. Cocked her head. "Tell me, Mr. Undercover, was some FBI slick shadowing me?"

His clinched jaw told her everything she needed to know.

"You lied to me."

Heavy rain rolled over the Prius again, and Jay stopped at another intersection. Let the car idle there.

"You've known all along who I am, and you played a game with me."

He wouldn't even look at her. "I had to. There are several HPD guys under suspicion."

"You knew Mac."

"No. I did not know him. But after his death, we suspected your husband must have been involved as a transport."

Her throat tightened and her temples throbbed. She shouldn't be able to even speak under such conditions, but the words came of their own force. "You suspected I worked with El Padrino. You have been scrutinizing me this whole time."

He tried hard to cover the truth with excuses. "Come on, you had to figure we were investigating Mac. He's killed on cartel territory out of his jurisdiction? Naturally, you were included on our watch list. Then you showed up here out of the blue? That looked suspicious."

"I didn't just show up here. You or your FBI guys planted a note in my car to lure me in."

He shot her a questionable look. "What note?"

"Oh, here we go, Actor Jay, covering his tracks." Man, she wanted to get out of that car.

"There are no tracks. I don't know anything about a note."

"Right."

"So okay, we watched you. Couldn't believe you showed up with keys to a building down the street from a cartel bar. Of course it looked like you and your husband were working side-by-side with the gang."

"So you planned the whole IRS audit, hoping I'd take the bait?"

"No." His denial took on an offended tone. "That was already underway."

The deluge, on its own roller coaster ride, let up again.

Jay shifted around in his seat. "We had an IRS audit planned before you arrived in town. But then you got pulled in, and everything flipped upside down." He glanced at her. "Everything."

None of this mattered. How. What. When. She'd been duped by her own kind.

"You lied to me." Another four words to add to the suffocating rock pile in her lap.

"No. I waited to see what you would do."

"You lied to me," she said louder.

His voice rose a couple of octaves, too. "I followed orders." His frustration climbed uphill to meet hers head-on. "You are the one who insisted on staying inside and playing undercover hero. Actually, you were cleared before you showed up in Albuquerque. Like I said, that looked suspicious, but it didn't take a Sherlock Holmes to figure out you were fumbling your way through an investigation attempt."

Fumbling? Wow, the blows keep coming.

His voice held that cynical tone again. "You tied our hands once you convinced El Padrino to let you stay. But me, I was willing to give you a shot at finding the money trail. It looked pretty doubtful, but hey, one can hope."

"It doesn't matter. You knew who I was. You knew El Padrino killed Mac." She thrust her finger at him. "You're a liar."

His response blind-sided her. "Get over it, Isa. You're in now. You got what you wanted."

Before she realized it, she'd drawn back her elbow, fingers balled into a fist. With the fury of fifteen enraged dragons, she let that fist fly and struck, landing her blow upside Jay's face.

CHAPTER 62

After he'd asked Oso to bring him the old woman they'd held in Sicily's now-vacant room, El Padrino did something he hadn't allowed himself to do in years. He walked to the minibar and poured himself a shot of tequila. He had certainly earned it.

In the early years of his climb to fortune, liquor could lure him into a state of stupor. That's why he'd given up drinking. Nothing and no one would make him act or appear less than the man he was destined to be.

Sometimes he felt the same way about humans. Useless frivolities that took energy and attention that rendered him no progress.

Perhaps Sophia had fallen to these depths. Lost her ability to challenge his passions.

But gripping the tequila bottle now, an old sensation roused. The gold liquid flowing into the shot glass enticed the boy within—a dreamer lying in that old field of grass miles away from the squalor of his village. A visionary letting the sun bake the fantasies of his mind into something palpable. That boy had achieved it all.

He chuckled. Of course he could control his liquor now.

Oso entered with the old woman following close behind. This woman. *She* was not a frivolous matter. He wanted to discover the reason one old woman could cause him unrest.

El Padrino saluted Oso with his glass.

"Jefe," Oso laughed, "my sister, she blows up my phone with texts demanding I return her spiritual mentor."

CALCULATED RISK

El Padrino offered a nod to Awena. "So you've made quite the impression on our family in Mexico."

He brought the shot glass to his mouth, letting the sharp scent of tequila entice his lips. "To my loyal friend," he said looking at Oso. He poured another tequila into a nearby glass. "We drink to our success and the future."

Oso took the glass.

Awena, olive skin sagging beneath deep-set eyes, looked from one to the other as El Padrino tilted his head back and tossed the tequila into his mouth. "You are troubled?" she asked.

Oso laughed again.

El Padrino grinned. "There is no trouble at all. We celebrate, and I've asked you here to join us." He took his seat in the wingback chair. "Would you like to live in luxury? Want for nothing?"

Awena hobbled across the floor. Without being offered a seat, she plopped down on the sofa and rested both hands on the top of her cane. That's when El Padrino noticed the carvings on the stick.

"I want for nothing now." She shrugged. "You cannot offer me anything that does not already belong to me accordingly."

He grinned, the tequila soothing the itch to show this woman what he was capable of. To show Miguel Lopez who he toyed with. To remind his wife that he was the master of their home.

"You are quite popular with my people. Oso's sister doesn't wish to let go of you and now, my wife has requested I return you to her." He held his glass out so Oso refill his glass.

"Your wife?" Awena asked. "Is your wife the one who took me to Isa Padilla's room one night?"

The soothing current of tequila flowing through his veins did little to prepare him for her statement. So, Sophia had played a little trick behind his back.

El Padrino drank the second shot. "Tell me about that night."

Awena examined the ceiling before saying, "She was very kind and concerned that Isa Padilla should know that I was doing well."

"And this was not Maria the cook, but an Italian woman with long hair?"

Awena hesitated.

He put on a knowing smile. "Do not be afraid. I'd like to acknowledge my lovely wife for her thoughtfulness."

"The woman who pointed me to Isa that night. She was not the cook. It was as you say. It was your wife," Awena said.

"And what did you and Isa discuss in her room, hm?" He motioned for Oso to bring the bottle on over.

Awena rested her chin on her cane. "God's plans. He has a plan for that one."

"Which one?"

"Isa Padilla."

"And tell me, what *are* his plans for her?"

"She is a revealer of truth."

He grimaced, not liking the implications made by this woman. Enough of the verbal banter.

"Oso, my laptop."

Oso left the room.

El Padrino pulled his phone from his pocket and pressed in Sophia's number. The call went to voicemail.

Awena's fingers drummed at her cane. She appeared collected in the middle of this burst of flurry. He hated her for that. Esteemed her for that. So like his mother.

Oso returned with the laptop, and El Padrino's fingers flew across the keyboard, pulling up his home camera app. He typed in his password.

Got it wrong.

Cursed and typed again.

Two more clicks and he had the right tab on the screen.

He hovered the mouse over it, lips twitching. Then he pressed, connecting his screen to the cameras in Isa's room.

The screen was black.

He punched another key, forcing the app to rewind to an earlier part of the day. Blank. The cameras weren't functioning. He slammed the cover down and dropped his laptop to the floor.

"Oso. Take her back to her room."

Oso went to the woman, and in a surprising gesture, held out his hand. El Padrino watched his best ally help the seer to her feet. Gentle gestures and helpful deeds were El Padrino's call, and not to be executed at the whim of his followers.

He poured another shot.

Awena kept her eyes on him long after she left the room. He could feel it.

The meetings with Miguel no-show Lopez were tabled for now. He had to settle his own business first. And he would settle it at home.

CHAPTER 63

Isa slapped her hands over her mouth, astonished she'd executed a roundhouse punch to Jay's jaw.

Thunder rumbled in the distance as the wrath of the rain moved east. The slapping wipers squeaked against the windshield.

Jay, unblinking, flipped the arm to turn the wipers off.

She held her breath for a couple of seconds before letting the air out of her lungs. "Jay ... I—"

He shot his hand up to silence her.

Shanking her own hand to relieve the sting at her knuckles, she said, "Come on, you had to see that coming. You really made me mad, and well, I probably needed to get that out."

He put the car in gear and let it roll forward, hollow words slipping through his teeth. "We're going back now."

That punch liberated some pent-up emotion. And even though regret poked at her conscious, she didn't want to let him off the hook of retribution. From here on out, they needed to stick to business. Nothing more. "Okay. But I think we need to talk about a couple of things first. I haven't told you everything yet."

Jay enforced his robot mode. "We're going to pick up Snake and Nick and go back to the compound."

"Would you listen for a minute?"

"No."

Regret stopped poking and started hitting. Jay had, after all, beat the drunk in the bar to protect her. When going for Ducktail, he hadn't looked like Captain America, but like Hulk—angry, outraged, and green with jealousy. If she didn't know better, she would say he cared about her wellbeing.

But they needed to be all business now—now that anything solid between them had disintegrated. "Jay. I apologize for hitting you."

At the intersection ahead, a green light switched to yellow. Instead of slowing down, the car picked up speed. She wasn't sure they would make it through the yellow light before it flipped red.

But he barreled for it anyway.

"Jay!" Isa shoved her foot into an imaginary brake. They approached too fast to stop now.

The light switched to red.

A car in the cross section started across.

Isa tensed, turning her face away.

Jay slammed on the brakes and their car fishtailed like a thrashing shark on the wet pavement.

Tires squealed.

The car jerked to a stop, inches from the other vehicle.

She gasped for air. "Are you ... crazy?"

Calmer than he should have been, Jay turned to glare at her. "I'm going to need you to follow my orders from here on out."

CHAPTER 64

The tequila ran through him like fire. El Padrino reached for another shot in the back seat of his SUV.

Looking in the visor mirror, Oso noticed. "Jefe, you've not slept in twenty-four hours. Try to get some shut-eye now."

He imagined his hands around Sophia's swanlike neck. Could feel his thumbs bear down into the curved notch at the center of her collarbone. Saw her eyes begging for mercy.

"You never know why the cameras might be off. Maybe they are broke," Oso offered.

There'd been times when El Padrino allowed Oso to speak logic into a situation. Let his loyal friend calm his scorched nerves. Not now. Discounted by Miguel Lopez and ignored by a deceptive wife, he figured himself due an eruption. Let the molten lava building up in his veins release all over the empire. Remind everyone what he was capable of.

Power surged right alongside the anger.

Oso tried again. "Maybe something's wrong with the security system."

When El Padrino did not give him a response, Oso put his head against the window. "Maybe ..." Oso's word trailed off into the space that El Padrino did not inhabit—the weak realm of excuses.

Just as well. No one could talk El Padrino down now. He glanced behind to see that the headlights of their second car, which carried Awena, were close, the fading lights of Las Cruces behind them now.

Another three hours and he'd be at his compound. *Honey, I'm home—and you'll be sorry.*

He picked up his cell again and punched in Sophia's number.

Voice mail.

CHAPTER 65

On top of everything, every single wrong thing, she now had near-wreck, post-traumatic stress disorder. And Jay? He had a bad case of moodiness, losing that professional trademark he was so proud of. If she hadn't witnessed it herself, she would have never believed that an FBI agent would nearly smash his car into another vehicle out of frustration.

He, in a haunting-like calm, put the car in reverse, backed away from the intersection, then took the street to their left.

Her vocabulary failed her. There were no words.

They were back at the Drake's Horn in what seemed like seconds. When she reached for the car-door handle, he growled, "Stay put." Then he threw the gear into park, yanked out the key, and opened the door—slamming it as he stormed away.

She was the hazardous liability? He needed to take stock of his own behaviors. She could help him count them up. Moody, entitled, manipulative, and a conversation hoarder. Basically, all the symptoms of a classic narcissist. Oh, and he was a terrible driver.

But she did as he ordered and stayed put.

Thought about that punch to his face. Sunk down in her seat. Truth was, Jay seemed to bring out the worst in her when all she wanted was for him to include her. Trust her. Okay, maybe she'd crossed lines and caused him trouble, but working as the lead accountant at HPD, she was used to calling the shots and doing so from a secluded office alone.

CALCULATED RISK

Convicting thoughts bounced through her head, knocking against long-held fortresses. Maybe trust couldn't be established unless one partner let another partner in. Inside. Where little girls hid behind protective dragons.

Isa pulled at her ponytail.

She counted cars in the parking lot waiting for Jay to return, because counting cars was much easier than cleaning up dragon fury.

After the car count, she decided to organize information and evidence. Up first? Tally all the lies Mac and Claire had used to deceive her.

Next on the list? El Padrino. Now there were some big potential numbers. Not knowing how many people he'd ordered murdered, she decided to estimate three per year for every year he'd been a known cartel leader. Eighteen. But how would she ever count the ripple effects of those murders? Or those who'd died of overdoses from the heroin, meth, and cocaine he manufactured? Had to be thousands and growing daily.

That's when Snake, Nick and a pink-haired girl in shorts and cowboy boots exited the side door of the bar, disrupting her assessments. Isa sat up straight. The trio sauntered over to the Prius and piled in—Nick and the girl in the back seat, Snake at the wheel.

"Jay will be right here," Nick said before she heard him lay a kiss somewhere on the girl. Where, she didn't want to imagine.

They purposely left her out of the conversation, speaking mostly Spanish, but Isa managed to catch a few words and phrases about drinking, motorcycles, and other women. Made her stomach turn ... and made her a little homesick for some normal, HPD cop conversations in the halls of those old black and yellowed vinyl tiles.

Her temperament fluctuated between mournful and hostile. And she had little control over it.

Another ten minutes of Spanglish and kissing sounds from the back seat, and Jay showed. Got in back with the two love birds. Nick started the car.

Isa pulled down the visor, hoping to make eye contact with Jay in the mirror. Undercover work had blurred her black and white lines and pulled some ghosts from her closets. When he finally glanced up at the mirror, she mouthed, *I'm sorry.*

But Jay, stone-faced, turned his head away.

CHAPTER 66

Sitting at the wrought-iron table on the patio outside her bedroom, Sophia took in the canyon view. She could smell the change, the seasonal rains moving up from the Albuquerque valley to the south. The rumbling thunder sounded like drums of revolution.

Oh, the things she'd witnessed on this patio. Here, she and José had shared their morning coffee. Here, she had watched him morph from a determined businessman to a power-hungry lunatic. Here, he had compared himself to history's great leaders and in the last couple of years, to God himself.

The man's ego had no limit.

But she'd learned while she listened, letting that self-image of his expand beyond reality. Discovered games she'd never seen played in Italy.

Like her father always told her, *In every situation, Sophia, one can find a diamond.* She'd found hers. Now, it was time to take her real estate plunder and disappear.

Her gaze wandered over the patio, and that's when she saw his discarded cigarette butt. Sophia got to her feet, picked it up, and tossed it over a boulder. José Ventura would come unglued if he knew she'd entertained someone on his patio—if he'd seen what they'd done.

Sophia lifted her eyes to the night sky, clouds making their way towards the mountains. A gust blew strands of hair from her face, and she thought of the coastal breezes of her beloved Italy.

CHAPTER 67

Isa couldn't get out of the car fast enough.

After Jay's revealing reaction to her apology, the ride back to the druggie compound had been miserable. She'd felt the invisible but icy darts he'd sent to the back of her head from the back seat of the car.

She had partnered with an artic glacier.

Hurrying to the garage, Isa exhaled some relief, glad to be out from under Jay's condemnation, but facing a whole new set of problems. She couldn't let what happened between them consume her. She had a case to wrap up, and that included getting photographs of the evidence on her desk, returning the computer and flash drives to Sophia, and coming up with a story that would protect Jay's cover, yet let Sophia know she was close to having solid evidence.

She glanced back to see Nick and Pink Hair disappear around the corner of the house, taking a walkway to one of the casitas. Snake headed toward the guard post down the drive. Jay stood next to the car, surveying the grounds.

He must have felt her gawking because in a sudden move, he pointed at her.

The absurd struggle between them wasn't going away.

He started for her. He looked crazed, pounding the pavement with his boots, eating up the ground between them.

She should have run, freeing herself from the insanity of Jay, El Padrino, Sophia, and the liars of her past. But for some unrealistic reason, his racing for her initiated a hope that she wouldn't finish this case alone. For the first time, maybe ever, she wanted help.

He got to her, gripped a piece of elbow, and pulled her toward the back of the garage.

She let him guide her, sensing his urgency and hoping this conversation would set them on a path of victory ... not shambles.

"No cameras in here," he said moving between a motorcycle and an ATV. "We'll talk."

"Okay." He *did* want to talk and that was a good sign.

"You need to listen for once."

She pursed her lips. The good sign flew out the opened garage door.

"Your gun, phone, identity papers, are in a box in El Padrino's office."

Was he telling her El Padrino absolutely knew who she was? Or ...

"He doesn't know anything is there."

She smacked her forehead. *Here we go again.* "He doesn't know that you put my gun and ID in his ... why would you ... I don't understand."

"His private rooms and this garage don't have cameras or receive searches. I really have to make this simple for you, don't I?"

She opened her mouth, but nothing came out.

Jay talked on. "My room gets searched daily and your room has probably had someone snooping around, too. I don't have access to his living quarters, so I stashed your gear in the bookshelf in his office. It's the perfect place to hide something you don't want cartel members coming across because nobody in this house knows how to read a book."

"Seriously?"

"Besides, no one's allowed to be in that office when El Padrino isn't there, so it's safe."

A little of the old Jay seemed to emerge, and though he was insulting and arrogant, at least he wasn't acting like RoboCop steering a Prius on a path of destruction.

"This information is an FYI only, in case something goes down before I get you out of here. Upper right cabinet in the bookcase."

Isa frowned. "What could go down?"

"We're dealing with hardened criminals here. Did I forget to mention that?"

Oh yeah, he was back to the old Jay. She scoffed.

"Now tell me how you got into El Padrino's books." He swiped at the hair twisting down on his forehead. "Talk fast."

He wanted it fast? She gave it to him fast. Already counted all the facts and she could roll them out like a calculator. But one fact alone mattered right now. "Sophia." She answered.

He raised his brows.

"She's in danger and wants out."

Looking at her like she needed a straitjacket, Jay said, "She told you this?"

"Yes."

"When?"

"Over breakfast."

"You had breakfast with Sophia Ventura?"

"Yes."

"Why?"

"I was invited."

He stared, his expression now a big, blank page.

Isa raised her chin. "I think Sophia planted those deeds I found among the expense receipts."

He cocked his head toward her. "You didn't tell her you were working for the feds, did you? I hope you haven't blown my cover."

"I'm not that stupid. But ..."

"Yeah?"

"She thinks I'm a vigilante. She researched me. Knows I'm Mac's wife and—"

"Stop."

She stopped. Didn't he say he wanted it fast?

"You're telling me that Sophia conducted an investigation on you. Did I hear that right?"

"Yes, that's what she said. She knew I worked for HPD."

Shaking his head, he moaned deep in his chest. "Not good. Not good at all, Isa."

"Why?"

"If she's researched one of us, she's interested enough to do her homework on all of us." Here came the finger in the face. "I don't trust her. You should have told me about this."

"I've been trying to tell you all night."

He ignored that fact. "I can't believe this. We'll have to move fast. Is what you have on the real estate claim thing enough to prove El Padrino's laundering money?"

"With some county record support, I think so."

"Are you at a ninety-percent *think so*, or a ten-percent *think so*?

"Seventy-five." She looked up. Played with a couple of ratios in her head. "Make that seventy-eight."

His face scrunched up like he'd swallowed something sour. Making little circles on his forehead with the butt of both palms, he shut his eyes and said, "Okay, here's how this will go." He opened one eye then the other. "I'm coming in your room tonight. Late. Same stage as we set before, like we're ..." he choked, struggling to say it. "Like we're together. I'll get photos of the evidence. Tomorrow we get you out, and our men set up for a raid here and in Las Cruces. El Padrino is camped out at a hotel there."

Okay, she could do this. Get all the ducks lined up. "I'll let Sophia know so she can prepare."

"You'll tell her nothing."

Isa's crossed her arms. "What? But I promised to help her."

"She's luring you into a confession about our case. We can't trust her."

"But you don't understand. There's a child involved, and I promised to help her if she brought Awena back."

"I don't trust her and I'm giving the orders." He backed between the car and motorcycle. "Get in the house and don't mess this up. Stay in your room until I get there."

"But what about Awena? Who will get her?"

"There's someone on that, Isa. Have you not heard our guys are the best in the world?"

She narrowed her eyes to mere slits in her head, so he'd get the message.

"Okay," he relented. "Your gal is not in a lockdown situation and should be easy to nab. The plan is to get her in the next couple of days, making it look like she wandered off. You need to trust me."

Her head shook back and forth, blocking Jay's incoming irrational directives. "I can't ignore Sophia and her child."

He kept backing up. "Tomorrow—everything will be sorted out tomorrow."

"Wait. Jay. Listen."

"I'm going to chat with the boys down there." He pointed behind him toward the guard shack at the bottom of the hill. "Make everything seem normal, since it hasn't seemed normal all day ... thanks to you."

"Wait ..."

He turned for the drive.

Isa kicked the motorcycle next to her. Did more damage to the rubber tip of her flip-flop than the bike's chrome. When would Jay trust *her* instincts?

Truth was, she'd pulled a pretty risky maneuver by pretending to be someone she wasn't—an undercover cop. Though he was a world-class actor, Jay liked his scenes to play out by the FBI book. And she'd managed to toss his book right out the window.

She got that. She was a spreadsheet girl, after all. Loved her defined, colored cells.

But today, they'd both have to play this outside their comfort zones. She couldn't wait for the FBI to sort things out tomorrow. She should help Sophia make a plan today.

CHAPTER 68

The Range Rover pulled to a stop. El Padrino sat up in the back seat, his vision blurred. "Where are we?"

Oso answered from the front. "The bar. Perhaps it is good to take a break before going up to the mountain."

Oso seemed a little too comfortable making decisions.

El Padrino's mouth felt like the desert and his head like waves in the ocean. "What have you done with the old woman?"

"I sent them on to the house. The brothers said she snored louder than a man." He opened his car door, got out, then opened El Padrino's door. "The guys will put her in her room. Now let's go unwind some already."

"Who is in there?" El Padrino asked, feeling around for the tequila bottle.

"The usual. Maybe it'd be nice for you to chill for a minute, get loose. Lopez has you worked up good."

He located his bottle. "I'm going in for another bottle, but you wait here." He scooted towards the door. "And when I return, you will take me home and I will put the fear of El Padrino into the ladies at the house."

"El Padrino."

"This is what I want to do, Oso, do you understand?"

Oso nodded.

CHAPTER 69

Regardless of Jay's quote-un-quote higher ranking orders, Isa couldn't ignore the agreement she'd made with Sophia. Not that she hadn't done her share of lying in this new covert role. But Sophia deserved to know things were in the works. Helping woman and child escape the clutches of a cartel could be her purpose. The ultimate purpose in all this from day one—her kidnapping at India Magic.

She crept down the hall past her bedroom door.

And, she needed to warn Maria, the cook. Somebody had to pay attention to the unsuspecting victims here.

Passing the bank of windows that opened to the grounds where she and Jay had played loving couple at the fiesta, she slipped into El Padrino's private area of the house. Back against the wall, she side-stepped up a narrow stairwell, the ground floor in this area of the house rising with the side of the mountain. Sliding around a corner, she entered a hall with three doors.

Isa leaned her ear to the first door. Thought she heard movement.

Hand poised to knock, behind her, another door opened.

She whirled around, heart jumping up into her throat.

Sophia's head stuck out of the door across the hall. "What ... what are you doing?" She asked, her brows high.

"Looking for you. We need to talk."

Sophia opened the door wide, glanced up at a camera in the hall, then motioned Isa over. "Come in. Come in."

Isa hustled across the hall.

CALCULATED RISK

In sweatpants and an oversized Maroon 5 T-shirt, Sophia looked like a perfectly ordinary soccer mom. Bright colors on the walls and toys scattered on the floor told Isa that she stood in El Padrino and Sophia's son's room. So very normal, yet not.

She saw him. A child who could not have been more than three years old ran up and grabbed his mother's leg.

"I ... I'm sorry," Isa stuttered. "I didn't mean to intrude."

Sophia ran a nervous hand through her son's dark hair. "It's not safe for you to wander the house at night. What are you doing here?"

The little boy whimpered, held his hands up to his mother.

"Back to bed with you," Sophia said, picking the child up then looking back at Isa. "He's not sleeping well lately."

Sophia carried the boy to a toddler's racecar bed. Tucking him in, she said, "I'm going to talk to this friend, and I'll be back to check on you in a few minutes."

That might be the most precious, innocent child Isa had ever laid eyes on. This boy would need to be away from the house during the coming FBI raid. A SWAT squad tearing through his home, automatic weapons in tow, could scar a child for life. Jay didn't understand the full picture.

A door opened and closed from somewhere down the hall. Left, right, north, south, Isa couldn't discern, but Sophia leaped over a mound of match-box cars and quietly closed the door that Isa had left ajar. She turned, put her finger to her lips, then whispered, "It's probably Nick or one of the guys, but keep your voice down."

Isa knew it wasn't Nick. Nick was with Pink Hair in one of the casitas. "I'll go back to my room." Isa started for the door.

"No," Sophia whispered. Put her hand out to stop Isa.

"It's okay, I seem to have gained the freedom to move about and it shouldn't shock anyone to see me walking in the halls. If I see somebody, I'll say I came by to tell you good night."

Sophia's shook her head hard, which got the boy's attention.

The toddler sprung up out of the bed howling, "Momma! Momma!"

Isa heard the footsteps of someone rushing up the hall.

CHAPTER 70

Isa watched Sophia leap back across the pile of toy vehicles and land beside her son's bed. She squatted next to him, murmuring motherly words of reassurance.

Seeing Sophia in mother mode nearly wrenched Isa's heart out of her chest. Only, it was still in her throat. The tender scene proved that even though Jay saw Isa as a problem, she had an important job to do here.

Isa put her hand over her heart. "I'm so sorry. But, Sophia, you need to get your boy and get out. Tonight."

Chaos broke out behind her.

The bedroom door flung open, hit the wall, and bounced back, almost slamming shut. Through the commotion, she saw an ogre crawled up out of the pit of hell. El Padrino.

Not good.

Another kick. Another crash.

The door flew wide again.

Isa shot a glance at mother and child near the bed. Saw the kid's chin quiver as he grasped for his mother's neck.

"José." Sophia pushed the boy back down into the bed. "You scare Luca. Get a hold of yourself." The wobble in her voice, the hesitation in her tone betrayed the command coming from her lips.

El Padrino did not get hold of himself.

He got a hold of Sophia. By the hair. In two steps he was across the room yanking Sophia to her feet so brutally she screeched, reaching behind to try and dislodge his hands from her head.

CALCULATED RISK

Isa got a distinct whiff of tequila.

She wanted to charge him but the fear-driven nails holding her feet to the floor wouldn't budge. Fixated in horror, she watched as El Padrino pulled Sophia's head back with one hand and slapped her hard across the face with the other.

Sophia let go a short cry, then she angled her head to face her husband, her expression daring him to strike.

Isa cringed. She jerked around to see Do-Rag step into the room, forehead down, his Frankenstein scowl warning her not to make a move.

The boy squealed for his mother.

El Padrino nodded toward his man. "Take Luca to Maria."

Slipping between Isa and El Padrino, Do-Rag grabbed the boy. Luca wailed and wiggled so hard the man almost dropped him.

Sophia's eyes went wild with rage as Do-Rag wrestled the frantic child out the door. That's when she screamed the scream of a thousand horrors, the word "no" starting deep in her chest and reverberating up through her throat, as the volume grew louder.

Every muscle in Isa's body stiffened. Her hands balled into fists.

El Padrino drew back a fist and landed it in Sophia's jaw. She buckled at the knees first. Her head fell forward, that long dark hair flopping over her face. Blood dripped to the floor.

Isa's own blood drained from her face. She entered a tunnel with narrowing walls. She'd be the next one down. Not because El Padrino had his sights on her—he'd barely noticed she was in the room. But because she felt the onrushing train that would take her to oblivion. That blood dripping on the floor ...

"Oso," El Padrino shouted.

The room spinning, Isa managed to glimpse Oso enter the scene.

"One," Isa said. *Not today. Not now.* She wasn't going to faint.

Oso did a double take.

"Two."

She had El Padrino's attention, too.

"Three."

"What's she doing?" Osa asked.

"Four," Isa yelled, her vision levelling up. Blood circulated again. Adrenalin raced. *Oh yeah,* she would do this.

Isa charged El Padrino before she could talk herself out of it.

She could take him. Pin the drunk to the wall. Anything to stop Sophia's brutal beating.

Oso yanked Isa up by the arms before she made it halfway across the room. She kicked at his shins, losing both flip-flops, but landing significant blows.

He grunted, his legs dancing to avoid more contact.

El Padrino's brows raised above his blood-shot eyes. "Take the accountant to her room for now. He glared at her. "I'll take care of you later."

Doubtful.

She'd get him first.

CHAPTER 71

Isa jerked out of Oso's grip. He didn't fight her once he had her in the hall. From there, he followed her as she rushed through the house toward her room. He seemed more resigned to than irritated by the events.

Arriving at her bedroom, she had the door opened before Oso caught up. She rushed in, closed the door, and leaned against it.

The sound of the thumb latch slipping the deadbolt into place let her know she was, once again, on lockdown.

What had happened? Had El Padrino and Sophia had a disagreement? Or worse? Had he somehow discovered she and Sophia were creating an exit strategy together?

Getting to El Padrino's office to find her gun would have to be the next step, so she could stop the mayhem going down. That and letting Jay know what was happening.

Unsure how she'd get out of her room, she started for her nightstand to switch on the light, but mid-step, heard the voice.

"I told you to stay in your room."

Startled, she stopped, but was oh so glad she wouldn't have to go find him. "Jay."

"Where have you been, Isa?" He flipped on the desk lamp.

Words piled up in her head so quickly, she could not put them in sentence order fast enough.

"I told you to stay put, and now you've got us both locked in here. Great move." He folded his arms neatly across his lap. "All I wanted you to do was to take pictures of your evidence."

"But—"

"It's impossible for you to follow orders, isn't it?"

"You don't understand. I ... Sophia—"

He posted his palm up to silence her. "Obviously, you are the one who lacks understanding."

"No. No." Isa pounded both fists to her forehead. "We don't have time for power struggles. We've got to do something, fast. Or he'll hurt her bad. He may *kill* her."

"You tend to run in headfirst. It's dangerous."

Her brain wanted to explode. And might if she didn't get the Sophia story out and through his thick skull. "El Padrino is here." Her hands shot back and forth as she tried to slice through the communication barrier between them. "And he is going to kill Sophia."

Jay glanced up to the camera, a flicker of concern in his eyes.

She gave Jay more. "The cameras are disabled. Or were. I'm not sure of anything now and it doesn't matter. El Padrino is coming for me next."

With eyes shut, he seemed to twist that around in his head.

"Listen to me," she pleaded. "He's knocked Sophia out cold, and it's going to get worse. That psycho is drunk."

Jay didn't move.

Houston, we have a problem here and I need you to do something fast. "Hello," she said snapping her fingers.

He opened his eyes and at last, joined the battle. "Show me what I need to snap pictures of. Or better ..." He got to his feet and shoved the phone at her. "You take the pictures."

She took his phone. Watched him head to the window, unlatch, and raise it.

"We have to stop El Padrino. What are you doing?"

Jay pulled at the screen's corners. "Get the pictures. Then you're going down this tree, into the woods, and waiting for me to wrap up some recon. You'll be safer out there if El Padrino comes looking for you."

"Sophia, Jay. We have a life in danger."

"Just get the pictures." Jay dropped the screen on the floor and stuck his head out. "See if you can follow those simple instructions."

She spread paperwork across the desk and started snapping shots. Behind her, Jay pulled the comforter off the bed, then the sheets.

Once she had pictures of her notes, she powered up the computer and snapped photos of the screens with quitclaim real estate records. Then, she slipped the flash drives into her front pant pocket.

There was more. Not more money-laundering evidence, but more to think through. Like springing Maria, who now had Luca.

When she reeled around to tell Jay she'd gotten the pictures, she found him crouched on the window seal, a twisted and knotted sheet in his hand.

Crazy Jay was about to jump from a second-floor window.

CHAPTER 72

In the beginning of their courtship, El Padrino reckoned Sophia a risk. Women like her—women with ambitions—would present challenges. Exotic challenges. Still, the thought of owning Sophia had been as exciting as the real estate territories he amassed.

But he'd forgotten that the attributes, which made her irresistible, could one day make her his enemy. He should have recognized the signs earlier.

After splashing her face with the cold water he had Oso bring, El Padrino got her to her feet, then half-dragged Sophia through the house. At his office door, he yanked her head back and asked, "Do you love me?"

She spat in his face.

Yet, he still wanted to love her. Wanted to force the devotion she'd shown him in the early years back into her. He wiped the spittle off his cheek.

What a fickle thing love turned out to be.

He looked into those dark Italian eyes of hers. "What have you done, my Sophia?"

Through swollen lips, she mumbled, "You've gone mad."

Pulling through the office door, he guided her to the chair opposite his desk. In the last couple of days, that chair had become the executioner's seat of judgement.

"What game do you play with your husband?" He moved hair from her face. "What are you up to, my beautiful liar?"

She grappled with words. "I don't know ... what you're ... talking about."

CALCULATED RISK

El Padrino walked behind his desk and opened the drawer holding his gun.

"You've got this wrong." Her breaths quickened, seeing the gavel of justice in his hand.

Sophia had been such a prize. What a shame the story ended here.

"José." The plea in her voice. The lovely Italian accent. It would be harder than any kill he'd ordered.

"Oso," he called, placing the loaded gun on his desk. "Remind my love what happens to those who betray me."

Behind him, he heard Oso enter the office. "El Padrino?"

"Come watch," said El Padrino. You can tell stories of how I tortured my own bride. Because this is what happens when anyone betrays El Padrino." He frowned at Oso. "I'm learning to trust no one."

Sophia made a weak play to stand but crumpled back into the chair again. His earlier punch had rearranged her equilibrium.

Oh, those eyes. Again, he fought the urge to scoop her up and hold her. He pulled a knife from his pocket, flipping it open.

Despite the swelling, her eyes opened wide. She shook her head back and forth in a frantic but silent plea.

Control. Death always put that factor in his hands.

CHAPTER 73

Before she could question the insane notion that Jay might jump from the second-floor window, he stretched forward and pushed himself out, sheet trailing behind him.

That's just what she needed. Jay impaled on the brush and boulders below.

She shoved his phone into her back pocket and rushed over to peer out. The sheet stretched from the foot of her bed to Jay, who was bouncing in the ponderosa pine a good six feet away from her window. Isa gasped, thinking his weight might snap the skinny limb he clung to.

He barked an order. "Turn off the bedroom lights."

"Why?" She couldn't help herself. Of all the things he could want her to do.

"Because I don't want anyone down there," he pointed to the ground "seeing you up here. Got that?"

"Oh."

"Try not to make this hard."

She hustled to the lamp, switched it off and got back to the window. "Now what?"

"Take the end of the sheet that's tied to the bed and secure it around your waist."

She looked at the knot of sheets stretched from Jay to the bed. "I'm not jumping. I'm barefoot."

"You're not going to jump. You're going to rappel."

She wanted to argue ... wanted to count pine tree limbs ... retie the knots in the sheet so they were spaced correctly. But she did as she was told and got the sheet secured around her waist. Next, she climbed up on the windowsill, toes gripping the edge.

"Atta girl." His lame encouragement helped. She braced herself.

"I want you to push off the window, aim your arms for the trunk."

"I can't get my arms around that trunk."

"I know. But aim for it. Shoot deep. You're going to get tangled in the branches. That will keep you in the tree."

"I'm allergic to pine needles." In the dark, she couldn't see his expression but felt every ounce of its disdain. "What if I miss?"

"That's what the sheet is for."

"The branches are too skinny."

"If these limbs can hold a mamma bear, they can hold you."

That, at least, was right. Bears climbed pine trees all the time in these mountains. She gulped. Closed her eyes—which wasn't the smartest thing to do—and sprung forward.

She heard Jay expel an "Oh," like he wasn't quite ready for her to take that leap of faith. Too late. Her hands grabbed at sticky branches and limbs as she crashed through what felt like heavy industrial scrub brushes.

Then a yank. Her face scraped the trunk. An arm caught a limb.

"Stay there," Jay said once she'd come to a halt.

Where would she go? Isa hoisted herself to get both armpits over the limb. Already her face and hands burned as her body reacted to the noxious pine. Step one, she told herself, was over. She could worry later about getting Benadryl for the welts already forming.

When Jay's feet were level with her arms, he instructed her to climb lower. To inch her way down. Easier said than done, she moved her tender feet from one lower branch to another, starting the descent.

In the time it took for them to pick their way down the tree, El Padrino could have killed Sophia, buried her body, and escaped to Mexico.

About five feet of space opened between her and the ground.

"How do you propose we get all the way down?" She looked up to see Jay wrapping the sheet another time around his waist. "Never mind. I see."

He nodded. "Jump. I'll break the fall."

"One." Before she hit two, she was airborne. No arguing. No counting. Just doing.

Jay took up slack in the sheet and slowed down the fall. Isa landed on her knees hard, barely missing a large rock jutting from the ground. She straightened, looked up to see Jay dropping down, crouched like a ninja warrior.

Seriously. Mission Impossible music should have played.

He landed on his feet, of course. Quickly untied the sheet and ordered her to the woods.

"What am I supposed to do in the woods?"

"Wait for me to come and find you."

"And what will you be doing?"

He pulled in what looked to be a patience-seeking breath. "Letting my guys know El Padrino is back at the compound and making sure that doesn't affect tomorrow's raid. Then, I'm going to gather some intel and buy you and me some time."

Isa hopped on one foot as she wiped at the pine needles stuck to her feet. "But what if El Padrino finds out I'm not in my room?"

"I'm going to cover our tracks." He held his hand out. "Give me the phone. I need to make those calls." She pulled his phone from her pocket and handed it over.

"Head downhill." He pointed where he wanted her to go.

"Shouldn't I go with you and help rescue Sophia?"

"I'll see what's happening in there, but I need you out here, safe. Understood?"

Safety. Why was Jay concerned for her safety? Sure, she was a mere bean counter, but she was a cop bean counter. "I ..." she stopped herself. "Okay."

Jay gave her a double take.

She nodded him on. "Go, already."

Jay sprang into a run and headed for the side of the house.

CALCULATED RISK

Isa crouched, keeping an eye on him until he was out of sight.

She would get inside and locate her Glock. Then she'd have the fire power to face an inebriated El Padrino. It would take super sleuth powers to move around in that house undetected. It would take a miracle for her find El Padrino and Sophia alone. But if this was her purpose ... if she could get one good shot ... she might have the chance to save that woman's life.

Waiting on Jay to pull his loose ends together wasn't an option.

CHAPTER 74

The chirping crickets and rustling breeze intensified the truth that she was on a solo mission. What would she do with Sophia once she killed El Padrino? Hide her in a bathroom and his body under a bed? Drag her out of the house and into the woods until the Feds showed up the next day? Trust that Jay wander over to El Padrino's private quarters in the nick of time and help?

What she'd learned in forensic accounting training, she would have to apply here. *Calculate possible damage.* Sophia's unnecessary death would be a big loss. *Uncover hidden assets.* She couldn't uncover anything waiting in the woods. All convicting assets were in the house and one of them was about to be murdered. *Expose the truth.* Her mouthpiece of truth was in the process of being silenced with vicious blows to her face.

Everything about this case and her being here pointed to one sum: interference for Sophia, whether Jay trusted the woman or not.

With God's help, she would do this.

Isa sent up a quick prayer for supernatural courage.

Logistically, entering the house through the garage made the most sense. To get in, she would have to cross the lawn and then walk up the drive, taking the chance she would be seen.

But if no one yet knew she had been banished to her room, she might stroll on into the house like nothing was wrong. Isa scratched at the red welts on her forearms.

CALCULATED RISK

She started walking—looking anything but natural—and made it across the lawn. But she came to an abrupt halt when she rounded a corner and saw a Range Rover behind a Nissan Sentra, both in the drive. *Uh-oh.*

Approaching with caution, she canvassed the interior of the Range Rover first.

The SUV looked to be empty.

Moving to the Sentra, she ducked, peeked in the back window.

Something slowly raised up in the back seat.

The natural reaction—the instinctive response to the sudden ghost-like appearing was to stop breathing. She didn't even blink, which gave her the opportunity to study who or what had just materialized in that car.

The thing couldn't be much more than five foot ... looked familiar ... braids.

Awena.

Providence. Isa's tension melted. Tears welled. Something in the crazed battles of cartel takedowns and strong-willed undercover agents finally went right.

She opened the door and slid in beside her friend.

Awena smiled wide. "God is good. I slept, I dreamed, and I awake to Isa Padilla at my side."

"I heard you were in Mexico. You okay?" Isa felt around on the woman's arms. Put her hands on that leather face. "Did they hurt you?"

Awena pulled Isa's hands into her lap. "I have been on my Beautiful Trail."

"Why are you back here and sleeping in the car?"

"Mr. Padrino said his wife wants me here. And I was tired."

Okay—now Awena was going to be in the middle of a big takedown because Isa, running ahead of things, had had her extracted from Mexico, where the FBI had a plan to rescue her. Uh-oh, again.

Isa glanced out the windows. "We've got to get you out of here. Some stuff is going down tonight."

"Going down?" She angled toward Isa. "What goes down tonight?"

"Federal agents are coming to arrest El Padrino tomorrow, but tonight, El Padrino is on a rampage. I need you out of harm's way." In the dark, Isa could see her friend's almond-shaped eyes widen.

"The Feds?" Awena swatted at the air like that was a crazy idea. "Who called in the Feds?"

"Long story. Let's get you tucked away in the woods." She reached for the car door.

But Awena grabbed her arm. "What of the wife?"

"Sophia?"

"The one who brought me to your room. It troubled her husband when I told him she'd done this. He is a man of fear."

So Awena had told El Padrino that Sophia had brought her to Isa's room.

Isa's *uh-ohs* were piling up quick.

"El Padrino has some seriously messed-up aggression and he is expressing that aggression against his wife right now." Isa opened the door and motioned her friend out.

"Where are we going?" Awena asked, scooting across the seat.

"You'll be safer in the woods." Isa said, and offered Awena her hand.

Awena took it, and the two walked back across the lawn, only this time Isa was crouched with her arm around Awena, looking even more unnatural than before. She scrutinized every foot of the premises around her, making sure no one wandered outside the garage for a smoke or for some Isa and Awena target practice.

Isa got Awena positioned behind a tree. "Sit here." She scanned the side of the house and nearby woods. "I'll be back for you."

"You have found your purpose, Isa Padilla?"

"I think so." Isa squeezed Awena's arm.

Awena reached up and patted Isa's cheek. "Me, too."

Isa made another trip across the lawns without seeing Nick or Snake or Pink Hair, or any other mobsters. She got through the garage and into the house.

CALCULATED RISK

Inside, things seemed eerily quiet. Like everybody might be dead kind of quiet. She made it to the back stairwell and up to the second floor, gluing herself to walls and peeking around corners. Progressing, she slipped around like a sleuth toward the front of the house where she figured El Padrino's office would be positioned for the best views. To the right and up a hall, she stepped onto a spacious landing above the first floor. Isa crouched. When she didn't hear movement below, she scooted to the railing, inspecting the grand entry for a side door that might lead to a library or office. She leaned over to get a better look. Couldn't get the right angle, so she got on her tip toes and hung her head low.

"Daughter."

Isa almost flipped, head-first over the railing.

"Awena, what are you doing here? You're supposed to be in the woods waiting for me."

"I received my instructions. So I followed you."

"Look, this isn't downtown Albuquerque when you can walk defiantly into oncoming traffic. This is real danger stuff. People have guns here. You have to go back to the woods." Isa noted the woman didn't have her cane.

"What are you looking for?" Awena rubbed her palms together a little too gleefully.

Oh dear. "I'm looking for El Padrino's office. My g—" she thought better of using the gun word. "There is something in there I need. But you. You promised to stay outside."

"I didn't promise. But his office is there." Awena pointed down the hall, the one Isa had just come through. "But take a right at the end. I'll show you."

"No—"

Awena whirled around and started trucking ... without her cane. *Unbelievable.*

Isa glanced around then hustled to catch up. But she put on the brakes when she heard muffled voices. Agitated, muffled voices. And Awena? She kept going and disappeared around the corner.

She'd counted on El Padrino being on the far and opposite end of the massive house. In his living quarters with Sophia. *Please don't let one of those voices be his.*

But she knew.

Isa peeked around the corner. No Awena. A carved wooden door stood ajar.

Good heavens, what had Awena walked into? No choice, then—she would walk into it too.

CHAPTER 75

El Padrino's voice got louder, each syllable shaking Isa's core.

She stalled—prayed for a plan of action.

Nothing of any substance materialized in her brain.

She pressed her sweaty palms into her forehead. *God, give me something here.*

But nothing … nothing. Arms dropped to her side in exasperation.

That's when she felt the flash drives in her pocket.

Whoa.

Peering around the corner again, she saw Do-Rag Mike approach from the other end of the hall. And he saw her. And probably knew she'd been banished to her room. And this … was … happening.

Isa stepped out to face him, gunfighter style. She pulled a flash drive out of her pocket. Leveled it at him.

He picked up his pace.

She trotted toward him, the two arriving at the office door simultaneously.

"I'm going in there," she declared.

Do-Rag snickered. Pulled a gun from somewhere behind him. "Try it."

"What I've got here, our boss will want to see." She shook the flash drive in his face.

"What the blimey is that?"

"Things you wouldn't understand."

Do-Rag held out his empty hand. "Give it to me."

CALCULATED RISK

She threw her head back and laughed. Admittedly, her attempt at evil scorn didn't sound near malicious enough, but she hoped he'd buy her bluff. "Oh no. The boss will want to hear what I've got to say." She lowered her voice. "'Cause there are more of these out there."

Do-rag looked appropriately stumped. "You packing?"

She wished. "Packing what? I don't have a gun. You know that. We're on the same team, idiot."

From the office, she heard El Padrino screech a foul word.

"Arms up," Do-Rag said. "No one gets in there without a search. I didn't make the rules."

So maybe he wasn't up to speed on all the latest developments—like the fact that she should be locked in her room right now.

Gritting her teeth, she lifted her arms and let him pat her down, including her pant pockets. All four of them. One at a time. Disgusting. He located the other two flash drives in her front pocket and reached in to retrieve them. Double disgusting.

Now she held *her* hand out. "You seriously want to explain to the boss why you took this secret information away from his top financial advisor?"

He slammed the drives into her hand, shook his fist in her face. "You better be careful, girl. Not everybody here likes you."

"Thanks for the employment tip." Isa turned and pushed the door open.

She took measurements at the threshold before entering. Awena stood dead-center in the chaos. Sophia looked like she'd been dumped in a chair with her head down, a bloodied towel in her lap, and a good-sized cut in her cheek. Oso stood at the window, apparently on surveillance detail. And El Padrino? He was at his desk with a gun in hand, but looking straight at Isa, brows up in surprise.

"She's clean." Do-Rag motioned her in. "Have fun," he whispered, and blew her a kiss.

Animals. The whole lot.

"Well, my accountant has found her way back to me after being told to stay in her room. What an interesting situation we have here."

His red face matched his bloodshot eyes. A near-empty bottle of tequila sat on the desk.

Isa tightened her grip on the flash drive.

"And your lover has joined us as well." El Padrino motioned behind her.

There, in a chair against the wall, sat Jay.

Isa couldn't discern if Jay were prisoner or participant in this meeting. His hard expression didn't budge when their eyes met.

Little beads of moisture collected on her upper lip.

CHAPTER 76

The sight of Jay's iced-over blue eyes gave her chills. What if Jay ... like Mac ... worked as a double agent and had simply managed to convince her that he was FBI all the way?

Awena, who must have been in the middle of a discourse when Isa entered, decided to keep talking. "And now that Isa Padilla is here, we can sort this out. Isa," Awena said, "tell them your purpose."

Isa wanted to combust. Awena was blowing any semblance of cover Isa had clung to. And Jay—didn't look like he would be coming to anyone's rescue.

"Isa's purpose?" El Padrino roared with laughter. "Old woman, now you have seen too much, and I am going to have deal with you, too."

Isa broke Jay's glare and swiveled around to watch El Padrino. Perpendicular to his desk was a bookcase with cabinets covering the entire wall. She wasn't sure if Jay had fed her a bogus line about her gun being stashed in that cabinet, but she was about to find out.

"Old woman," El Padrino emptied the tequila bottle into a nearby glass. "You remind me of my mother. Did I tell you that? I never liked her much."

Isa cast an eye back at Jay. The guy looked like a statue, not even blinking his eyes.

"I told you, no?" El Padrino swung his arm across the room. "And tonight, it seems my family doesn't like *me* much. Look at my betraying wife."

CALCULATED RISK

Sophia lifted her head, which let Isa know she was, at least, conscious.

"Let's see," El Padrino continued, swiveling in his chair, "There's my life-long brother Oso."

Isa watched Oso shift. The slight discomfort in his posture made her wonder where Oso's true allegiance lay.

Then El Padrino considered Jay and Isa. "But these two I am not so sure about. Tell me Isa, are you and this coyote my family? Or no? This is your chance to convince me."

Isa swallowed dry air.

"Coyote." El Padrino narrowed his red-hot gaze on Jay. "This woman of yours has conspired with my betraying wife." The drunk man pushed out of his chair and stood. "Oh, what to do with my family. Shall I acquire new ones?"

"José," Sophia said, slurring his name. All eyes went to her pale face and puffed-up lips. "Don't."

"Hush, my love," he said, puckering his lips in a mocking kiss. "I'm choosing new family members now." He twirled the gun around in his hand. "Who shall be first? Hm? Who will tell me the truth about what goes on in my house and with my properties?"

Awena backed up and began to chant ... out loud ... in Navajo. She even pulled a couple of Indian stomp moves.

No doubt, Awena pleaded intervention from God Almighty.

"Stop that!" El Padrino ordered.

Everyone in the room stiffened. Except Awena. She kept right on chanting and dancing.

El Padrino then flipped his frustration to Isa, aiming his gun for her chest. "What have you and my wife planned against me?"

Isa held up the flash drive.

Awena, concern all over her, quietened down.

Dead silence took the stage for a good three seconds before Isa heard Jay rise to his feet behind her.

Impulse or instinct, she wasn't sure, but she threw her impromptu plan out there before Jay had a chance to stop her.

"This." Isa said, teeth bared. "We need to talk about *this*. Not Sophia."

She sensed Jay encroach from behind and from the corner of her eye, she saw Oso reach for Awena.

But she stood her ground.

El Padrino snickered. "What is that?"

"Legal, county records," she shot back.

An evil grin lifted his red cheeks. "What records have you garnished, Accountant? Something for me to fear?" He slid his eyes to the side to get a twenty on Jay, then he moved them right back to Isa. "So you've come to make a deal. Well tell me, Accountant, what do you have that I might want?"

"Property. India Magic."

"India Magic? I've already promised you that building. For this you interrupt my meeting?"

"There's more."

"More?" Glancing over to Oso, he seemed to lose a slight footing in the game. "What is more?"

Osa pulled Awena toward a corner in the room, appearing oddly protective.

"Isa." Jay moved in. "Stop."

She fabricated on the spot. "The properties. All of them. Transferred into my name, like India Magic was transferred to Mac's name."

She heard Jay moan.

El Padrino jerked sideways to address his bleeding bride. "You have conspired with her to use my money and property against me?"

"No." Isa lied. "It's not Sophia ... I've worked with others. Mac. Juan. And Sicily. We had an alliance for months." She pulled the flash drive into her chest, working her fist around it. "These properties were quitclaimed to me. Right now, I'm the owner and I am *your* landlord.

He snarled. "I should kill you now."

"But then, how would you get the deeds back? I alone can quitclaim them to you. County records have already been filed."

"Isa?" Jay drew her name out in a *what do you think you're doing* fashion.

"You want to play like one of the big boys? Let's play," El Padrino mocked. "Jay, are you part of our game?"

CALCULATED RISK

"Sure," Jay answered sounding resolute. He stepped beside her, pulled his gun from behind his back, then pointed his weapon right at her. "Let's hear what she has to say."

Isa's pulse quickened. *Turncoat Jay.*

She couldn't see Oso but heard him shifting around. Knew he'd pulled out a weapon, too. All chicken-men and their guns accounted for.

It was Isa versus the boys.

She made a visual check on Sophia. The injured woman's mouth was agape, eyes trained on Isa.

"Well?" El Padrino seemed to love the fact that Jay had turned on her. "Looks like you have the floor, Accountant. Convince me why I should not blow you away now. There's no real estate record I can't fix."

"Let Sophia and Awena leave unharmed, and I'll go to the county offices tomorrow and file claims to deed all the properties back to you," Isa said.

"You must think me stupid. I have no guarantee that you'll do it. My counter offer is this. First thing tomorrow, you go to the county records and sign the deeds back to their rightful owner, *then* I'll let these women go."

At least they were negotiating. Maybe she could pull this off and get the innocent victims out of there.

That's when Awena wrenched out of Oso's grip and marched across the room. She grabbed the tequila bottle on El Padrino's desk and sent it flying. The bottle connected to the cabinets, and glass blasted across the room. El Padrino went for Awena, but Oso got to her first.

CHAPTER 77

At the sight of Awena struggling between the two cartel animals, Isa shoved the flash drive in her pocket and made for the trio. Oso tried to chuck her off, but with a gun in his hand, he couldn't keep a grip on Awena and hold Isa at bay. El Padrino stumbled to the side, and Jay looked to be moving in on the ruckus.

Then something cracked. Or exploded.

Slapping at Oso and grasping for Awena, Isa stopped at the sudden sound.

A shot. Someone had pulled a trigger.

That's when everything bounced from confusing to chaos.

The gun blast pulled Oso off guard because Isa was able to jerk Awena from his grip and ease her to the floor in case of other gunfire. She hovered over her friend, trying to make sense of the turmoil around her.

Sophia had her arms over her head.

Jay was stumbling backwards, his left shoulder oozing blood.

El Padrino—it looked like he was going to pull the trigger ... and shoot Jay again.

"No," Isa yelled and scrambled upright.

With one hand, Oso commandeered Awena from the floor, and tossed her to the side. Then he leveled *his* weapon on Jay.

Jay's wound didn't keep him from meeting their threats head on. He lifted his gun, switching his aim from El Padrino to Oso and back.

CALCULATED RISK

So Jay was on her side. And now he needed her help.

Then Do-Rag tore through the door and guns swung at the perceived intruder. Another explosion. Another shot.

Isa dove for the floor.

El Padrino cursed. He'd shot his own man.

Jay ordered everyone to put their weapons down, sounding very FBI. Nobody listened.

With all the attention on Do-Rag's body, Isa scrambled to her feet and made for the bookcase. She managed to get her hand on a cabinet door and pull it open.

"You shot Mike!" Oso cried. It sounded like he'd just accused El Padrino of a stupid move.

El Padrino had an endless inventory of obscene words. He let them fly.

If she didn't get her Glock out of the cabinet, she'd be the next one down. Isa tugged at books and files.

"Stop!" El Padrino ordered.

She glanced back to see who he threatened. The stage had changed. Jay was sliding down the wall. Oso flipped Do-Rag over. Awena pulled Sophia out of the chair. And El Padrino—he gawked at one person then another, so very unsure of his former controlling self.

Isa saw a box at the back, just out of reach. She jumped, her fingertips touching the side.

"I said, stop." El Padrino sounded like a maniac.

Isa checked the scene again.

Jay's arm lay limp in his lap. But he watched Isa and he nodded.

Oso seized Do-Rag's weapon and straightened to full height, a gun in each hand. Eyes on her.

El Padrino growled.

Isa put her sights on the box again. Jumped. Got the tips of her fingers under the lid.

She heard another shot. *Who was shooting who?* She jumped, pulling at the lid. This time she got it and the box crashed to the ground.

On the floor—her wallet, her phone, and her beautiful Glock 19.

She dove for it. Cocked it as she rolled over on her back, gun up and ready to aim.

Jay, still slumped against the wall, had his working arm up with his weapon in position.

Oso was down.

How he'd done it, she didn't know, but Jay had shot Oso.

El Padrino paid no mind to what happened around him. He'd gotten to Awena and Sophia. Put his revolver against Sophia's head.

Before he could get his index finger on the trigger, Isa squeezed hers.

As the firing pin connected with the cartridge in her Glock, the energy burst kicked her gun upwards, but she held it tight, pulling her arms back into position for another shot.

El Padrino yelped and dropped his gun. She'd hit him in the arm.

Aiming for his leg, she squeezed the trigger again.

The monster crumbled.

CHAPTER 78

Isa watched as El Padrino fell to his knees then flopped back on the floor. She hurried over to kick his gun out of reach.

The monster looked up at her, not as a wicked villain, but as a confused, disoriented, drunken slob. What a difference a few seconds could make.

El Padrino moaned. His eyes rolled back in his head.

Expecting to see a grateful Sophia, Isa glanced up to find the woman's puffed lips pursed. Sophia wiggled out from beneath Awena's caring hands, stumbled over her husband, and got to his desk, fumbling around like a woman gone mad. She pulled a drawer open.

Isa turned and rushed to Jay. Dropped beside him.

Eyes squeezed shut and face taking on a sickly shade of gray, Jay sucked in deep breaths.

With her gun still in her grasp, she felt around his arms and legs with her free hand, checking for other wounds. Aside from his shoulder, there didn't appear to be other injuries.

Isa poked her finger at his face. Wanted to hear him say something mean.

She got her wish.

He lifted one eye lid then let it drift shut. "I had this. Didn't need you busting in here." He grimaced. Gripped his shoulder.

"You put a gun to my head," Isa said, removing his hand from the bloody wound and pressing her own into it.

He gasped but opened his eyes and watched her face. "I bought you time."

Isa scooted closer. "Whatever."

"Don't you know undercover rules?"

Though she could see he labored to get words out, he kept dishing up the smack.

He said, "Rule number six. To create confusion in the enemy's mind, pull your weapon on your partner."

"Are you calling me your partner?" She asked, bloody fingers scratching at a new ponderosa pine welt rising on her chin.

He rolled his head to the right. "So you killed a cartel leader. Guess you'll want me to tell you how smart you are."

"I didn't kill him. I left him alive so the law could do its work."

"Didn't they teach you anything over at HPD? You're supposed to go for the kill. Especially when they're drunk with a gun in their hand."

She pulled Jay forward to see if the bullet had gone through the back of his shoulder blade. Clean exit wound. "Looks like you'll live to see José Ventura put away. I know that makes you happy."

Awena eased down beside them. "He will be okay?" she asked, putting her weathered hand on the side of his face.

"I think they'll get him fixed up." Isa smiled at that thought.

"I knew he was a good one." Awena nodded at Jay's arm. "The tattoo speaks."

The flaming sword.

Jay glanced at his tat. "This? It's a long story." Then he slid his gaze back to Isa. "Good job, partner."

Her ragged nerves took on a warm sensation. Which was ridiculous. They'd just finished a gun battle, for goodness sake. Why was she feeling all cozy with Jay?

There would be lots of therapy sessions in her future.

Isa looked up to see Sophia making for the exit.

But the door blew open and guys decked out in SWAT gear knocked her to the ground.

The United States Federal Bureau of Investigators made a grand entrance, guns drawn, heads down, and everyone a suspect.

"Drop your weapons," one of them commanded.

Isa laid her Glock on the floor. Stood slowly and raised both hands over her head. Awena followed suit.

"We have wounded." Isa nodded toward Jay on the floor then Sophia at the desk.

"She's with me." Jay pointed at Isa. "But I had this."

CHAPTER 79

When the FBI secured Sophia's hands behind her back, Isa's heart pinched with guilt. So much for the great rescue. Tonight, the woman's child had been ripped from her arms, she had been beaten and threatened within an inch of life, and probably suffered from a concussion. And now, she was getting hauled off to jail.

Sophia gave Isa a mournful look as they escorted her out the door.

She had failed Sophia. To top that off, she wasn't able to keep mother and child together and out of harm's way. But if the law did its work, Sophia would have a good chance at being released, considering she had provided Isa with incriminating evidence against her husband. They would just need to step through the processes of the court system.

When the guys in charge brought up Maria, Isa explained who she was and that she could possibly look after Luca for a few days. But then one of the men in blue mentioned checking Maria's legal status, and Maria made herself scarce. The social workers from CPS eventually showed up. Took the traumatized child away.

Awena, of course, schooled agents with talk of the real problem—the unseen forces at play. The Feds wanted to question her separately before anyone had a chance to corroborate stories or be influenced by remarks about the crime scene. Imagining what the conversation between Awena and the official-looking female agent would sound like, Isa chuckled.

CALCULATED RISK

While the feds snapped photos and gathered evidence, she paced from Jay to the unconscious El Padrino, to the FBI agent in charge. Jay's *she's with me* endorsement had bought her the privilege of staying at the scene.

The first ambulance to arrive carried José Ventura to the hospital. Because of the alcohol level coursing through his veins at the time Isa shot him, he'd likely felt little pain. He'd probably passed out from consumption, not trauma. If he hadn't been plastered, he might have thought quicker, moved faster, and the day would have ended very differently. It didn't matter that he was sloppy drunk when she shot him, though. She'd taken down a drug lord.

When the ambulance carrying Ventura pulled down the drive, Isa watched the lights splay red and blue across the pine and rock from the window upstairs.

She looked back at the horrific mess of blood splattered across the office. Oso and Do- Rag's bodies still lay on the floor. Agents asked Jay dozens of questions while paramedics fastened him to a stretcher. Her thoughts rewound to the beginning when she found the deed to the old India Magic building in Mac's bank box. He must have taken quite the risk to not quitclaim that property back to El Padrino. Had Claire known? Had they worked together?

There were still questions that needed answers.

When the med team got Jay in the hall, he yelled back at her to not touch anything.

She rolled her eyes, then watched the guys from the morgue bag up Oso and Do-Rag. "Who called you guys in?" she asked as they zipped Oso's bag.

"Your partner," one answered.

Isa bit down into her bottom lip. Jay had believed her after all.

Downstairs, she could hear agents giving commands to the other 96 members they'd rounded up.

After three different agents took her statement and one questioned her a second time, the FBI guys stepped through their processes—snapping pictures, outlining bodies, and trying to make sense of the scene. A surreal quietness drifted in. She seemed to observe from somewhere outside and not from the middle of the chaos. Isa looked up and studied the ceiling where, according to Awena, the real battle had taken place. What was there and how much influence did it have on the people who were now dead or headed to jail? And how much influence had these unseen instigators had on her?

"Ma'am?"

Isa whirled around. "Yeah?"

"We've got to secure the scene now. Your partner asked that you not forget about the evidence you have on you."

Isa dug in her pocket. Pulled out the flash drives. "Tell him I'll be right there."

CHAPTER 80

Always, the smells in hospitals reminded Isa of Angel. After her brother's overdose, he had lived on life support for five days before the doctors convinced her mother that he was brain dead. Three of those hard days, their mother had shown up drunk.

Isa quietly pushed the door to Jay's room open. Expected to find him sleeping. But no. He sat upright and punching at his phone screen.

"Hey." He only glanced at her and got right back to texting. "What's the word?"

She stepped to the end of his bed, hand rubbing up and down her purse shoulder strap. "You tell me. You're Captain America."

"You're a funny girl."

Jay looked good. Left shoulder moving good, lots of color in his face, and hair messier than ever.

Isa gazed about the room to keep her eyes off the thin hospital gown across his chest. "No, really. I thought you might have a couple of updates for *me*."

"I find it hard to believe that you haven't found a way to get your hands all over this case. It's big news."

She shrugged. "I might have one or two fingers on it. But a whole hand? Nah."

One side of his mouth lifted in a crooked grin. "Give me a second, here." He swiped through a couple of screens.

"What are you doing?" She pulled a stool on wheels over to the side of the bed and sat, hands still hanging onto that purse strap.

CALCULATED RISK

"Scheduling a tattoo removal." He touched the 96 on his neck. "Second removal since I started undercover."

Isa pointed at the flaming sword on his forearm "How long have you had that one?"

"This?" He laid the phone beside him on the bed and lifted his arm for Isa to get a better look.

"Yeah." She refrained from reaching out and touching it, touching him. "I meant to ask."

"I got this flaming blade in my early twenties." He rubbed his hand across the sword. "College."

To date, small talk hadn't been their vibe. It felt weird. And good. Both. "Well, Awena certainly liked it." She leaned closer. "What does it mean?"

Jay pushed back against piled up pillows behind him. He blinked a couple times as a somber shadow settled across his face. It was one of those regret clouds that brings a rain of memories. "It was a time," he said, as he seemed to peer into a past occurrence. "A time I wanted to remember. But I've let the memory fade."

Isa adjusted on the stool and a wheel squeaked.

Absorbed in the past, he didn't notice. "I had a salvation experience through a campus Bible study. That's when I got the call to seek justice. To fight bad guys." He patted the phone beside him, coming back from wherever his thoughts had taken him. Shifting those blue eyes to peer at her, he said, "That's when I changed my major from a blow-off business degree to criminology. I put my sights on the FBI and never looked back."

"Like it was your purpose?"

"Something like that. Yeah."

She nodded knowingly.

She hadn't considered Jay's past. Their times together had been stressful, complicated, and unfettered with common curiosities. So now she had questions.

"Why the sword?"

He touched the tattoo again. "Cherubim. The guardians of Eden. I saw myself as a guardian of what's right in the world."

Isa let the purse on her shoulder slide to the floor. The conversation felt like an invitation to stay awhile. "I didn't know you were religious."

"I'm not. Was never religious. But I am a believer. Worn down a bit, I guess."

Oh man, she needed to make an Excel sheet of queries. "What's the difference?"

"You ask too many questions." Jay stated, stoic armor falling into place. "Hey, did you hear they found several kilos of heroin and 200 pounds of cannabis in a wall in that old building you own? Guess El Padrino used the place as a storehouse."

"Awena claimed to see a demon guarding something in that building."

"It guarded a gold mine, then." Jay didn't miss a beat. "El Padrino will have arraignment as soon as he is able to get in a wheel chair, thanks to you." He offered her a genuine, appreciative smile. "Sophia's arraignment is next week."

"That I knew. My sergeant told me as much."

Jay cocked his head. "Your sergeant? I guess you are giving up civilian life now that you got a taste of real action."

"Sergeant Caba never turned in my resignation. On the day I walked out, he said he wouldn't accept my notice and was extending me a leave instead. Come to find out, he did exactly what he threatened to do." She shrugged. "Guess I worked undercover as a real agent all along, covered by insurance and everything." She pulled her pony tail tight. "Caba told me that when I walked out, he was already looking into Claire as a suspect. They suspected Mac and one of his partners, too. And that the two of them were communicating with your agency. Of course, he couldn't reveal that to me back then." She sighed. "They've taken in a couple of other Houston officers. Looks like there was an alliance going down inside HPD."

"Then you *are* still on the case."

A hint, a trace of optimism hung in his voice.

"I'll examine the quitclaims. There are some financial questions hanging out there."

"But you'll ... eventually head back to Houston?" He said it slowly, like he had a mouth full of caution to work the words around.

Isa paused. "I'm not sure what I'm going to do yet. The India Magic building will go up for auction after all the real estate is sorted out. I might be an interested buyer. I've always wanted to bake professionally and serve up gourmet coffees."

He tapped his fingers on his phone looking, for the first time ever, like he didn't know what to do with the incoming information. "India Magic. *Coffee Magic.*" He chuckled but then his gaze turned soft. "If you buy that building, I wouldn't mind stopping in for a cup of coffee, you know ... giving you a hard time. If you stick around.

Possibilities fluttered across her chest. His mentioning a future encounter should not be affecting her this way. But it affected her this way.

Jay wanting to stop by for coffee meant nothing.

Except it did. It meant he would like to see her outside of a work relationship.

"I think I'd like you to stop by."

His eyes dropped to his phone. "Yeah, me, too. You know, things got stormy between us and I'd like to ..." he let the unfinished sentence hang there.

She found herself on the edge of that stool.

The following six seconds passed uneasily.

"I don't know," he finally said with a shake of his head. "I have to figure a thing or two out."

"Jay." She heard herself speaking but couldn't believe the words forming. She wanted to swallow them down, but they tumbled out anyway. "Sometimes when we were acting, it didn't feel like pretending."

"Yeah. I know." His regret cloud hovered again. "But Isa."

The way he said *Isa.*

"Jay?"

"My name is Jacob. Jacob Lahache."

All this time and she'd not yet considered once that he'd been using an undercover name. "Jacob." She whispered it. Tried the feel of it. Fit nice in her mouth.

He wrenched around in his bed. "And ..."

She waited, expecting.

"I'm engaged."

She flinched. "Engaged?"

"I'm getting married in six months."

CHAPTER 81

Sitting on a bench outside the court room where Sophia Evelina Ricci Ventura faced the judge, Isa mentally sorted people and the clothes they wore. So far, thirteen men and women wore various forms of black and white while eight chose blue as their color of the day. Three shirts in shades of green accompanied by gray or black trousers rushed by. And there were two reds—one of the red shirts pecking at a phone, stopped in front of Isa.

Isa's gaze wandered down the hall in casual pursuit of something in yellow. She'd count anything to keep from thinking of Jay. She hadn't spoken with him since he'd announced his upcoming marriage, and she had no idea if he'd fully recovered from his injury, been assigned to another case, or would show up today for Sophia's arraignment.

A woman in an orange, flowy dress whizzed by. One for sunny orange.

When two men—one in a dark blue suite and one in jeans, gang symbols blaring—stopped in front of her to discuss something that looked to be crucial, she thought of the gangsters she'd encountered while living at the cartel compound. Oso had been a fierce guard for El Padrino, his provider, but when he sheltered Awena in that final confrontation, he proved he had a protective nature at heart. Too bad the warped life of a cartel member altered his God-given gift. He would have made an awesome cop. And Nick, who was probably going to join a gang of another type in prison, would have been one keen team player on a football squad, or maybe a construction crew, serving as the social glue that kept men working together. Each one of those guys had been misguided and deceived.

And according to Awena, the deception came from demons.

The Drake's Horn had closed indefinitely. Asset forfeiture allowed the FBI to seize it and several properties owned by El Padrino, including the old India Magic building. But not before Awena got in the building and evicted the resident demon. Isa didn't know the details of how the eviction transpired, but Awena had given Isa the all-clear in case her inheritance wasn't deemed a criminal enterprise.

No such luck. Now it belonged to the federal government. She hadn't decided if she would show up when the place went to auction. Maybe her purpose in unearthing hidden things wasn't over and she'd go back to her sarge and the HPD. *Lord knows the sarge needs help with the vacant slots the arrests left on the force.*

She reached for her purse. Dug around and pulled out the tattered note she'd carried around for months now. Unfolded it. Lost count of how many times she'd read it.

Nothing is covered up that will not be revealed, or hidden that will not be made known.

No doubt now. Claire had planted that note. Her grandmother had called Isa, trying to make sense of her granddaughter's death. Between bouts of sobbing, she had explained that Claire kept a diary. Within the pages, Claire recorded a private war between knowing the right thing to do and finding it difficult to stop. She had even written the realization that to get out of the situation she'd gotten herself into, she would be harming others. *She was scared,* her grandmama said, and she'd turned to the Bible, writing out verses on the pages.

"My Claire," her grandmother had cried. "She knew the Lord, and I know she is with Him now."

After that call, Isa determined to look positively at the imprint Claire left behind. Her friend had walked into a trap, albeit knowingly, and ended up a victim. Her attempt to get Isa involved through a cryptic note without implicating others had been a gesture of goodness. And considering the words on that note had led Isa to ponder her purpose and the providence of God, well, that meant Claire's note had honorable rippled effects that would continue for a lifetime.

Isa hoped, even prayed, God would continue to use Claire's final and brave act to his glory.

One side of the massive courtroom door opened, and the bailiff motioned Isa off her bench. "Judge is ready for you."

Isa folded the note, placed it back into the envelope, then slipped it into her purse strapped across her shoulder. She followed the man through a second set of doors. Sophia's lawyer approached and opened the little gate that separated spectators from the law-room characters. Behind him sat Sophia, her face saturated with relief. Isa knew Sophia's lawyer had filled her in on the plan.

"Approach the bench, Ms. Phillips," the judge announced. "It's not an official trial and there's no need to put you on the witness stand."

"Yes, your honor."

This was new. She'd been a prosecution's expert witness before, but never a witness for the accused. The judge made note of that right away. "Ms. Phillips, it is my understanding that you will be called as a witness in the prosecution of Mrs. Ventura's husband—the case of one José Ventura. Is that correct?"

"Yes, your honor." Isa straightened her navy suit's lapel. "I uncovered illegal financial activities."

"It is highly unusual to have you serve in different capacities for two people charged with similar offenses in the same ..." he peered down at her from over his glasses, "in the same overall case, if you will."

"I understand the confusion, your honor. Working as an undercover agent, I uncovered financial fraud, but I did it with the help of the defendant."

"For the record, please state the name of the defendant

and what she did to help you."

"Yes, sir. Sophia Ventura aided my undercover investigation by giving me information on real estate fraud that could lead to the arrest of her husband."

"I see here you've worked out of jurisdiction. I trust all the paperwork and records are being handled accordingly. If this goes to trial, the appointed judge will want your ducks in row." He peered over his glasses again.

"Your honor," Sophia's lawyer interrupted. "It's our hope that Mrs. Ventura will go into the witness protection program."

"It is a little early for that decision," the judge said. "So, Ms. Phillips, I've been told it is your recommendation I release the defendant on bail."

"Yes, sir. She proved to be a reliable informant."

"But, your honor." The district attorney's number one man stood. "I believe she's at risk for flight. Our sources are finding evidence she planned to leave the country."

"To protect herself." Sophia's lawyer pointed at her. "Her husband was and remains a major threat."

The prosecutor shot back, "We're not offering Mrs. Ventura a deal as a witness at this time. Our sources show she may have been amassing—"

The judge interrupted. "I don't make determinations based on maybes. Ms. Phillips, it seems I've only you to vouch for Mrs. Ventura at the moment. So I am going to ask you again. What is your recommendation and on what basis?"

"I believe Sophia Ventura was in a dangerous situation. While I've not yet been able to verify all aspects of the financial crimes she and her husband are accused of, I can say she made it possible for me to identify the quitclaim real estate offense. She helped me, your honor. I believe she wishes to serve justice."

The judge pounded his gavel onto the bench. "Defendant is ordered not to leave the state of New Mexico. The defendant is ordered to not speak with anyone besides her lawyer and the prosecution about her aid in disclosing criminal offenses to the state and federal government until trial date is determined. Bail is set at $150,000.00. Court dismissed."

Isa turned to face a tearful Sophia.

Thank you, Sophia mouthed. She would make bail. Having to put up a mere 10% of the stated amount, she'd have no problem being free within hours.

Luca would be reunited with his mom.

The law was doing its work.

Isa nodded back to Sophia. She walked out with an unexpected and keen sense of resolution. Her purpose in law enforcement, she determined with each step leading her away from the court room, had been fulfilled. She could see muffins in her future.

Making her way from the courthouse to the parking lot, she thought about walking the extra nine blocks to pass by India Magic and take time to imagine the color she would paint over the hot pink trim outside. She picked up speed, a nice summer breeze brushing against her face as people passed.

Then she saw him.

Jacob Lahache crossed the street in front of her, heading toward the courthouse behind her.

Isa's head turned as she watched him until he reached the steps that stretched up to the halls where the law did its work.

She bit her lip and smiled. *Coffee Magic.* She turned and hurried up the street. A destiny waited across town.

CHAPTER 82

Six weeks later.

Sophia watched Luca push a plastic firetruck along the white railing of the second-floor balcony. From her deck lounge, she could see the first glimmer of Monterrey's evening lights in the valley below. Life on La Silla Pico Sur wasn't bad at all. Surrounded by Mexican white oaks and armed guards, she would have a haven, far from the grasp of US officials.

Monterrey looked to be lovely. The fast-paced city at the mountain's base offered things Albuquerque never would. Arts, entertainment, the opportunity to rub elbows with Mexico's elite. She'd moved a notch closer to her goal, leaving New Mexico and its class C syndicated crimes behind. Jumping bail, she'd landed in the next phase.

A red-headed woodpecker chipped away at a towering oak that reached past the balcony patio. "Luca," she said, pulling her sunglasses to the bridge of her nose. "Look there." She pointed at the bird.

Wide-eyed, Luca followed the track of her finger and ran to the rail. She slid her glasses back up and looked to the bright blue skies.

This affair, this season, would be a side visit in her journey. A short stop along the way, as Italy remained the ultimate destination. It was her destiny. It was Luca's destiny. She'd been planning her return since the day she'd left, ousted from the family business by an ambitious and threatened cousin.

CALCULATED RISK

Luca trotted back to his firetruck, making engine sounds. Smart and gorgeous and so much like the men in her family, he'd be the perfect apprentice when the time came.

The door behind her opened. Luca's new nanny stepped across the balcony and scooped him into her arms. "*Comida ahora?*" she asked, planting him on her hip.

"Yes," Sophia answered. "Dinner, then a bath, and then bed." She swung her bare legs off the lounge and stood. Made her way to the outdoor bar to make herself a martini. Miguel Lopez, master of this home and head of the largest drug smuggling racket at the US southern border, would be home any minute.

In the coming months, he'd have a few surprises.

She heard the door open again. Loosened her coverup so he'd notice her curves in the two-piece swim suite. "Miguel," she cooed when he rounded the corner and headed for her. "I've waited for you all day."

Dropping his unfinished cigarette to the ground, he murmured, "Mi querida."

CHAPTER 83

Awena lifted her cane to show Isa the Scripture reference carved beneath the sun symbol near the handle. Psalm 19:1. "The heavens declare the glory of God, the skies proclaim the work of his hands." She ran her fingers across the deep grooves. "See, in this way, we see the sun represents our Savior."

"I get it." Isa had said that sixteen times since Awena had begun to explain the symbols carved into her cane over the last few weeks.

"Nothing can live without the sun." Her slanted eyes radiated wisdom most days, but when Awena talked about her faith, Isa swore Awena's almond eyes radiated light. "The sun gives life," Awena continued. "Yet is also a dangerous ball of fire."

Isa's looked up to watch a large, tatted-up, bald guy lumber down the sidewalk. She thought of Nick.

Awena elbowed Isa. "See, Christ gives us life, yet he is also a powerful fire, ready to consume. So in this way, the sun teaches us of Christ."

"*Híjole!*" Maria passed behind them with a tray of dirty coffee mugs. It hadn't taken but a couple of days for Isa and Awena to determine *híjole* was Maria's favorite word when impatient. Or irritable. Or hungry.

Twilight eased down early in December. Isa glanced out the front windows again to see a low-riding car outside. The glitter on the fuzzy-dice mirror ornaments caught the setting sun. "Maria, your grandson's here. You better go. I'll get the mugs."

CALCULATED RISK

Maria's apron was off and she, out the door before Isa finished her sentence.

Awena, ignoring the interruption, pulled a Bible from beneath the counter. "There are more references to the sun as a symbol for the light that came to the world."

"Let's get you to the bus stop before it gets darker. We're past closing time already."

Awena flipped a couple of pages. "Here, Daughter. See. The sun is a bridegroom, coming out of his chamber."

Isa took the book. Scanned the reference beneath Awena's crooked finger. She loved this woman. Loved prickly Maria, too. Found a place of peace between the elder women she'd hired to help her with Coffee Magic.

In the last forty-four days, Isa had come to see her need for both these women. If Maria was the fiery spark they needed to keep Coffee Magic lively, Awena was the calming waters that flowed over the hectic days.

Gently, Isa closed the Bible and pushed it back into Awena's hands. "I'll walk you to the bus stop."

"I walk myself. There are no more demons around here."

"Right. Thanks for that."

"No problem."

"I will walk you anyway. I need fresh air before I hit the bookwork." She pulled Awena's patched coat from the hooks along the wall. "Come on. We'll continue this study on Monday or tomorrow when I meet you for church." Church was a small gathering of people in one of Albquerque's south side laundromats.

Awena slipped her arms into the coat.

On their way out the door, Isa stopped to flip the lights off.

The two walked down the street, the crisp, high desert air filling Isa's lungs. "We'll have to plan a Christmas celebration next week."

"No elf on the shelf," Awena said. "Elves creep me out."

"Me, too."

At the bus stop, Isa kissed Awena on the cheek, said good night, and turned.

"Isa."

Isa looked back over her shoulder to see Awena watching her. The look on her face as serious as she'd ever seen. "You chose well."

"Chose what?" Isa shrugged.

"Your Beautiful Trail."

Isa nodded. Tucked her hands in her coat pockets. "Goodnight, Awena."

The Saturday night bar crowd trickled onto the streets from nearby parking lots and office buildings. A car playing "All I Want for Christmas is You" battled for air dominance with another car blaring some unknown rap tune, the bass turned to depths the human ear couldn't process.

Home. She could feel the beginning of it. She imagined that first step onto a sidewalk of the classic *Home for the Holidays* portrait. Only her homecoming streets were in the middle of downtown Albuquerque.

She opened the door but didn't flip on the lights, not wanting to attract street wanderers.

At table one, she adjusted a chair. Lined it up perfectly with the seat on the opposite side. A coffee mug sat on table three. She picked it up.

But the shadow at table four near the corner wasn't supposed to be there.

Isa stopped. Instinct drove her hand to the back of her jeans where her gun should be. But no. She'd stopped packing weeks ago, convinced the Drake's Horn down the street was, at last, exterminated of all roaches.

Squinting, Isa wanted to believe that what took shape before her eyes was not really taking form and was an illusion from light filtering through the windows.

But someone sat there. Still. Poised like a spider waiting for its prey.

She swallowed, her mind running through several scenarios while her right foot slid back for a defensive kick if whoever—if whatever—attacked.

"Hello, Isa Phillips."

The last person she expected to see in Coffee Magic. "Well, Jay Hernandez—"

He waited a beat. "That's Jacob Lahache."

She sat the cup on table five. "That's right. You're a man of many faces and names. An undercover—"

"Bounty Hunter."

She almost laughed. Had Captain America gone rogue? "You're kidding."

Jacob uncrossed his legs and leaned forward, the light angling across his face. He'd grown a beard.

"I'm going after Sophia."

"Pshaw." Isa had already heard all the news about Sophia skipping town. Her old sarge back at HPD was part gossip, part informant. "She's a bail jumper. Getting Sophia won't make you a hero. She's a scared victim. That's all."

"She's the daughter of a big crime boss in Italy."

"You've lost it." She started for the counter and bumped a chair at table six, knocking it over.

"El Padrino didn't kill your husband."

She picked up the chair. Pushed it under the table. "You don't know what you're talking about."

"Sophia had him executed. He worked for her behind El Padrino's back."

Isa froze, but the dormant dragon inside stirred.

Jacob talked on. "I've done some research. She's amassing a fortune that stretches from here to Europe."

Mad. Crazed. Insane.

"I don't know what you've been drinking, but you've lost your mind. Besides, is your new wife going to let you chase drug dealers across the planet?"

She heard him pull in a breath.

"There is no new wife."

Her palms got sweaty a little too fast. "What do you mean?"

"You heard me. Thanks to you, Isa, the wedding didn't happen.

"What? I ... I ..." Isa tried to land the flight of ideas flailing in her brain so she could make sense of his statement. "I don't know what you're talking about, and why are you telling me all this now?"

One side of his mouth lifted in a mischievous grin. "I thought you'd like to join me."

ABOUT THE AUTHOR

Award-winning author L. G. Westlake writes fun, action-packed suspense with characters who are clever, fearless, and sometimes quirky, but always heroes. Her debut novel, *Quest for the Life Tree*, received recognition as the publisher's top eight books of the year and she has been writing suspense novels and encouraging blogs ever since.

L. G. and her husband originally hail from Texas where she served as founding director of a Crisis Pregnancy Center. Since that time, she and her husband have served in short and long-term missions in seven countries, and now live in the Land of Enchantment where L. G. works as the marketing manager of a ministry that shares God's Word with the world. She also enjoys cooking, gardening, and hanging out with hubby on her patio overlooking the city of Albuquerque. But the thing that gives L. G. her biggest thrill is inspiring readers to unearth their God-given gifts and become superheroes for the Lord. She and her husband have three grown children and four grandchildren (superheroes in the making).

Check out L. G.'s blogs and books at LaurieGreenWestlake. com

Made in the USA
Monee, IL
03 July 2021

72326163R00197